TEXAS DEAD

A SEASON OF DEATH

WILLIAM GENSBURGER

PRAISE FOR TEXAS DEAD

Winner - Readers' Favorite Book Award
Winner - Literary Titan Silver Book Award
Winner of Indies Today Best Mystery Winner - National
Indie Book Award Winner

"I found it to have **suspense, mystery, humor, romance, charming** and **lovable characters,** and **a very real plot.**" *~Trudi LoPreto, Reader's Favorite*

"Texas Dead is a **foot-jammed-on-the-gas-pedal crime novel with a solid plot and stellar characters.** Maxie is a terrific lead who is strong enough to take on bad guys, yet soft enough to use 'hun' as a term of endearment. It's the **small little touches** that Gensburger adds that truly make **the characters jump off the pages.** As for plotting, perfectly timed clues, leads, and suspects are revealed to readers seamlessly as the story's current races forward to its comfortable conclusion. With **twists, turns, and surprises galore,** along with a few hearty laughs, Texas Dead is **the perfect high-octane mystery.** *~Steve Quade, Indies Today*

"Texas Dead by Willian Gensburger is **an epic crime novel** filled with suspense and murder and a tender, unexpected love story. Gensburger did **an excellent job** of developing the characters in this story.... What I liked most about this book was Maxie's character. The violent aspect of the story was not overdone. Typically, I am offended by all three; however, the few situations present in this book did not bother me. I recommend this book to adult readers who enjoy **a good crime novel with some romance thrown in**." *~B. Creech, Online Book Club*

"William's Gensburger narrative is something that we have to praise because not many authors can "keep up" with their own narratives, that is, without swaying or deviating from the story. The **consistent, pleasant, fast-paced narrative** in this book, is well used, and every character has a moment of spotlight, allowing the readers to connect to them. Gensburger takes his time in telling the mystery and… he **makes our waiting worth the while.** *~Julio Carlos, Scribble's Worth Book Reviews.*

"Looking for a **great summer read**? Check out William Gensburger's new book, "Texas Dead". It's terrific-**very clever and engaging**." *~Dan Ashley, ABC7 News, SF Bay Area*

"A **fabulous page-turner.** Fans of Marcia Miller's 'Sharon McCone' series, and readers who enjoy Ray Bradbury's style of writing, will enjoy this book." *~Jill Hedgecock, The Diablo Gazette newspaper, Concord, California*

"An **epic crime novel** filled with suspense and murder and a tender, unexpected love story. Gensburger did an **excellent job of developing the characters** in this story. I recommend this book to adult readers who enjoy a good crime novel with some romance thrown in." *~B. Creech, OnlineBookClub.org*

"**Not your average gritty murder mystery**—plenty of humor injected into the story to make this hard-boiled mystery feel light and fun as well as **deeply intriguing. Vivid scenes and backdrops**…really bring the story to life. "A variety of **interesting characters**…kept me curious and **captivated the whole time.** This is a **thrilling crime fiction** novel with **brave-hearted characters**, intelligent decisions, and shocking revelations." ~ *Thomas Anderson, Editor In Chief, Literary Titan*

"It's **so cinematic**…crying out for that screenplay," ~Alex Lewczuk of Siren Radio (UK).

"Looking for **a great read?** Check out William Gensburger's new book, "Texas Dead". It's **terrific- very clever and engaging**." ~*Dan Ashley, ABC7 News Anchor, San Francisco Bay Area, California*

"This is a **fast-paced exciting book** that takes place in Corpus Christi, Texas. It has **a solid mystery** and a blooming romance. There is also comic snark between detectives Michaels and Jameson that breaks up the high drama of the story. I can't wait for future books in the series." ~ **Mollien Fote Osterman**, Reviewer

"…I was **totally hooked** and could not put it down. The book has **good suspense** and an interesting backdrop and story line. I loved the ending…tell me more! **Very interesting characters**, I could picture each of them, I particularly liked Jameson. Can't wait for the next Mackenzie Michaels mystery….."

~**Jane Blomstrand**, Author, 'Meet the Principal: My Journey Beyond the Curriculum'

"I just finished 'Texas Dead'. William's **character detail is incredible**. I felt like I really knew Maxie and Devin, Kobe and Hank. I'm looking forward to the next book."
~**Cliff Hitchcock**, Insurance Agency

A SEASON OF DEATH by William Gensburger

Updated version of Texas Dead.

First printing: June 2021

Revised edition: June 2025

Published by B&P Books, LLC

©2025 William Gensburger. William@Misterwriter.com

ISBN: 9798988973768 (print)

AUTHOR'S NOTE

This is a revised version of 'Texas Dead." Along with another few rounds of editing and many adjustments.

And watch for my all-new novel "A Splinter of Justice" coming soon.

Enjoy!

~William Gensburger

Email: *William@BNPBooks.com*

1

THE DEAD MAN

The pretty detective was late, not that it mattered—the corpse, which had been face down in the alley for quite some time, wasn't going anywhere. Although she had known since seven in the morning, despite the break in the rain and an abundance of cabs, she arrived after the last reporter on the scene. This annoyed her more than anything else; her car was in the shop—new brakes—leaving her no way to get here.

Maxie preferred to be at crime scenes before the reporters arrived. It gave the image of professionalism; she was a firm believer in professionalism. It also allowed her a chance to examine the scene free of distractions, even before the medical examiner. Clues were to be found everywhere. From the position of the body, items around, skin mottling, as well as the attire of the victim, all were clues that could be useful in her *first look.*

The city was Corpus Christi, Texas, the name a literal translation meaning *the body of Christ,* which, as she approached, she thought ironic, given this body, along with the others she had recently encountered, would experience no resurrection. Worse, this was the fifteenth body of the year, and it was only April. Usually, Corpus Christi had between five and ten murders a year. This was, she considered, a *spate of killings* and out of the norm, a very ominous sign.

Her partner, Kobe Jameson, a thirty-something Jamaican man with a smoothly shaved head and equally smooth, dark skin, was already on the scene. He nodded at her as she approached. Kobe had been her right hand for the past nine years; she relied on him to keep her—as she liked to call it—*balanced,* especially during the heat of the cases when things happened quickly, as tempers boiled over. Kobe had a keen eye, a knack for following leads, and, more critical to Maxie, a sense of humor. *In this line of work, you need a sense of humor or the life gets sucked right out of you,* she thought. Burnout rates were high.

The camera crews were finishing up their background shots. *Reporters are like birds on a phone line,* she considered, *all looking the same, moving the same, with similar gestures. All were trying to be relevant in their moment of fame.*

Her full name was MacKenzie Michaels, but everyone called her 'Maxie.' Tall, slender, shoulder-length light-brown hair with a hint of added color, usually auburn. She was thirty-eight, attractive, with a contagious smile and an even more infectious laugh; a seasoned detective with many cases under her belt—not just cases, but solved cases, something that earned her praise from the higher-ups, giving her a degree of autonomy and political clout. Everyone wanted to be close to Maxie. Maxie was the standard to which they aspired.

Today, she wore a linen skirt, collared blouse, with her trademark pale blue silk scarf. Maxie always believed in looking her best, part of the charm that captivated the public, the paparazzi, and the local celebrities. *Because you deal in homicides for a living doesn't mean you can't look good*, she thought.

"Detective MacKenzie Michaels has arrived on the scene of the latest in a string of bizarre murders that have the police baffled," one of the reporters, a woman named Jilweena Davis, told the camera, filling in the front matter of the story already completed before Maxie's arrival. "The victim, an approximately thirty-five-year-old caucasian male, has not yet been identified. It is believed, however, like the others murdered last week, a connection to organized crime cannot be ruled out." Seeing Maxie walking close to her, the reporter reached out with a hand, waving her closer. "Maxie, can you share any information?"

Maxie stopped and smiled at her. "Good morning, Jilweena," she said, noting Jilweena appreciated the first name recognition; it made it appear, to the viewing public, they were friends, though they were not. "We're in the process of identifying the victim. Of course, this is another tragedy for Corpus Christi. We are actively pursuing all leads and will make a statement as soon as possible. Thank you."

Jilweena smiled at Maxie, then turned back to the camera. "As you can see, information is not yet forthcoming in what some have called a gang-style killing spree. Hopefully, we will learn more shortly. This is Jilweena Davis for Channel Six News. Back to you in the studio."

"We're clear," the cameraman told her, already dismantling the camera couplings to load back into the van. The equipment was compact enough that one man could load, unload, set up, and take down everything quickly within a few minutes.

The medical examiner's assistant zipped up the corpse in a standard heavy, dark, body-sized duffel bag. Chief M.E. Sammy Yatsuki moved closer to Maxie. "The vic is Curtis Delaney per his driver's license. Cause of death: blunt force trauma to the back of the head."

"When?"

"Given skin mottling and liver temp, I'd say sometime late last night, maybe ten or eleven."

Sammy had been a transplant from Tokyo, Japan. His family had moved during his teen years, so he had the benefit of dual cultures, the former pushing him, along with his parents, to excel in his degree course in Forensic Pathology.

Jameson handed Maxie the wallet with the license. She pulled out the contents—a business card with his name and company name: **Stanton Investments, Corpus Christi, Texas**. On the back, it read: **In Case of Emergency**: **Devin Parker (361) 886-2600**

"Not like the others," Jameson said. "No gunshot wound." Maxie nodded. She had noticed that as well. At this stage of the investigation, it could mean anything. Still, given the consistency of the other killings, this one could well be unrelated. *Great, just what we need, a different killer*, she thought.

"Sammy, anything else I should know?"

The M.E. nodded. "He didn't die here. He was already dead when the body was dropped."

"Thanks. We'll check video feeds from security cameras to see what we can learn."

"I will get started," Jameson said.

Maxie moved closer to where Jameson was standing. "You're looking at me strangely."

"You look very stylish," Jameson replied with a smile. "That is all."

"Thank you, Kobe. It's nice to be appreciated." She smiled, brushed back some hair, then handed him back the wallet. "Be a doll and drop me at Bud's Garage on Costa—they're holding my Audi hostage?"

Bud Harringer was the owner of Bud's Garage. Her car had broken down the morning after she arrived six years ago. Bud, who was still driving their tow vehicle at the time, rescued her. Bud's had been her go-to for car work ever since, treated her fairly, and knew a lot about the goings-on in Corpus Christi.

"Of course, I will," Jameson replied. "The public thinks all these killings are related. It is not a positive for the city. Will you advise the chief to issue a statement?"

"Not yet. What we need is to find a solid lead and a decent plan of attack," Maxie replied. She got into his car, a small Ford Fusion. "It's the million-dollar trick," she added. "I feel like I'm missing something obvious."

The killing had taken place downtown, although she did not yet know that, in an alleyway on People's Street, connected to Water Street, next to Shoreline Boulevard, by the Marina. The area was not a lower-class neighborhood, recently revitalized with upgrades to infrastructure—roadways resurfaced so tourists, some of the lifeblood of the city, could enjoy what many Corpus Christi residents—and Texans in general—could not; smooth roads to drive on, free of the usual potholes. She used to joke that you needed a military Humvee to avoid ruining your alignment or your tires with all the potholes.

Homes along this part of the city were expensive. As you moved along the coastline, huge mansions—money mansions, as she called them—lined the roadway, each architecturally different from the others. Some homes were in an opulent Spanish style, while others next door might appear more like a medieval castle complete with turrets. It amused her how people with money often lacked taste, especially in their home designs. The color schemes! She wouldn't be caught dead living there; she considered it gaudy, not to mention exposed—exposed to the ever-increasing traffic, for one thing. There was a lot more crime since COVID-19 changed the world. But these homes all had one thing in common—the view of the bay, Mustang Island, and, though they could not see it except from the highest of rooftops, the Gulf of Mexico, a large basin that was an adjunct to the Atlantic Ocean, stretching from Mexico to the Florida Keys. The view of the bay was amazing, usually clear, with a massive variety of marine birds flying by. The water itself was shallow for quite some distance out before dropping into deeper water, allowing the fisherman to wade out a few hundred yards, waist deep, yet still be able to catch a lot of fish. On the Gulf side of Mustang Island, you could take a fishing boat farther out to find all manner of fish from trout to marlin, the cold water variety available in abundance, although strictly enforced limits were in place to protect the species from over-fishing—licenses with Fish and Game enforcement.

Of course, the Gulf of Mexico was regularly home to seasonal hurricanes, many of which managed to rotate further south, past Louisiana, slamming into the Texas coast right at Corpus Christi. Hurricane Katrina was one hurricane that hit Louisiana in 2005, with sustained winds exceeding 125 mph. The damage there lasted through the last two decades, with a quarter of the state still impacted. The extent of the damage forced many residents to be relocated to Houston, Texas, where they still remained.

Hurricane Harvey, in 2017, was the last Category 4 hurricane to impact Corpus Christi, slamming into Louisiana and Texas, making landfall at Port Aransas and Rockport, causing tidal swells of over ten feet. This resulted in 69 deaths as a direct result. Corpus Christi suffered wind damage to roofs, trees, power lines, and backups to storm drains, causing flooding.

This was during Maxie's second year in Corpus Christi. The city issued a voluntary evacuation order, with most businesses shutting down for a week.

Eighty percent of the homes in Aransas Pass, Rockport, and Port Aransas, homes not built to withstand such an onslaught, were destroyed. Elsewhere, homes had storm shutters that residents would screw into place, removing any items that could be dislodged and thrown by the force of the winds to become projectiles, causing further damage.

It had been a trial-by-fire introduction for Maxie, who found great purpose in assisting residents, many of whom had been displaced. It also gave her a chance to get to know many people—people you help in emergencies, never forget every small act of kindness. She brought meals to those families with children, still without power. She worked with emergency crews, extricating people trapped.

If you followed Shoreline further down, you reached the Marina and the berth of the USS Lexington aircraft carrier, a twice-retired World War II carrier that had seen plenty of action before it was finally retired to Corpus Christi. It was now open to the public for tours. For a small donation to their museum, you could walk through the main hangar deck, up precarious walkways, bulkheads, up tight, steep, metal stairs to the various levels, including the flight deck. When she had gone there, it made her feel claustrophobic, not to mention trying to go up the skinny ladders in a skirt with heels on. She could have switched to walking shoes, but not Maxie—style above all else.

Further up deck was the primary flight control, the bridge, where the captain and navigator sat, complete with an adjacent map room. Lower, the ready rooms where flight briefings were held before missions, CVIC, where the intelligence planning would occur, next to crew berths, tightly packed sleeping quarters, Maxie never imagined experiencing. It was a man's world—more toys for the boys, though women were serving aboard other carriers in ever-increasing numbers.

Maxie knew all this—she solved a murder on the Lex two years earlier and, in the process, received a solid education about the grand dame. But the vessel still smelled of oil, not the fragrance she would have enjoyed daily. Oil from the engines, oil from the aircraft, and the work areas. Quite utilitarian. Equally permeating. And while Maxie appreciated the history of the ship, the practical aspect hardly thrilled her.

On the drive to Bud's, she joked about it with Jameson. Then, she fell silent. He would notice after a few minutes, glance over at her to see if she was all right. She pretended not to notice. After a few more minutes of silence, he gave up and awaited the inevitable play.

"Did you kill him, Kobe?" she asked her partner, matter-of-factly. Kobe laughed. He knew this game; she played it often, especially if she had time to kill. "Where were you last night between the hours of ten and midnight?" She did this with no facial expression. He chuckled again. "You're a spy, aren't you?" she added. "You're working for the Russians? Or is it the Chinese?"

"You got me there," he answered. "But, I do have an alibi."

"What might that be?"

He looked at her. "Were we not playing poker on your deck last night?"

"Ah," she said, a massive grin on her face. "*That* is your excuse? You left at nine, as I recall. Nice try, though."

"So am I under arrest?" he asked resignedly.

"I'm mulling it over. It might be necessary for me to have you wear the cuffs, though."

Jameson shook his head. "It would make my driving quite dangerous."

"I suppose. Well, don't leave town. I may have more questions later."

"I will not leave," he assured her. "I have nowhere else to go."

AFTER THEY REACHED the repair shop, while she waited for her car to be brought out, she dialed the number on Curtis Delaney's wallet card to leave a message.

"Mr. Devin Parker, this is Detective Michaels at CCPD. I need to speak with you at your earliest convenience. Could you please come down to the station at 321 John Sartain Street, at the corner of North Chaparral? You can call me at this number if you can't find it. Thank you."

"It will not be a pleasant day for him," Jameson said.

"Can't be helped. He needs to identify the body. I have an odd feeling about this one, Kobe. It isn't straightforward like the others."

The lot boy, an eighteen-something with shaggy hair tied into a man-bun, brought out her Galaxy-Blue Metallic Audi Q7. "You washed her," she gushed. "You guys are too much. Thank you."

"It's a beautiful color," the lot boy told her with a hint of envy in his voice. He would have loved to own the car, unlike the heavily used Dodge truck he had bought for five hundred dollars, systematically replacing the alternator, fuel pump, tires, and rebuilding the engine over three weeks, using money earned from his job.

"It truly is," Maxie replied. She turned to Jameson. "Thanks for the ride."

"You are welcome. I will see you at the office after you...?"

"After I what?"

"You know what," he said. "You always stop."

"Stop where?" she said coyly. "Kobe, I have no idea what you are talking about."

"You know where," he laughed, his prominent teeth white against his skin. "You can bring me a Danish as a thank you for driving you around."

Now it was her turn to laugh. He did know her well. She nodded and watched as he started up his car and drove off. She waved after him.

A quarter-mile up the street, on the way to the *office*, as they both called it, was a quaint pastry shop. It was called *Just A Taste*. It occupied what must have been, at one time, an older private residence fully converted for commercial use. It was a mother-daughter operation: Judy and Teresa Valencia had the best coffee and the tastiest treats Maxie had found in her entire time in Corpus Christi.

The outside of the building had an ornate pink trim with its sign firmly centered. Soft curtains framed the windows. A series of small bistro tables were arranged in what once was a dining room, while on the left, the refrigerated glass counter displayed anything perishable.

As usual, both were working, Judy bringing out fresh pastries and cakes while Teresa was handling the register and serving the customers. The aroma of the coffee was comforting, making you want to order some even if you hated coffee.

"Hola Maxie," Theresa called out. Judy turned back and put her tray down to wave at Maxie, who was approaching the counter.

"You look fabulous, Maxie," Judy told her. "Always younger each time I see you. I'm envious."

Maxie beamed. "You both lie so well," she said. "That's why I always come back."

"Your usual?" Theresa asked. Maxie nodded. "Coming right up. Have a seat."

Maxie scanned for open seats. The place wasn't packed today, which was a plus. The area, in what must have been a former breakfast nook, held her favorite table. Teresa and Judy both looked at each other, smiling. "You always take this table," Teresa told her as she brought out espresso and a chocolate croissant on a small plate, placing them before her.

"It's such a peaceful spot," Maxie replied. "I always love sitting here." The truth was that she liked to imagine the house as her own, not that she disliked her home. This one held a rustic quality. If nothing else, it was a nice place to escape from time to time.

Judy approached with a paper bag, placing it on the table. "For Señor Jameson," she said. "Must not forget him."

"You're so kind to remember," Maxie said, reaching for her espresso to take a sip. *Fantastic coffee,* she thought. It took her mind from the murders to thoughts of relaxing on her deck overlooking the canals.

For Maxie, moments like these allowed her to unwind and process the information percolating. Though the owners knew her and always fussed over her, she could remain anonymous, not bothered by anyone else. The chocolate croissant was a bonus.

A half-hour later, she was done. She never waited for the bill—had a vague idea of the pricing, always left a twenty-dollar bill on the table, more than enough for her espresso and snacks, along with a hefty tip. The small espresso spoon stopped it from blowing off. She grabbed the bag, turned to the women as she walked out, and waved.

"Bye, Maxie," both chimed.

2

DEVIN PARKER

Jameson met her back at the station. She had an actual office there, unlike other detectives with desks in the central area. This was because she had asked for one. It was a no-brainer. Maxie had solved more cases in her time on the force than most people. Her tenacity, style, and—despite ruffling some feathers of her colleagues—her open-ended way of dealing with the media, the public, and city officials, made her invaluable. When it came to Maxie, there were no limitations. Maxie could have whatever she wanted, not that she was demanding, nor did she take advantage of her status.

Maxie was astute. Professionally, personally, and financially. Wise investments in the stock market had netted her enough for a luxurious, two-story waterfront house on Padre Island, complete with a boat dock and her sailboat. She had named it: *Lady Tears*, had the name painted in gold lettering and outlined in black across the stern. The boat was a 1982 Bristol 40, centerboard/sloop, sleek, fast, with a shallow draft and a waterline length of twenty-seven and a half feet.

Reddish-brown mahogany interior colors, a small galley, and room for a handful of people to sleep. She loved taking her out on the bay and hoisting sails after using the Westerbeke motor to first get out of the channel. Sailing offered a sense of peace rather than the convenience of just the engine.

She used the boat frequently, finding the change of scenery conducive to solving crime and schmoozing with everyone from the police chief, city council members, city mayors, and others seeking her counsel. It was her home away from home and her retreat. She could handle the sails alone and with relative ease, to a point where she considered herself proficient.

"He is in your office," Jameson told her as she walked in, handing him the small brown bag with his Danish inside. "I gave him a coffee." She nodded, strode past after casting him a *'you didn't give him that awful swill, did you?'* look, then entered her corner office.

It had been painted a light peach, and she had decorated it with her two favorite things: tall, lush plants and ornaments with a nautical theme. On her desk, a small wooden sailboat served to remind her of her boat. A wooden inbox was now a tiny beach oasis; she added sand, shells, and a small plastic dolphin. Large paintings of various beach scenes, one with an abandoned wooden lifeboat and another with two images of pelicans, adorned the walls. It was less an office than a sanctuary. And she had left an open invitation for any other detectives needing a place to retreat, to use without asking permission, something that had ingratiated her with them even more than her charm. At least no one openly seemed to resent her for it.

Devin was sitting on one of the twin chairs by the desk, flipping through his phone messages. She closed the door.

"Mr. Parker, Maxie Michaels," she said, extending a hand

for him to shake. "Thanks for coming in." He started to stand, but she waved him back down, instead lifting the paper coffee cup and placing it on the opposite edge of the desk. "Trust me, you don't want to drink this," she said quietly.

Devin was in his late thirties, six feet tall, and muscular in the right places. He had a shock of dark hair that fell over his face—he swept it back. His eyes were a compelling, deep-blue color. "No one would tell me why I'm here."

"I asked them to let me do that," she said, pulling out her chair and sitting down. "I apologize. There's no easy way for me to say this, but we found Curtis Delaney dead this morning." She held out the business card they had retrieved from the body.

Devin's face fell, the blood draining from the shock of what he had just heard. "Curtis...that's not possible. I just spoke with him yesterday."

"I am so sorry for your loss. We got your name from this card." She flipped it over. "He carried it in his wallet. How exactly are you related?"

"We're cousins. Long story. How...? What happened?" Devin could barely get the words out. His head felt suddenly waterlogged, and he could not clear his thoughts.

He hadn't seen Curtis for some time, each promising to arrange a dinner or a weekend away fishing, but both were always extremely busy, and time mercilessly slipped by unnoticed.

Maxie sat upright and leaned closer, her hand reaching for the box of Kleenex she kept on the side of the desk, and moved it closer to him. Devin's face, she noted, was frozen, and she knew he was struggling to process the information.

"Murdered," she explained. "Blunt force to the back of the head." She let it sink in for a moment. "Do you know anyone who would want to hurt him?"

Devin shook his head. "Curtis is...was...the most honest person I knew. He always treated everyone fairly."

Maxie watched his expressions for any telltale signs of a lie or deception. There were none—he was genuinely distraught and caught off-guard, and she felt sorry for him, for the pain she knew he was experiencing. It never got any easier having to tell people that a loved one was dead, let alone murdered—that was the only news she delivered as a homicide detective.

"No enemies?"

"God, no," Devin said.

"What line of work was he in—Stanton Investments. What is that?"

"Financial advisor. He was always good with money, finances, and stocks. He advised so many people where to put their money. He was considered somewhat of a genius with money."

"Could someone have been seeking revenge for a bad investment?" Maxie asked.

Devin shook his head. "There were not many bad investments. People knew Curtis put his money where his mouth was—he always invested where he advised his clients to invest. If they lost money, so did he. God, this is terrible." He put his face into his hands, felt the tears surging, and quickly grabbed a Kleenex, fighting them back.

"I am sorry," Maxie said. "I know this is difficult." She was sizing him up, noting how his body hunched over as he fought back the tears. She studied how he sat, what he wore—a tailored, open-collared shirt, high-quality cotton and well-ironed, tailored slacks, Allen Edmonds Cap Toe Oxford shoes—stylish, she thought.

His mannerisms confirmed what her gut had already assessed: Devin Parker was not involved in the death of

Curtis Delaney in any way. And this made her job much more straightforward—she would remove him from her suspect list rather than having to ferret out information had he been trying to be deceptive. "We'll talk more about Curtis later as I learn more, but now, I'm afraid I need to ask you to do something uncomfortable. I need you to positively identify the body for me. Can you do that?"

Devin's face answered the question. A look of horror—he would have to look upon the lifeless body of his cousin, let alone how he had been murdered. But he knew he had to do it—there was no other family to do so. He nodded slowly.

Maxie stood and came around to help him up. "Take a moment if you need it," she said softly.

He shook his head, brushed his hair back, and took a deep breath. "It's okay," he said. "There's no avoiding it. I'd rather get this done."

"Good," she said reassuringly. "We'll take my car—it's a short slog to the Medical Examiner's office."

They walked together through the precinct, the bright overhead neons hiding the plain look of the place. The walls had the usual OSHA safety notices, some Wanted posters, and two walls devoted to awards—an Officer of the Year plaque covering the last ten years, and an enclosed glass bookcase with older artifacts from earlier days of Corpus law enforcement, such as old handcuffs, uniforms, and defunct weaponry.

They avoided the eyes of the curious, down the stairs to the lobby, and out the rear door where her car was parked. She unlocked it remotely. "Where'd *you* park?"

He pointed to a jet-black Ducati Multistrada 1200 Enduro motorcycle in the visitor lot. It was a beautiful bike to look at, designed for adventure riding. Devin didn't go off-road with it, so he did not have mud tires; nonetheless, it was the kind of bike that would catch your eye as it passed you on the road.

"Nice," she said. "I thought about getting one, what with traffic and all." But really, she had not—bikes were not her style, besides which, she loved her Audi, had custom-picked the color, and no way would she part with it voluntarily.

A handful of minutes later, they passed under the Crosstown Freeway and headed south on 17th Street. Devin had been silent the whole way, and Maxie knew the shock of the news had cemented itself.

"Doing okay?"

"Does it ever get easier?" he asked her.

"Does what get easier?"

"Dealing with death?"

Maxie considered the question. She had certainly seen her fair share of death since joining the force. Almost none were from natural causes, such as heart failure or hospital illness deaths. Only the homicides came her way.

"The day it does is the day I quit," she answered. "Death should always affect you; remind you how precious life is."

Devin glanced at her. "It's a shame people forget that. I see a lot of death as an investigative reporter."

THE ME's office was on Hospital Drive, just up the Street from the large Christus Spohn Hospital. It was an older building, built in 1995, with the same sand-colored exterior as the Police Station. When first built, it had a capacity for only 12 bodies, and yet this office now covered 19 counties, nowhere near enough. A new building of 5,200 square feet was in the works—approval to negotiate bids had passed the

Commissioners Court. But that would be years away. Meanwhile, the county had purchased a 53-foot refrigerated truck that could hold an additional 40 bodies. The necessity of this arrived, like a hard slap, with the mass of Covid-19 deaths, most from area nursing homes. The M.E. office was overworked, often causing delays in death certificate issuance. Now, things had lightened somewhat, and deaths from Covid-19 had dropped to single digits.

Sammy Yatsuki was expecting them. The facility smelled. The bite of cold antiseptic with a trace of formaldehyde permeating everything. It had no decor, just neutral walls, long and thin corridors, and bright, overhead neon lights, cold like death itself.

Curtis's body was on the main table in the morgue, a sheet covering him. Sammy had just finished his physical autopsy and was writing up the notes as they walked in. Across the back wall were several other rolling tables—these bodies were fully covered, awaiting disposition or movement to the truck outside. Sammy missed the days of fewer bodies.

"Sammy, this is Devin Parker. He's the deceased's cousin, here to identify the body."

"My condolences," Sammy said to Devin, motioning them to move closer to the table. He gently pulled back the covering to expose Curtis's head. Devin looked at the face and then quickly nodded. "It's him." He turned away. It was too hard to look at Curtis and realize he was gone. His face was pale, drained of blood, and expressionless. Not at all like he was sleeping—more like a body unoccupied by a soul—his living energy missing. It almost didn't seem like the body belonged to Curtis, more like a mannequin with inanimate facial features.

"I'm sorry," Maxie said, patting his arm. "This is the hardest part. It's never easy."

"He doesn't look real," Devin said, turning back and looking once again. His face was clean, with no sign of injury, no blood or bruising. "How exactly did he die?"

"He was hit on the back of the head with a heavy object," Sammy explained. "Death would have been instantaneous. He likely felt no pain. Based on my examination, I would guess a large tire iron, a large wrench, pipe, something along those lines. I'll have more information in my report. We took impressions of the wound and will match them up."

"Toxicology?" Maxie asked.

Sammy shook his head. "Results are not back yet, Maxie, but I am confident in ruling it out. Mr. Delaney was in good physical shape at the time of his death. There were no indications of substance use or abuse. His medical records show no use of prescriptions, and he was not a smoker, either."

"Thanks, Sammy," Maxie said.

Devin looked at Sammy. "Thank you for taking care of him. I guess the mortuary will come to pick him up."

"It shouldn't be much longer," Sammy said. "We'll let you know when they call."

Maxie led Devin outside to the front lobby. "Wait here a sec?"

She returned to Sammy's lab.

"Seems like a nice guy," she noted. "What do you think?"

"In your line of work, they all are nice until they aren't," Sammy noted sarcastically, turning back to Curtis's body and fully covering it again.

"True. Anything else from the autopsy he didn't need to hear?"

"No signs of defensive wounds. It was swift. He didn't know what hit him—literally."

"And struck from behind. A crime of deception. Is it tied into the other killings?"

"Hard to say. The way he was killed was different, but that might have been an outlier. He was seemingly unaffiliated with gangs, no tattoos at all—which is unusual these days."

"It's been a crazy few months, Sammy," she said with a sigh. "I need a break to figure it out."

Back in the lobby, she motioned for Devin to follow her to the car.

"You okay?"

Devin nodded. "As well as I can be," he said. "Have you spoken with Robert Meeker?"

"Who's that?"

"His business partner at Stanton Investments. And his best friend."

Maxie shook her head. "Not yet."

"I should go with you if that's okay?" he offered. "I should be there when he learns about Curtis." Maxie agreed.

3

ROB MEEKER

The offices of Stanton Investments were at the corner of Staples Street and Everhart Road, and the drive took under ten minutes. Next door to the office was Schlotzsky's, a chain sandwich and burger joint, Devin told Maxie Curtis had often frequented. Curtis had taken Devin there a few months before, insisting he try the Fiesta Chicken, a tasty and calorie-rich sandwich, burger-style, complete with a Jalapeño-cheese bun. Devin remembered seeing the whopping 1450 calories on the menu and wondered whether he could order a kid's portion instead.

It was made worse by the fact that Curtis was not overweight—one would think a regular diet of fast food would kill you, but Curtis worked out, jogged daily, and kept his other meals at a lower calorie count to offset his lunch. Devin pondered the irony as they parked.

Two police cars were out front blocking traffic. Maxie pulled up behind one, put up her magnetic roof beacon, and got out.

"What's going on?" she asked, clipping her badge to her waist belt.

"Looks like a break-in. The place has been tossed."

"Oh really," Maxie said, thinking, *that's interesting timing.* "Let's go in," she told Devin, motioning him to follow.

Inside, Robert Meeker was speaking with another police officer when he spotted Devin and a woman he did not know and waved them closer. "Hey buddy, long time no see. Excuse the mess—we got robbed while I was at lunch."

Meeker was tall, just over six feet, and solidly built, although not at all athletic. *For a financial guy, he always looks like he has just stepped out of bed, hair ruffled, with a slight beard stubble. Would you give money to this man?* Devin thought.

"Rob, this is Detective Michaels," Devin told him. "You'd better have a seat."

The floor was littered with files, paper, photo frames, and other objects from the office. The receptionist's desk was empty—everything had been swept aside.

Maxie pointed at a chair on the floor, and Rob lifted it up and dutifully sat down. "What's going on?"

Devin picked up the other and motioned for Maxie to sit.

"Curtis is dead," Devin said. "Murdered. Last night."

Rob looked shocked. His face whitened, and his eyes darted between Maxie and Devin. "You're kidding me, right? This is just a sick joke?"

"I wish it were. I've just come from the morgue."

"Mr. Meeker," Maxie said. "When did you see Curtis last?"

Rob, still in shock, looked up at the ceiling in thought. His eyes caught sight of a pencil hanging by the nib from one of the insulation squares. It was one of Curtis's many pranks.

"Lunchtime...yesterday. He went across the street for lunch. He never came back, so I just assumed he had a meeting. Didn't think twice about it. How did he... I mean, why? Do you have leads?"

"We're still investigating. Did Curtis have any enemies? Any recent problems he might have shared with you? Money problems?" Maxie stopped to give him a chance to reply. Rob shook his head.

Maxie was studying his facial expressions. *Hard to read.* He seemed genuinely surprised, but then again, *people have been known to lie well,* she thought. She had certainly known enough liars in her time as a detective—they usually were relatively easy to read, although some had perfected the art of deception enough that it would only be unexpected mistakes that would reveal the truth.

"Curtis was—well, you know Devin—not that kind of guy. Everyone liked him."

"What about the burglary here?" Maxie asked. "Anything taken?"

"Someone went through the computers, but everything seems to be here still." He pointed at the pencil hanging from the ceiling. "Curtis," he said. Devin and Maxie both glanced up. He stood and moved about the room, shaking his head. "I can't believe that he's... gone."

Devin got up and walked to Curtis's office. The furniture and files had also been overturned. He'd been in this office many times over the years, knew the layout, where items of furniture went, and pictures on the walls. There had been many an evening sitting with Curtis after hours, discussing their lives and how they had meandered since they first met. *Lots of wonderful memories,* Devin thought, and then sadness crept back in as he remembered that Curtis was gone.

He lifted up Curtis's chair and put it back behind the desk, then sat in it and looked out at the office as though it were his own. *Why would someone ransack the place and not take anything? What was going on?* He heard Maxie ask other questions just outside the door.

"Do you keep money here—large currency that someone might want to steal?"

"Very rarely," Rob said. "Usually, transactions are all digital."

Devin glanced at the desktop. It was empty—everything that had been on it now lay on the floor to the left of the desk. Someone had been sitting here and brushed it all off with one hand. He leaned over and retrieved what he could reach— the phone, a small table lamp, Curtis's business card holder—the cards were strewn across the floor. And a small four-inch by four-inch stone picture frame. Devin turned it over. It was a snapshot of Curtis, Devin, and their grandparents, Reid and Doris Stanton, taken two years earlier. Reid, who was always well-dressed, stood taller than Curtis and Devin. He was six feet four inches tall, making him tower over his wife, who seemed diminutive by comparison.

Devin smiled at the memory. *Reid and Doris have been gone a year next month,* he thought. Now with Curtis gone, Devin was all that was left. He felt alone.

Rob and Maxie walked in. Devin held up the picture to Rob. "Mind if I take this?" Rob looked at the photo and smiled, the gap in his front teeth suddenly showing.

"He loved that picture. Always said it was good times. Of course, take it. In fact, take anything you want. He was my friend, but he was your family."

"Thanks, Rob," Devin said. "I realize this is hard on you as well. You were his best friend."

"I don't know what's going to happen now?" Rob said. He

moved closer to Devin and placed a reassuring hand on his shoulder. "Curtis was the lifeblood of this place. I can't see running it without him, you know?"

Maxie turned to Rob. "Whatever you do, don't make any decisions until you've had a chance to process this. Don't rush to something you might regret. It's been my experience that people need time to process their true feelings after a tragedy. You have my sincere condolences."

She wasn't sure whether she believed the last part; her suspicions were still active about Rob—it just didn't feel right, and she could not express that in a verbal way that would make sense to anyone else. "Women's intuition," she had explained once to Jameson. He was more of a tangible proof kind of guy, but he seemed to appreciate her instincts.

Rob nodded.

"I have what I need," Maxie told Devin. "I'll wait for you outside. Take your time."

Devin nodded. "What can I say. It's... surreal," he told Rob. "I can't fathom who would want to hurt Curtis, of all people."

"I know."

"Did you see anything that wasn't...well...normal for him? I can't figure out any motive here. It certainly wasn't theft."

Rob pulled up the other chair and sat beside Devin. "Nothing. It was just another day. Aside from the break-in. Do you think they're related?"

"I don't know. They must have been after something to turn the place upside down."

"I'll keep looking," Rob said. "If I do find something missing, I'll let you know."

Devin got up. "Thanks. Curtis wanted to be cremated."

Rob nodded. "That or being launched into space." He smiled at the memory. Curtis was a huge SpaceX supporter, as well as an early investor in Tesla stock, both Elon Musk's creations, and loved the idea that travel to Mars was rapidly becoming a reality.

"I thought, perhaps, a small memorial at a crematorium. I don't think he'd want to have a large crowd, but aside from you and me, there's no family left."

"I'll be there," Rob said. "Just tell me when and where."

"I will." Devin extended a hand to shake, but Rob, instead, pulled him in for a hug, wrapping his arms around Devin and patting him on the back.

When he let go, Devin nodded and started for the door.

"Hey, Devin," Rob called after him. Devin turned and saw that Rob was holding the picture frame. "Don't forget this." He handed it to him.

"Almost forgot," Devin said sheepishly. "Thank you."

From the lobby, Rob watched as Devin got in Maxie's car. She retrieved the police beacon and then pulled away. Even after the car was out of sight, he stood there, staring aimlessly out front.

Across the road, parked in a small, nondescript pale blue Ford Fiesta, a man watched, unseen by Rob. He was middle-aged, with darker skin, perhaps Middle Eastern. His eyes were a piercing blue, bright, and they seemed to shine against the dark of his eye sockets and bushy eyebrows. Many fine lines seemed etched around both eyes. These looked as though they had been drawn on, rather than the signs of age leaving their mark. Regardless, he had been watching the whole visit take place.

He noted Maxie leaving, noticed her outfit, her hair, and the way her scarf moved in the slight breeze. *Classy lady*, he thought. Then, a short time after her, Devin emerged to get into her car. The man observed him as well. *This one was close to the victim*, he knew. Even after they had left, the man remained. He had a small notebook which he wrote in with a short pencil. He noted the time and Maxie's license plate. He added the word: *confident.*

Next to him, a small laptop was open. On the screen, some code was spilling down. He checked it, seemed to understand what it meant, then returned his gaze to the office Devin had just left.

He already knew who Devin was, had read previous articles he had written, and so his natural inclination was to believe that Devin was just an innocent bystander caught up in the murder, a person following leads, trying to uncover the truth himself. He was not certain, yet, how that would fit into what he was there for. It was the other one in which the man took an interest. He resolved to take the first opportunity to plant a listening device in the office and also to tap into the computer system, per instructions, to see any email exchanges. Only then could he learn the extent of his suspicions. That would dictate the next course of action.

The man had met Curtis briefly just before his untimely death. They had met once, for ten minutes, in the park the day before. The man had been sitting on a bench by the pond, watching the fish, when Curtis had approached him and asked permission to sit. It had been no coincidence. They sat far apart enough to look like strangers, and yet Curtis looked troubled. The man asked why he looked troubled, and Curtis just shook his head. The man wondered whether he felt endangered by the question, certainly enough to not trust a stranger with so big a secret? The man already knew the secret and what troubled Curtis, but for him, the man knew there was no solution. It was not his responsibility.

When he had confirmed Curtis's death the following day, he drove downtown just as the body was being removed from the alleyway and watched through binoculars until there was nothing left to see. *Corpus Christi*, he thought, *never loses an opportunity to surprise in both positive and negative ways.*

The world had changed here over the past year, and not in ways he considered positive. It was not just here; the whole country—and even other countries—appeared to be in a declining spiral; the values of years gone by had been discarded. *If it continues,* he considered, *we will all be at the bottom with nowhere left to go.* Not that his job was to help in any way to effect change. He was, after all, just doing his job, a single cog in the whole system. He interfered only when instructed. The rest of the time, he observed, filed reports, and often liked to sit and contemplate what it all really meant; what importance it really held. Beyond that, he had other plans for the future, things that were well past this time with his current employer. These things were never discussed; he knew better than to trust anyone. The seeds for this future were already firmly planted.

He looked at the code on the laptop again, then closed the laptop lid and started up his car.

SEVERAL HOURS LATER, the man entered the offices. No security system was active to stop him; it had been deactivated remotely. From the time he was young, he enjoyed sneaking around in the dark. There was an air of mystery about it, outside of the norm, away from regular people; here in the dark, he was the watcher, set apart from humanity in general. He wasn't sure if it was the control he felt, being able to do these things, or just some strange need to be nosey about the lives of other people, certainly quite different from his own. Whatever it was, after a moment of enjoyment, he swept the thoughts from his mind and got to work.

Swiftly, he planted the bugs on the phone and computer in Rob's office, then, after looking around once more, left the building and returned to his car. Within a day, he would know if there were other secrets to be found. His employer wanted to be sure that there were not. *Patience*, he reminded himself.

4

HANK REMSTED

The Corpus Christi Tribune was an old newspaper that occupied an even older building downtown. Founded in 1899, it had served as one of several large circulation dailies for decades, focused on unbiased reporting and trustworthy journalism, and with a team of in-house professionals, held much success before the advent of the Internet.

And the exterior façade of the building was an ornate mid-1920s art deco style architecture, designed by the contemporaries of architects Raymond Hood and John Mead Howells, famous for The Daily News building in Manhattan.

As Google and social media became the public's primary source of information and news, regardless of accuracy, the *Tribune*, like most papers, saw a massive decline in subscriptions. For a time, it appeared that digital versions of the paper could allay print and delivery costs. However, the public, having a taste of all things online being free, resisted paying for something available elsewhere at no charge.

And, of course, the accusing voice of environmentalists

was ever-present to point out how many trees had to be killed to print each newspaper.

Devin remembered arguing with a friend who had questioned why he still worked in a profession that no longer needed accuracy, that accuracy took time, and that was anathema to timeliness in the age where everyone expected instant gratification. Devin had asked his friend if he would be comfortable seeing a doctor who hadn't finished medical school or a pilot who had learned to fly from a book?

It was a valid point, although it did little to sway the impact.

As a result of declining sales, the once independent *Tribune* was purchased by the Dewey Media Group out of Cincinnati. The *Tribune* was one of the many struggling newspapers they bought. The new owners immediately went about trimming anything that failed to produce a profit, cut back on the reporting staff, relied more heavily on the Associated Press feeds that junior reporters tweaked into semi-custom stories, and focused heavily on advertising sales. And so the paper had shrunk to an almost embarrassing size, most of its content advertising, sports, as well as a lot of regurgitated national news. One thing the editor refused to do was lose local coverage. Its primary audience had dwindled to the older, less computer-savvy generation, people who still read their news with their morning coffee. No spies hung around street corners anymore, with folded newspapers under their arms and a smoldering cigarette dangling from their lips. This was, after all, a time of—reported—progress.

Devin, however, was lucky. In no small measure, thanks to his investigative journalism—old school beat-walking for leads and the truth—he secured his employment and garnered positive attention from the *Tribune's* owners. Even old man Robert

Dewey, the DMG CEO, sent him a personal letter letting Devin know that he held 'favored son' status. And this was, in no small part, due to recognition he commanded for the exposé on secret child labor in America. That piece had caught the attention of the country and brought about a firestorm of other investigations, arrests, and prosecutions, as well as a new spate of legislation designed to protect children from further exploitation.

Were one to ask Devin, however, whether the changes were adequate, he would politely smile and suggest more needed to be done. "So much goes on in front of our faces, disguised as good intentions or charitable acts that would incense you," he was quoted as saying in response.

Hank Remsted was Devin's boss. As editor of the *Tribune*, he saw himself as a kind of Perry White, the editor-in-chief of 'The Daily Planet' in the Superman serial. Of course, the allusion mainly was for his ego, yet it seemed to give him a modicum of respectability.

Hank was in his mid-sixties, medium height and build. He had short hair that was more military cut than styled, a pencil mustache that looped down the sides of his mouth. His family had immigrated from Sweden when Hank was a boy, not so much to escape the turmoils of Europe as to ensure a better future for their son. America was the land of opportunity, welcoming all willing to work hard.

And Hank had worked hard, mostly because it was expected of him. In their new homeland, his immigrant parents were eager to assimilate and ensure a decent future for their son. As a result, Hank had to work harder than those who had been born in America. He had risen to the top from the bottom, the last forty years with the *Tribune*, starting in the mailroom, then as a beat reporter, and through every job possible with the paper. By the time he became editor in his late forties, he had a full understanding of all aspects that made the paper run.

AFTER MAXIE HAD BROUGHT him back to his motorcycle, Devin decided it was time to bring Hank into the loop. Devin needed to have his blessing to pursue the story, even though he was emotionally compromised. Hank, however, knew him well enough to believe that Devin's objectivity wouldn't be clouded—one of the pet peeves the editor had with the current world of journalism was the abject lack of objectivity. Everything seemed simplified, biased, and rarely factual. He missed the days of the black and white presentation of fact, allowing the reader—or viewer, when it came to TV—to decide for themselves.

Back then, the news was *reported*, not analyzed or injected with opinion. Nowadays, with fewer resources and heavily relying on the feeds of Reuters News Agency or the Associated Press, reporters—both print and television— felt compelled to add *flavor* in order to boost ratings, turning the whole thing into an entertainment forum rather than the austere reporting it needed to be.

Devin entered from the main lobby. The shiny marbled flooring, freshly mopped, weathered but strong, always made him feel he was a part of something larger, a place with history, solid, not flimsy.

An old security guard was seated by the entrance. His name was Lee. He had worked for the paper since his teens, first in the mail room, like Hank, then later, as part of private security. It was an easy job. So far, there had been no lunatics shooting up the place, as had happened in some other larger cities. Lee was glad of that. His wife, Jane, now dead for several years, as well as their daughter Tisha, had enjoyed the stability of his job.

As Devin approached, he called out. "How are you, Lee?"

"Just fine, young man," was Lee's standard answer. He never got to know the faces that came or went, although he did recognize Devin. Devin was one of the few people from the paper who had attended his wife's funeral, and Lee appreciated that. Still, Devin's name eluded him.

The short elevator ride brought Devin to the sixth floor, where the executive offices were. This included Hank Remsted, Devin, who had an office on one corner, and Percival Wald, the controller who handled the financial matters of the paper, on the other.

Seeing through the glass walls that Hank was alone in his office, Devin knocked once and then let himself in.

"Hey, boss."

"Devin," Hank said, standing and extending a hand. "I am very sorry to hear about your loss. Heard it on the police band and called in for details. Have a seat. Drink?"

Hank loved his whiskey; he kept a bottle of Jack Daniels in the lower-left drawer along with some shot glasses. He used to tell Devin, "A shot is a great way to get visitors to start talking," and over the years, Devin had seen many a politician talking in his office. Interestingly, no matter the length of the drinking time, Devin had never seen Hank drunk.

Hank was gregarious and had a deep laugh that seemed to come from within his belly, reverberating its way up and out. Today, he had a serious look. He knew his star reporter was hurting, and he was determined to be supportive.

Devin declined, glancing at his watch.

He didn't push. "You doing okay?"

"I've been better," Devin told him. "It's quite surreal."

"I bet," he said. "Sit. You're making me nervous."

Devin obeyed. "I want to investigate the murder."

Hank nodded. "Of course you do. Gotta be careful, though. I don't need to remind you. Any leads?"

"No. The police are working on it, and I'll keep following up. I just came from the morgue."

"Sorry. Never a great experience, that. What do you have to go on?" He got up and opened his window, then sat back and pulled a cigarette from a silver box on his desk and lit it.

"Just the murder and Curtis's office was ransacked." Devin was watching the cigarette smoke spiral up, then across, currents of air teasing it in random directions.

Devin glanced at the journalism awards Hank had accumulated as editor. Each had been framed and neatly placed, evenly spaced.

"Someone looking for something?"

Devin nodded. "Something for sure. Has to be."

"Gang related? Like the other killings?"

"I can't see how. Curtis wasn't that type."

"I agree. Besides, I have a suspicion about this."

"Like what?"

"A series of killings. Some seemingly random. Others with gang affiliation. It seems very convenient that suddenly a lot of murders are happening here."

"I'm still unsure what you're getting at," Devin said.

"My gut as a newspaper man tells me this is bigger. Did you ever watch 'The Godfather' movies?

"Mafia? You think it's mafia? You hate conspiracies, Hank."

"I'm not saying it is," Hank said, defending himself. "Consider this, if you wanted to set up a crime organization in a place with relatively low crime, aside from gangs, what would you have to do?"

Devin considered the question. "First, I would have to get rid of the gangs. Or at least their leaders."

"Exactly," Hank said, balancing the cigarette on the window ledge and grabbing the pad and pen from his desk. He scribbled down a name and cellphone number, then handed it to Devin before retrieving his smoke. "I've got someone I think you should work with."

Devin glanced at it. "Detective Maxie?"

He nodded. "The best of the best. She's a no-nonsense, old-school detective for a young stunner. Worked on a case for me a few years back. Call her. Tell her I sent you."

"We've already met. She's lead on this case." He folded the paper and pocketed it.

Hank broke into a grin. "Excellent. Then you're in good hands. She'll take care of you." A cloud of smoke rose to the ceiling and did not go out the open window. "Maxie's like a bulldog—she won't let go until she gets her man."

"I hope so. I really want this solved. I need to understand why Curtis lost his life. Someone has to pay."

Hank leaned forward and forcefully butted out the cigarette in the ashtray. He spoke measuredly. "Let me tell you something, Devin. I've always been straight with you. Always supported you. You just tell me what you need, and I'll make it happen. But, if I'm right about his, well, God help us all if Maxie can't put an end to it."

"Thanks, Boss. I appreciate that. And hopefully, in the end, there'll be an award-winning story in it once the truth is found."

"I'll look forward to that, too. Meantime, I suggest you take some time off— compassionate leave—get your head straight. You might be acting fine, but this sort of thing almost always catches up to you when you least expect it. If you are going to investigate, you need to make sure your emotions don't cloud your judgment."

Devin nodded.

"Will there be a funeral service?" Hank asked.

"A small service at the crematorium, when I get that arranged."

"Keep me updated, will ya? I'd like to be there to offer support, if that's okay with you, of course."

"Sure thing."

Devin shook Hank's hand and left the office. The phone rang as he closed the door, and Devin glanced back. Hank was already on the call, his hands waving emphatically as he spoke. Devin felt comforted in the knowledge that he had Hank's support. That said, he had no intention of taking time off; there was too much to do, and he knew, as with any investigation, time was of the essence. He did not want to lose any clues.

5

THE N.P.Z

It wasn't the best part of town, not that Jameson was deterred by the neighborhood, a mostly poorer part of the city, older homes, many in need of work, chain link fencing, debris in the yards, and, perhaps more of a clue, the few unsavory types walking around aimlessly. Now and then, one would stop, stare at some random object, and remain transfixed. Jameson recognized that look. They were under the influence of a drug like crack, PCP, heroin—the list was long these days.

Jameson called this area the NPZ—the No Pool Zone. When you looked at aerial footage or maps, you would see there were no privately owned pools to be found anywhere here. The money just wasn't there, unlike other neighboring areas further out, closer to the water.

Jameson was familiar with this area. *It is like many neighborhoods across America,* he thought. People forget that many Americans have to live well below the poverty line, their kids growing up in gang-infested neighborhoods, having less of a chance to escape undamaged. Whether arrested for petty theft, drugs, or gang-related activities from break-ins, assault through to harder crimes like abduction, rape, and murder, the young kids in these urban areas were at much higher risk than those in more affluent areas.

It was not so visible during the day, although at certain public parks, groups of youth would congregate, hidden from view by buildings, trees, and pathways that would disguise their activities.

These days, gangs are found in every community, no matter the economic status of the neighborhoods. The mindset of these communities had been trained not to fight back against the media consensus of a national systemic racism, something that now blamed all white people for the sins of the past. It was an easy blame. Politicians had jumped on the bandwagon—all causes are political bandwagons—demanding restitution and compensation for slavery. California, ironically, was in the lead on this, and had not achieved statehood at the time of slavery, and had held no slaves. California, however, always operated to its own drumbeat. No one seemed to mind.

And then Chicago managed to pass legislation awarding many millions in restitution to those who had been affected by slavery. Jameson wasn't sure how they would calculate who would be receiving the cash handouts. *Would they need to prove their ancestors were slaves?* He wondered.

Logic seemed far removed from the state of the country these days. Everything seemed to have been turned upside-down. The influx of unlawful migrants from open border policies has resulted in thousands of undocumented people, many with criminal backgrounds, and most, no longer screened for illnesses, placed randomly and without notice in cities throughout the country. That alone seemed a recipe for disaster. The politicians, however, always held firm to the argument of America as a melting pot in order to justify the surge of migration; after all, it benefited the redrawing of districts, voting rolls, and, ultimately, would help keep certain parties in office. But at what cost? The current Congress even wanted Washington, DC, to be granted statehood to become the fifty-first state.

Jameson cared little for the politics or the politicians unless it directly affected his ability to do the job. For that, he was glad to be teamed with Maxie, who had no qualms going head to head with officials, politicians, or anyone who got in her way. He recalled one time that ended in a shouting match with a now-defunct city mayor.

"If you want me to look the other way like you do, then have me fired; otherwise, shut up," she had told the official. That mayor tried his best to have her fired, but instead, discovered her connections, as well as a successful recall petition against him. It also helped that she had the backing of the police chief. Maxie had those kinds of connections.

Jameson was born in Chicago's East Side to a single mother, Gladys. Gladys had held two jobs to afford the rent of their tiny apartment. They lived with Jameson's grandmother, Pearl, who remembered the days of segregation, and reminded both her daughter and grandson to stand up for what they believed in and to never accept a handout as a tool to silence them. Jameson remembered her as a *feisty fighter*.

"Blame, blame, blame, blame, blame," Pearl would often say to him. "Everyone gotta blame somebody for their failing. Can't just be their own damn fault. Your granddaddy, God rest his soul, never blamed anyone. He just did the work, did it well, made sure the bosses saw that. And they did. Raised him up. More pay."

"Different times, grandma," he would tell her.

"Not so different, boy," she replied. "Just different people. Nowadays, it's everybody else's fault. Never their own."

"Alleluia, praise the Lord," Gladys would say, walking into the room at the tail end of the conversation. "That's so true. If you want a fair go to a circus."

Growing up, Jameson did, like most non-whites, experience racism. He wasn't just Black—he was Jamaican Black, and he did not want to fall into the same trap of gangs that he saw his friends getting pulled into, talking him into being 'sumbody,' and dissing him when he told them he had chores to do, homework to finish, or that his mother expected him home.

He also watched as, over time, many of his friends were arrested or went to prison, while a few others were killed in rival gang drive-by shootings, straight-on battles over territory, or other 'causes' Jameson just did not believe in. Friends died of drug overdoses. One such friend, Rizzy, had died in his arms, crying out loud, lamenting his choices as his breathing shallowed, until finally, after a few harsh gasps, his body froze, eyes and mouth open wide like a fish out of water. It was a wasted life and left a solid imprint on Jameson.

Jameson swore he would never live like that. When he turned eighteen, he joined the army on the promise of money for college upon completion of service. Pearl, suffering from emphysema, and his mother Gladys, while sad, were proud to see him doing something that would give him the opportunity for a better life.

A year into his service, Pearl died in her sleep. Gladys, not wanting to break his progress, kept it a secret from him until he came home on leave that Christmas, several months later. By then, Pearl had long been buried, and while Jameson held no ill will for his mother's secret, he made her promise there would be no more surprises like that. She agreed.

Once his tour in the military ended, and using the college funds available from it, he obtained a bachelor's degree in criminal justice from the University of Illinois at Chicago and, after four years, applied for a police officer position in San Antonio, Texas. He was accepted and moved there with his mother into a nicer apartment in the Leon Valley suburb of the city.

Starting out as a rookie cop on a one-year probation, like all other cops, he incrementally passed through multiple training opportunities that included patrol, traffic detail, crime prevention, street crime, bomb squad, and K-9, each giving him a sense of his strengths and weaknesses. Most importantly—and a motto of the SAPD—Jameson had to offer a level-headed, courteous, and efficient approach to whatever situation he faced. It was called 'community policing in order to foster better relationships between law enforcement and the community. In this, Jameson excelled; he had a calm demeanor, did not fluster easily, and reacted consistently and fairly, even in the face of hostility. This earned him the respect of his superiors, peers, and even those whom he arrested. A few arrestees even thanked him for his courtesy. He received numerous letters of appreciation, including recognition and commendations for his diligence and skill.

After five years, he was eligible to apply to be a detective. The exam included a polygraph test, which he passed easily, a medical screening, and a background investigation. His commanding officer, at the time, offered a written recommendation that simply stated: 'You'd be stupid to not snap this one up. Kobe Jameson is as good as they get.' A month later, Detective Kobe Jameson was sworn in before Chief Patrick Ramsey and Deputy Chief Shaun Flugle.

He was partnered with an up-and-coming female detective, Mackenzie Michaels, a street-smart, sassy, stylish force of nature who went by the name Maxie. They worked well together and clicked almost immediately. They enjoyed intellectual discussions on all subjects, free of bias or superiority, and he came to admire her boldness in tackling anything difficult. She also had a terrific sense of humor, which she employed continuously. One time, Jameson had asked what she thought about the issue of race and how it affected their work. Maxie had simply smiled at him, playfully punching him in the shoulder before replying, "Kobe, I won't race you if you won't race me. Deal?"

It was only when Maxie wanted to leave San Antonio for Corpus Christi, potentially breaking up their partnership, that Jameson thought long and hard about the future. His mother had passed away peacefully a year earlier, happy in the knowledge that her son had succeeded. Gladys had met Maxie, approved of the dynamic, and realized that they had each other's backs. Now, with his mother gone and no other family, Jameson pondered his future.

"You're gonna miss me, aren't you?" Maxie asked him. Jameson nodded.

"Well, just say the word, and I'll make that a joint transfer."

"You can do that?"

"Let's just say that the Corpus Police Chief wants me there, and I want you there. Wanna see what happens with that?"

Jameson beamed. "Yes. I like that."

"Me, too."

And that was that. The truth was that Maxie would not

have left without him. But she failed to mention that part
to him.

JAMESON RECALLED ALL this as he walked toward X-Gym on
Trojan Street, in the Central City part of Corpus Christi, past
the high school and the Nueces County Corrections Department that served as a probation office. X-Gym wasn't much
to look at, but Jameson considered it a vital part of Corpus
Christi. The owner was a muscular former Green Beret
named Lamar Jackson. Like Jameson, Lamar believed in
grounding a change in the youth before they had the opportunity to get into trouble.

Lamar had started the gym using his savings, taking a run
down building and having community volunteers help get it
up to code, paint it, add equipment, weights, a boxing ring,
and even tee-shirts with the enlarged X-Gym logo, a fist
within a circle crossed by an X. It was a symbol of freedom,
empowerment, and, above all, honesty and trust.

The rules were simple. Lamar operated on donations to
pay costs. The gym was free to local kids, most of whom he
considered at risk of joining gangs, getting into drugs, or
worse. They were welcome there before and after school, and
on weekends, at no charge. Lamar would coach them, boxing,
weights, running, wrestling, and life lessons, turning aggres-
sion into controlled skills, focus, challenging them to rise
above whatever obstacles life had put their way. So long as
they took his pledge: No drugs. No gangs. No crime. And a
'C-plus average' at school. They had to show him progress
reports. He would randomly check them for drugs, handing
them a cup in which to urinate, and he would test it himself.

The kids knew he meant business. And because he was friends with the local police, many officers would come volunteer, and Lamar would get regular updates about the kids, further ensuring that they were on the straight path.

The kids loved it. They respected Lamar, a huge, Schwarzenegger-bulk of a man, and pushed themselves to limits they never realized they could reach.

Jameson had met Lamar when he first arrived in Corpus Christi, working with the Police Department's 'Save Our Streets' program to which Lamar was assigned. Lamar needed volunteers to come and coach alongside him—the popularity of the gym and the needs it served were too great for one man. So Jameson volunteered and brought some other officers in as well.

The kids loved Jameson. He projected confidence and strength without the need to be intimidating. He smiled a lot, held a high level of expectation, and took an interest in each kid beyond the gym. They would share personal details of their lives with him, and he would offer suggestions. He remembered their birthdays, important events, and even showed up at school events after hours. And while many kids had low respect for police in general, Jameson was accepted. He was one authority figure whom they recognized as fair.

Inside the gym, there was a changing area with a set of lockers. No locks. Lamar had announced that inside the gym, they were family, and family had to have trust. Break the trust, and Lamar would find out. Break the trust, and you would be banned from the gym. Simple. No second chances. He had no thefts. The gym remained free of graffiti tags. It was *their* gym, and they wanted it kept clean.

As Jameson entered, Lamar greeted him with a wave, happy to see him back. Lamar was in the boxing ring working with three students, each taking turns jabbing at him. He would duck and dodge appropriately. They all turned to look at Jameson as he approached. One of the kids, a 15-year-old named Tyson, stepped out of the ring and rushed over to him, bumping fists, a large grin on his face.

"Hey man, glad you made it."

"Wouldn't miss it," Jameson said. Today was a semi-tournament day, and Tyson was going to go a few rounds with a classmate. Over the previous months, Tyson had become quite close with Jameson; he was always excited to be around him.

Tyson came from a broken home; his father abandoned the family, and his mother was often hungover and unable to provide for her son's emotional needs. Tyson wasn't physically built for a fight, a near six-foot-tall scrawny Black kid who, until recently, had a very bad temper, which often resulted in fights, most of which he would lose. He didn't do drugs, didn't do particularly well in school, and Jameson took a liking to him immediately, offering advice, coaching, tutoring, and getting the boy to promise to raise his grades so he would earn the right to remain at the gym.

"When do you fight?"

"I'm up next. Maybe a few minutes. I'm glad you came."

"Remember what I told you," Jameson said. "Keep moving, do not let your opponent see what you're doing." Tyson nodded and moved back.

Lamar motioned the other boys to get out of the ring. Everyone was ready. They lined the edge of the ring, trying not to touch the ropes because Lamar didn't like that, and anxiously waited for the first fight to be called.

"First up, Tyson G and Bobby S," Lamar called out. Both boys climbed in, inserted mouth guards, and practiced jabs in their respective corners. "Fair fight. Three rounds. Ready?"

Tyson and Bobby approached each other. Compared to

Tyson, Bobby was a brick. But that meant he moved more slowly. He also packed a meaner punch, and Tyson knew he needed to avoid getting it full force. The boys bumped gloves, then retreated to their corners. Lamar rang the bell, and both came out fast. Tyson glanced at Jameson, who nodded back, motioned for Tyson to focus on his opponent. Bobby moved in, raised his fist for a power punch, only to realize that Tyson had already moved aside, the fist finding empty air. Tyson took the moment to dart in and body punch Bobby twice in the side before backing out. Bobby caught his breath.

The others were cheering. Jameson heard them rooting for Bobby, so he shouted above them, "You've got this, Tyson. Focus."

Lamar smiled. It was unlikely that Tyson would prevail, but he had to pit the boys together. The first rule of the gym was no favorites, no special treatment, everybody equal. If that meant that you had your ass handed to you, then you took that gracefully and accepted it as a lesson to be learned. With enough practice and over time, even the weakest boxer would win a fight. The difference was that the win was earned and never given.

This was one of the things that Jameson really liked about the lessons here. Life was not fair, and anybody expecting that it would be, or that the rules needed to be changed in order to make everyone win, was just fooling themselves. Life always favored the strongest, and the opportunity to become strong was just that, something to be cultivated, earned, respected, and hopefully attained. Even the strongest fighter will not win all fights. But if you want integrity and you want lessons that inner-city kids were able to learn, then you need to forget about fairness and deal with effort and practice. Those were the real-life skills.

Even if Tyson won this fight, the lesson was the same: one of personal strength, meeting the obstacles that life presented, and learning how to handle them. Graciously.

In the real world, this translated to kids who made efforts, understood their weaknesses, and were able to avoid gangs, drugs, and other pitfalls that others wouldn't or couldn't. The hope was that this would translate to jobs and better opportunities, breaking the cycle of poverty and welfare.

Tyson dodged Bobby's fist, managing to get a punch in just as the bell rang. First round over. Jameson joined him in the corner as he rinsed with some water.

"You move fast. Make him think you're going to move, but hold back, let him come to you. Then strike," Jameson advised. "His momentum will increase the power of your punch."

Tyson nodded, replaced the mouth guard, and, as the bell rang, leaped up and toward his opponent. For a few more minutes, Tyson led Bobby around, ducking in and out of range, long enough for Bobby to learn the pattern. Each time Bobby tried to anticipate, pushing himself further forward, exposing himself. Finally, after a half-dozen attempts, Tyson followed Jameson's advice and, on the move he would have made, held back. Bobby lunged forward, anticipating the move, right into Tyson's space. With his arm ready, he let off as hard a punch as he was able, straight to Bobby's stomach. His fist made solid contact, and the air left Bobby's lungs. Without waiting, Tyson repeated the punch with the other hand. Bobby staggered for breath, dazed, then fell to the floor, clutching at his stomach. Lamar knelt down beside him for the count. "One...two...." *Ding Ding!* Lamar stood, grabbed Tyson's left hand, and held it high into the air. "Tyson G!"

The group of boys, all seriously surprised, began to yelp

and cheer. Tyson, stunned that he had won, looked at Jameson, who was beaming. Jameson gave him a thumbs up!

Lamar exited the ring and approached Jameson. "You've brought out the best in that boy. You should be proud."

Jameson nodded. "He just needed someone to steer him in the right direction. We all do."

"True enough," Lamar replied with a throaty laugh. "I think your partner does most of the steering, though!" He winked.

"She does keep me on my toes, for sure."

"You should bring her down sometime."

"Maxie? Boxing?" Jameson laughed. That was quite the visual.

Tyson walked up to him. "You did well," he told the boy.

"Thanks for the advice."

"You did all the work," Jameson said. "Just remember, in life, like that fight, sometimes you will feel like you just cannot win. But instead of getting angry, learn what the weakness of those against you is. Bide your time. Find your opportunity. Then strike."

Tyson wiped the sweat from his forehead that had trickled into his eyes. "Is that what you do when you work?"

"Sometimes. Being a detective means learning everything you can learn. Watch everything. You cannot rush. You must learn patience."

"I'll work on that," Tyson said. "May I get a ride home after the next fight?"

"Sure," Jameson said. "Your mom will be really proud of your win."

Tyson rolled his eyes. "If she's sober," he said, walking off before Jameson replied. It wasn't that the boy was wrong; his mother was an alcoholic. In Jameson's eyes, however, she was still Tyson's mother. Better or worse, she was doing what she was able. After Tyson's father had abandoned them, she took it hard. That she was able to hold a job at all amazed Jameson. She worked as a bagger at the nearby HEB supermarket, a job that was just barely enough to pay their rent and utilities, let alone food. Local charitable groups brought in food, in addition to her welfare food stamps. If any kid was at risk of running to the gangs for some sense of order, Tyson would be it.

It took almost a month before Tyson would even open up to him. Tyson's opinion of do-gooders, as he had labeled Jameson, was that they served to satisfy their need to do something, then left once that need was satisfied. But Jameson didn't leave. Instead, he pushed harder. He showed up at Tyson's apartment, spoke with his mother, and offered to work with Tyson one-on-one.

On days he worked at the gym, he would give Tyson a ride home. Tyson was aware of that, but he always asked, never wanting Jameson to think he was being taken for granted.

"How long you gonna be around?" he asked Jameson one day.

"Ten minutes," Jameson replied jokingly, then, seeing that the boy was not laughing, nodded and said simply, "As long as you want me around."

"How long is that?"

Jameson took out his business card, turned it over, and scribbled his cell phone number, then handed it to Tyson. "That's my cell. It is for you. If you need to talk. If you're in a situation. If you feel sad. There is no time limit. I will be around as long as you want me to be."

Tyson stared at the card. No one had ever done anything that made him feel important. This small business card meant the world to him. "I'll ask your mom to add me to your school contact. They can list me as your uncle. How's that?"

Tyson smiled. "That's excellent." He stared at the card. "That's very good. Uncle J," he said with a broad grin.

Jameson grinned. "Uncle J, yeah, that's cool."

Tyson had only called him one time. It was six months earlier, late one night. He had been in the park on his skateboard and had been ambushed by young gang members from the neighborhood. He had tried leaving, but they stopped him. One punched him in the face and stole his skateboard. To avoid the beating that was coming if he stayed, Tyson ran. He was built for speed. He managed to elude the teens, found a phone booth outside a gas station, and called Jameson. Jameson had instructed him to keep out of sight, arriving soon after to take Tyson home. Tyson nursed a black eye. Jameson gave him some ice wrapped in a towel and told him to press it against the eye.

Once he felt confident that Tyson was fine, Jameson drove to the park where the assault had happened. The teens were still there. They stood looking at Jameson defiantly as he got out of his car. Jameson shook his head, all the while staring at them. They knew who he was and recognized that he was a cop. He saw by the slight shift in their body positions that they understood they had just been marked. Their demeanor softened, becoming more submissive, and they scurried off.

Two days later, Jameson showed up at Tyson's apartment with a new skateboard and a flip phone. He advised Tyson to avoid being on the street at night, but if he was in trouble, he could at least make a call. He also suggested Tyson get serious about the boxing program at the X-Gym.

ON THE RIDE HOME, little was said. Jameson broke the silence.

"I was proud of the way you handled yourself today."

"Thanks."

"You okay?"

Tyson nodded. "I just wanted to thank you for what you do for me. I know you don't have to." Jameson looked at the boy.

"I like being a part of your life. Uncle J, remember?"

Tyson stifled a laugh. He nodded.

"And thank you for always doing your best. I realize that it is not always easy. I know you wish some things were different. But I promised you that I would always be there for you. Because I *want* to. I care about you." He reached over and ruffled Tyson's hair.

"I never thought I would win that fight."

"See, if you think you cannot do something, it will not happen. You have to believe you can do it. Then you figure out how you can do it. That is what you did today."

As he pulled over in front of Tyson's apartment, they both got out. "You okay?"

Tyson nodded and wiped at his eyes with the back of his hand. Jameson extended an arm for a fist bump, but instead, Tyson leaned in for a full hug. Jameson closed his arms around the boy and held him tightly before letting go.

Tyson bounded up the steps to the first-floor apartment, waved once to Jameson before ducking inside. For a moment, Jameson stood there relishing the moment. It felt empowering to make a difference in Tyson's life. It was the closest thing to having a family of his own. *One kid. One life. You cannot save them all,* he reminded himself, getting back into his car and driving off. *But you can always try!*

6

ARRANGEMENTS TO MAKE

After leaving the *Tribune*, Devin had stopped at the store to grab a frozen meal for dinner. It wasn't that he couldn't cook; just that his usual day would be long, and by the time he got home, cooking was the last thing on his mind.

He lived on the top floor in a small three-story building—Baypoint Apartments on Ennis-Joslin Road. The apartment complex was pleasant—an excellent bay view, pool, on-site gym, as well as a convenient location. The rent wasn't cheap, but with his job, he did get to enjoy a few perks. That and the fact that he was a single guy, his expenses were kept to a minimum.

And yet, since he had learned of Curtis's murder, his mind wouldn't stop exploring the possible reasons and suspects, so much so that he was exhausted early. He had carelessly tossed the frozen dinner into the microwave, guessing at the time. When it notified him it was done, he grabbed it and put it on a plate, turning it upside down so the contents would come out, grabbed a beer, sat at his small dinette, and wolfed the meal down. It took no time to finish. For a moment, he wished he had bought two meals—one seemed small, but after a few more swigs of beer, he felt full. He tossed the remnants into the trash can and decided to turn in.

The plan was to get up early and handle all the cremation arrangements. He hoped that it could happen the same day or, at the latest, the next day, even though it was short notice.

Despite his exhaustion, Devin had another near-sleepless night. Tossing fitfully, he resisted the urge to just get up and call it quits. He'd drift in and out of a light sleep—REM, that part with rapid eye movements and vivid dreams that felt like they lasted hours when, in fact, only minutes had passed. There were dreams of Curtis, older memories of time spent at the Stanton's Austin, Texas home. Then the images distorted into nonsensical fragments, much as dreams tend to do, leaving only the realism of the emotions felt. Again, he snapped awake, staring at the ceiling before deciding to get up.

He made a coffee and sat on his balcony, watching the darkness outside slowly give way to morning.

As soon as they were open, he called various crematoriums to check on price and availability, and to ensure they didn't sound like they would be inflating prices or taking advantage of his grief. Reid, his grandfather, had warned him of this in one of their many conversations about life. "Watch out for people who take advantage of emotionally difficult times," he had said. At the time, he was talking with Devin about the plans when he and Doris passed on. Reid, always the conscientious one, had made as many arrangements as possible, believing that those left behind should be free to grieve without having to worry about the details of funerals or cremations. And so he had arranged everything, including a short video message to Curtis and Devin. He wanted it done right, and he wanted to spare them the added burden of decisions he had already made.

When they died the previous year, days apart from each other, Devin and Curtis had little to arrange. They held a small service, and both Reid and Doris had elected cremation over burial. Reid firmly believed that at the end of the day, cemeteries would be dug up to make room for condos. That, and the futility of making loved ones come to cry over a piece of manicured grass. "Our souls won't be there, you know?" he had explained.

Devin ultimately settled on the same company that handled Reid and Doris—*Silent Dreams Cremations*. He called and left the contact information for the coroner, asking only that they do something nice for Curtis. Leroy Spindler, the owner and lead mortician, promised that he would, thanking Devin for thinking of them.

And that's that, Devin thought after he had ended the call. It seemed so easy, almost casual, even though he knew that it was not. *Dust to dust... and all that,* he thought.

It gave Devin a chance to reflect on his own life. Looking back, weren't the years spent chasing leads for stories just Devin passing through the motions of making a difference, being relevant in an ever-changing world? It was a question that often plagued him. *What was it that Shakespeare said, he wondered?*

"All the world's a stage,
And all the men and women merely players;
They have their exits and their entrances;
And one man in his time plays many parts...."

It seemed to be accurate enough. At least to Devin. Life was so fleeting. He would never have imagined that he would be here, struggling to find Curtis's murderer, fighting to avoid falling down the rabbit hole of lies and deception that seemed to permeate everything.

Spindler called Devin back within the hour. He had all the plans ready for Curtis's service and cremation. "Is four this afternoon too late?"

"That's fine," Devin said.

"I've spoken with the coroner, and we will be picking up his body soon. Do you have any special requests?"

"No. It will be a closed casket. Respectful. Decent," Devin said.

"Of course."

The call ended. Devin sent Rob a text giving him the information. Then he left a message with Hank's assistant.

The sun was bright against a cloudless sky. He saw the calm water. A variety of birds were flying over the boats: cranes, seagulls, and pelicans were the main ones, all vying for their fish meals. By far, the pelicans were the most dramatic, lazily ascending to the sky, then suddenly folding their wings and dive-bombing the water. Devin watched. It wasn't the most effective method of fishing, with a score ratio of one in four tries. Nonetheless, it was hypnotic watching the show they created.

There was an element of peace watching them. It was survival. *If only life were that pure,* he thought. *No lies, no deceptions. What you saw was what you got, with no pretense.*

He fetched a soda from the fridge and sat down again. Below, he saw the pool. A few kids with some scantily-clad women attempting to tan in the new sunlight of the day occupied the area. In the time he had lived here, he had never used the pool. It wasn't that he didn't like the pool; he just found it difficult to sit still doing nothing. *It's called relaxing,* he reminded himself. *Something people did here and there to recharge their minds and bodies.* Just not his style.

If he didn't have a story to follow, he felt restless. The world was brimming with stories, everything from complex and sinister plots to heartwarming moments. And Devin enjoyed the art of storytelling. There was a purity in the telling, weaving the words to express a viewpoint, a visual, or a character trait, bringing the subjects to life, finding the angle of relevance that would elevate the story from the mundane to the powerful.

So much time was spent pursuing the stories that he hadn't dated for quite some time, either. Dating was majorly time-consuming, and for the most part, the women he had asked out lacked the depth he was seeking. He assumed he would meet the right person at some point and reminded himself not to get obsessed with it until then.

The eulogy he would write about Curtis, he knew, would be a tribute to a family member. Curtis had been a decent guy and lived a decent life. And while he was not one whose life had drama assaulting him at every turn, Devin believed that the life Curtis had led was one of honesty and decency in a world where both qualities seemed ever harder to find.

This was Devin's superpower, if it could be said that he had one. He visualized stories as emotions and words swirling together, a vast ocean of this alternate language that defied simplification. *How do you feel a flower?* He pondered. *Or a smile?* Music was far easier; music affected something in the brain that was affiliated with emotions, and music had that tendency to bind reality together. Devin noted that a motion picture without a soundtrack was incomplete. Likewise, a story with the wrong words failed in its primary purpose.

He had his notebook open and was free-flowing words about Curtis to use, but at this stage, they were just a bank of words without form. In his mind, he saw how he wished them framed, then felt the underlying emotional pull that would allow him to select choice words. Finally, almost intuitively, he would settle on the phrasing, intonation, and flow, and the writing would begin, a symphony of that which explained reality, without explaining anything at all.

Curtis Delaney knew that the pulse of life demanded him to constantly strive to improve, not just the standard of work, which itself was already extremely high, but also his connection to the work and the people with whom he worked.

Devin read the passage back. "Pulse of life," he said. "Ugh!" He drew a line through that part.

Curtis Delaney held himself to a standard most people could never attain. His intuition, rich and balanced, not unlike a symphony, compelled him to always assume the needs of his family and friends over his own, and to provide everyone he encountered with honesty and decency above all else. He did this not because he had to. He did so because that is how he had been created. It was not a decision he would make. It just was the way it was, and all who met him were made better as a result.

He read it over again, then closed his notebook. That was not the final version, he knew. In the same way, Curtis was intuitive about all things financial. Devin was the same way with what he wrote.

He took another sip of the soda and stared out at the windsurfers skimming the water, their curved chutes pulling them on their boards where the wind decreed. Periodically, a strong gust would lift one out of the water, twenty or so feet in the air, before they would fall back again, sometimes unceremoniously losing their balance.

Curtis parasailed, Devin thought. *Poor Curtis.*

THE STRANGE MAN was again in the shadows. This time, he had left his car off to one side and, with binoculars in hand, had walked to the front side of Devin's apartment complex, just outside the fencing, where he was out of sight but could see Devin's balcony and Devin sitting nursing a soda as he gazed out.

The man also lived in an apartment complex, just not this one—he could not afford this level of rent. Instead, he lived closer to the Crosstown Parkway, in an area that was somewhat rundown, not at all *glitzy* like these apartments and condominiums, not that the man held any resentment toward those who enjoyed such a lifestyle. It was just not convenient for what he did, with so little time spent there.

The man's apartment was dark. He lived alone. He had purchased a large wall painting of a sailboat to fill one wall and another of a horse for the adjacent wall. Burgundy curtains were closed, keeping the rooms cool but dark. To one side, a dehumidifier was running—many people used them to keep the moisture level at a more comfortable level without the cost of constantly running an air conditioner.

Dishes were piled in the sink—he was never home long enough to keep them clean, so he resorted to getting fed up and spending a few hours washing them, doing laundry, and any other housekeeping that needed to be done.

He was not so interested in Devin at this time as he was in anyone else who might come visit. Devin was easy to predict, the man had concluded. But as far as this murder was concerned, others were involved and would be problematic for him. He needed to understand as much about Devin's life as possible and leave nothing to chance.

After a time, seeing nothing unusual, the man left, driving further down Ennis Joslin until the intersection of Nile Rd. There, on his right, was a parking lot to a nature preserve, a place to walk along wooden guide paths a few hundred yards toward the bay. The path allowed visitors to explore wild bird habitats along the way. He enjoyed this spot as it gave him a sense of peace when he had so little peace the rest of the time.

As he walked further along the wooden trail, the sounds of the birds increased until, at the end of the trail, the sound was very loud. The gulls packed the muddy flats of the bay. Others were flying around. He leaned over the wooden observation deck and stared out at the water. There was no one to disturb him here. Surrounded by greenery on one side and water on the other, as well as the cacophony of sounds from a variety of birds, he could think clearly, assess what he had learned, and formulate a plan.

He would wait in this area until night fell and then return to the office building to retrieve the surveillance devices he would need to document his investigation. After a half-hour enjoying the solitude, he returned to his car, a pale blue Ford Fiesta, slipped on a night shade to block out the light, then pushed his car seat back and went to sleep. By the time he awoke, it was dark outside. He took a moment to orient himself and gather his thoughts.

He checked his watch. Six-thirty. He would have plenty of time to drive over to the office, stopping and picking up a coffee on the way. Once there, he would have to pick the lock on the back door, hack into the communication box, disable the alarm, and then be able to take his time. He had to be thorough.

He needed access to the computer and phone logs, which he hoped would lead to some information he could use. Curtis had known the truth, and any evidence would have been there unless Curtis had managed to pass it along to someone else. Someone like Devin. So far, his observations of

Devin led the man to doubt that anything was in his possession. And the man's earlier efforts, when he had ransacked the office, had also proved fruitless.

Whether the information was still in the office somewhere or whether Meeker had it, he had to discover. That was the purpose of this part of the investigation. *Trust no one,* he reminded himself.

His cellphone chimed with the arrival of a message. He glanced at it. *Anything new?* The message read.

Patience, he typed back.

"*I have none left,*" the reply said.

"*I know,*" he cautiously typed back. "Soon."

7

GOODBYE, CURTIS

The crematorium was simple and nondescript. An outer lobby was for the family to sit comfortably while the body was prepared. Burgundy-colored, velvet curtains acted as wall coverings, muting any sound. From two small speakers mounted to the wall, Muzak was softly playing.

Leroy Spindler, the owner and operator, greeted Devin in the lobby. He was a short man, dark hair slicked back, cleanly shaved, simple black suit and tie. "It is regrettable to have to see you again so soon," he said, his facial expression bending into what he considered an appropriate gesture of remorse. *He's wearing makeup*, Devin noted, seeing the face powder and eyeliner, giving the man's face a rubbery look.

"Thank you," Devin replied. "This is Rob Meeker, Curtis's friend and business partner."

Spindler shook his hand. "Condolences."

Hank joined them, shook Devin's hand, patted him on the shoulder, and Devin motioned for him to sit.

"Do you know how many visitors we will have today?" Spindler asked.

"This is it," Devin said. "Curtis wanted small."

"Very well. If you'll all follow me inside." He turned and walked through a doorway that led into the small chapel. There were no windows here; more of the burgundy curtains hung on each wall. Chairs had been set out, several rows of ten. This permitted the crematorium to adjust to the size of the mourners rather than looking like a church.

A metal guide rail with rollers across the length extended from the right side of the room to the left. Here, the coffin would travel, stopping in the center, next to the altar, where family and friends could express their final sentiments, before continuing on the track and exiting the room on the other side via a small door that rose up and down again once the coffin had passed through. The whole thing seemed bizarre to Devin, not at all like the last service that he attended here.

The coffin seemed a totally unnecessary touch. The body would be cremated. The encasement was merely a transport vessel that would be cleaned, reused, opened for some viewings, and otherwise closed.

While the back of the chapel was darkened, the front was brightly illuminated from overhead spotlights, the beam aimed at the altar. Behind it, Curtis's coffin was already in place, dark brown wood with a deep green wreath atop. The rail on each side was draped with a burgundy covering matching the wall curtains. This would all be removed at the end of the service before the actual cremation.

"Mr. Parker, if you would like to say a few words," Spindler suggested. Devin nodded and moved to the altar. From his jacket pocket, he removed a folded piece of paper.

He smoothed it against the altar, then looked up at Rob and Hank.

"There's nothing I can say that Rob doesn't already know. Hank, thank you for coming and being supportive. Curtis was my cousin, although we had no blood relationship. We were raised more as brothers than as cousins and spent many years together. So I can attest to his character. Curtis Delaney held himself to a standard most people could never attain. His intuition, rich and balanced, not unlike a symphony, compelled him to always assume the needs of his family and friends over his own and to provide everyone he encountered with honesty and decency above all else. He did this not because he had to. He did so because he had been created that way. It was not a decision he would make. It was the way it was, and all who encountered him were made better as a result."

Devin dabbed at his eyes. Even though he had written the words, the emotions now hit him, as though he had heard them for the first time, as though he had only now learned Curtis had died. "I'll miss you, brother. And I will find your killer. You have my promise. You deserved so much better."

Devin stood there, at a loss for more words, numbed to the realization of the finality of this moment. Soon, the body would be subjected to 1,600 degrees of heat produced by the furnace into which it would go. After the process was done, in just under three hours, what remained would be the skeleton in crumbled ash form—about six pounds worth. This crematorium, Devin recalled, provided the remains in a burgundy-colored velvet pouch placed inside a small, tasteful porcelain jar.

Devin remembered Curtis asking, "Would it be strange if I kept Pops and Gram on the mantle?" Devin had not thought it strange at all. After six months, Curtis called him up one morning and asked if Devin would join him at their property in Austin; he had decided they should be scattered on the land they loved. Curtis still owned the place, all two hundred acres of countryside. They scattered the ashes by the gardens Gram had spent countless hours nurturing. Curtis had left the pots on each side of the archway leading to their front door.

Devin wondered whether he should scatter Curtis there as well. It was not something he had thought about, and he knew at some point he would need to, although there was no rush.

He nodded, looking out at the empty seats, Rob, and Hank. *Curtis had so many friends*, he thought, that *we could have filled three rooms this size*. But, of course, it was not his wish. Instead, he had arranged for them all to receive a notice in the mail, along with the words he had just read, typed on a card. He would end it with a personal message reminding them how important each had been to Curtis.

Curtis believed time should be spent with loved ones while alive. Having a service after death seemed, to him, like an afterthought. Devin hoped he would have approved of this small one.

He stepped down. Rob stood as though he would speak, but then stopped cold, shaking his head. "I can't, man," he said. "Can't."

"It's fine, Rob," Devin assured him. "There's no need. I know what you meant to each other."

Spindler approached Devin. "Excellent words," he said. Devin nodded. "We have no formality, as you remember from before, from this point. Last time, you and Mr. Curtis left. You are welcome, however, to press the button on the podium, which will send Mr. Curtis through the gateway."

Devin nodded. Spindler removed the covering from the

rails and dropped them to rest on the floor beneath, then checked that the coffin was firmly on the tracks before motioning Devin closer, pointing at the button underneath the podium. Devin felt for it, found and pressed it. The coffin began to slowly move to the door on the left. As it approached, the door opened, and the coffin passed through. The doors closed again. The whole process seemed more like a contrived Disneyland ride rather than an actual part of a funeral.

Spindler nodded his approval. He had devised this system. It was peaceful, efficient, and he had named each part. There was 'the reflection' when the body first arrived at the podium. 'The gateway' was where it would pass through. And he termed the final process "the transition."

"Mr. Curtis will *transition* for several hours. We can deliver his remains to you at your convenience, or you may come to pick them up tomorrow."

"Thank you," Devin answered. "I'm not sure when I will be home, so better I come tomorrow to collect him."

"We shall be ready for you," Spindler said. "Thank you all for being here. I am certain Mr. Curtis would have been touched."

Hank patted Devin on the shoulder. "A fine eulogy. You okay?"

Devin nodded. "A bit numb. Thanks for coming, Hank. I appreciate it."

"Of course. Can I give you a lift?"

"I have my bike outside, but thanks just the same."

He watched Hank leave. Rob said nothing. He extended his hand as he passed. Devin shook it. "It will be okay," he said. "It will take some time, but we will survive this."

Rob nodded. "Whenever you're ready to go through his things at the office—anytime, man."

"I appreciate that." Devin realized he would also have to go through Curtis's house—there was no other family to do that, either."

Devin was the last one to leave. Outside, he got on his bike and stared at the building for a few moments. He had seen enough of death over the last few years. Once he had found Curtis's killer, he hoped he would be able to enjoy some peace, maybe take a trip abroad—a change of scenery would be priceless.

ACROSS THE STREET, the man in the pale blue Ford Fiesta was watching through binoculars. He had seen Hank come out, light up a cigarette, and then Rob leave. He knew Devin was still inside and was waiting to see if anyone else would come out, but no one did. He jotted a few notes, the day and time, then waited for Devin to leave before he did. But first, he made a phone call.

"It seems I am not making much progress," he said impatiently. "You should probably intervene. Unless you want me to." He ended the call.

SEARCHING FOR CLUES

Jameson had the CCTV footage on the computer when Maxie returned from a coffee run. She handed him his cup, then sat down and sipped at her latte. He thanked her and stared at her. She looked back at him.

"Yes, I know what you're thinking, and you're right. The office coffee tastes like crap, and no self-respecting person should drink it," she said with a smile and took a sip. "All better now?"

He laughed. "So, what did you think of the cousin and the business partner?"

"What did you think, Kobe?" she fired back.

Jameson looked thoughtful. "The cousin was genuine. I do not think he was involved. The business partner...."

"Yes, go on...."

"Something was not right."

Maxie nodded. "Agreed. Not only that, but what are the chances that they would have a break-in with nothing stolen, just as we are starting our investigation?"

"Are you saying that it was staged?"

Maxie shook her head. "I'm just saying—no such thing as a coincidence, Kobe. There is more to this. And I will discover it."

"You always do," he replied, turning back to start the video footage.

"What have we got?"

The video was shot from a camera across the alley. An informant had tipped them off that this was the place of the murder. The field of view showed the street and the alleyway. A light-colored car pulled up. A man got out of the driver's side and went to the passenger side. He opened the door and pulled out a body—Curtis—and dragged him into the alley. Then he left. The darkness impeded facial recognition. The video was grainy. There would be no enlarging it.

Maxie and Jameson were still watching the feed. After the car had driven off, Jameson reached over to shut off the feed.

"Wait!" Maxie said, pointing at the screen. "Just wait." She had spotted a shadow from the streetlamp. A figure was coming into view. A woman, a homeless woman, pushing a shopping cart. The video quality was poor, but she was wearing clothing that seemed too loose. She turned her head furtively, checking that no one was around, then scurried past the body, pushing her cart, not stopping to examine the scene for anything useful to her.

"She looks scared," Maxie said. "Knew better than to hang around."

"I would be, too, if I had just seen someone dump a body," Jameson said.

"Play it again. We have to find her. She may be able to identify the killer."

The video replayed. Maxie scrutinized the images. "We're going to have to hit the streets and see if anyone can direct us to her. Do you have any other feeds?"

"There is one camera a block further up, but it showed no car and...I did not wait to look for the woman," he said, noticing her look. "She may have been delayed."

"Good idea," Maxie said, settling back and enjoying her coffee.

Jameson located the identification code for the camera he was looking for, entered his own code, selected the time stamp, and waited for the feed to start. There was no car, as he had already observed. He allowed the video to play out, then realized that Maxie was watching over his shoulder. After five minutes had elapsed, she tapped him on the shoulder to let him know that it was enough.

"That should help us narrow the search."

"It is still a lot of territory."

"It is. But we can do it with style. Yes?"

Jameson smiled. "Yes."

THE AREA around People's Street and Water Street was not a low-class area by any means. You had a smattering of smaller buildings, most no taller than 10 stories, spread out unevenly so as not to appear densely packed.

On every corner, there were restaurants, pubs, coffee shops, and hotels of one kind or another—ornate fronts with palm trees spaced evenly throughout. Traffic was light. The streets were clean. Hardly the place to dump a body. But, like every city, homelessness was an ongoing issue. These unfortunate people lived in hidden alcoves, under bridges or overpasses, and were also walking the streets, some with shopping carts carrying their only possessions. Periodically, you would pass one of them and, unlike the scammers holding cardboard signs at intersections while hiding their cell phones, when faced with genuine homelessness, there was no mistaking it. Beyond the worn or torn clothing, dirtied skin, matted hair, they had little life in their eyes—most people didn't even bother to look. Most people preferred to look away, pretending they were a blip on the normalcy of their own lives, failing to realize that the line between normal and homeless was hair-thin.

Maxie and Jameson were looking for one person in particular: the woman with the cart that had walked by the CCTV cameras moments after Curtis's body was dumped. They had a vague idea from the out-of-focus video of what she looked like. Whether she would look the same today remained to be seen.

They walked into a coffee shop and showed the grainy photo print from the video to the manager. He seemed annoyed that his routine was being interrupted, but he obliged and examined the image. He shook his head and announced he had never seen her. Next, they tried the hotel next door. One of the janitors, a younger Hispanic male, had been on duty the night of the murder. He recognized the woman. She was often seen walking by the hotel, sometimes asking the patrons for "spare change."

"What is spare change, anyway?" he asked.

"Do you know where I can find her?" Maxie asked. The man shrugged. "Most of the regulars hang out behind the diner, up one street. There's an alley behind that's dark and away from the street, so the cops don't bother them."

Maxie thanked him, gave him ten bucks for his time, and they left, walking over to the next street, as the janitor had described. Walking toward the back, they could see a few people—they had set up camp with tents in the opposite corner against a fence, and a few shopping carts parked haphazardly.

The woman from the video feed was sorting her cart. She couldn't have been older than forty, her hair matted and her face stained with dirt. She spotted Maxie and Jameson and scurried off to one side, trying to make herself invisible to them.

"It's okay," Maxie said. "We're not here to hurt you. May I speak with you for a minute?" Maxie had her hand outstretched.

The woman stared at her, then reluctantly nodded. "It's about the body, isn't it?" she said. She was missing one of her front teeth. Maxie nodded.

"What's your name?"

"Marjorie," the woman said.

"Marjorie, would you tell us what you saw?"

Jameson opened his notepad and started to jot down what transpired.

"Didn't see much," Marjorie said, going back to sorting. "I was walking along, minding my own when a car comes up past me. Going fast it was. Thought it would hit the wall, but it didn't. Scared me. A man got out one side and pulled the body from the other side. He took it up just in the alley, then left it there."

"Did he see you?"

The woman shook her head. "Don't want him to know either."

"Can you describe him?"

"Big man. White, I think. Had a red cap with a big fishing hook."

"The Hooks," Jameson muttered. That was the Corpus Christi Baseball team. Jameson followed them.

"Do you think you could recognize him if you saw him again?"

"Maybe." A shocked look crossed her face. "I ain't gonna testify, if that's what you're getting at. I won't."

Maxie tried to calm her. "It's fine. I understand he scared you. But if I showed you some photographs, do you think you could identify him that way?"

Marjorie thought about it for a moment and nodded. "So long as I don't have to testify. No way. You have to promise."

Maxie nodded. "I promise. Marjorie, but I have to get the photos from my office. If I come back later, will you be here?"

Marjorie nodded. "This is my home."

"Terrific. I really appreciate your help, Marjorie." Maxie reached for her purse and pulled out a twenty-dollar bill. She handed it to Marjorie. "Get something nice to eat, okay?" Marjorie nodded and smiled, exposing the gap in her teeth. "Good. I'll see you soon." Marjorie nodded again.

Maxie and Jameson walked back to the car.

"Why didn't you just show Marjorie the mugshots from your phone?" Jameson asked. He knew she would have a reason; she rarely acted on impulse.

"I need to add another photo I don't have on my phone, yet," she replied.

"Who?"

Maxie smiled. "Patience, grasshopper. You'll see."

9

TARGET DEVIN

When Devin arrived home, he parked his bike and meandered through the complex, past the pool area, to the mailboxes by the office. With the few envelopes—mostly bills—in hand, he walked back to the elevator. It seemed almost silly to take an elevator up two levels, but it was something he didn't think about until he was already inside. Even then, only because it was a painstakingly slow ride, he reminded himself to *start taking the stairs.* Not to mention that the elevator was frequently inoperative.

In many ways, his apartment complex served as his castle, a place where he felt safe, surrounded by others, especially people who did not realize he was a reporter, or that, some years back, he *almost* received a Pulitzer Prize for the exposé of the secret world of child labor inside the United States.

Almost winning a Pulitzer is much like nearly winning an Olympic medal, Devin thought. *No one remembered the runner-up.* There was also no celebrity involved, *thankfully,* he thought, although he was often recognized due to his other articles in the local paper.

He got out of the elevator and walked to his door. He noticed it was ajar. Carefully, with his foot, he pushed it open further. No one was inside that he could tell, but the place was in shambles. And dark. His furniture had been turned over, books dumped. It was a mess.

African wall carvings he had collected, which used to line the walls by the entry, were now scattered across the floor, one broken. The intruder must have carelessly stepped on it. As he walked in further, he realized his laptop was gone. After heading down the hall, checking his bedroom, he placed his mail on the small table next to the couch—the only thing still standing— then closed the front door.

He was feeling angry—more angry than violated. Instinctively, he knew this was connected to Curtis, and the anger was more at the fact that he was missing what was really behind this.

The fridge door was also open. He pulled out a beer, popped the cap, then slammed the fridge shut. He put down his satchel, remembering that he still had the photo he had taken from Curtis's office—he had forgotten to take it out. Despite the chaos, he now placed it on the mantle. *It belongs there*, he thought, finding the image lightened his mood. *Those were wonderful days.*

He walked out on his deck, sat down, and admired the view of the marina. The weather was bright, sunny, unlike the rest of his day. *This day has been a nightmare*, he told himself. Sitting there, he looked back, surveying the damage while sipping his beer. *Could this day get any worse?*

He pulled out his phone, looked up his call log, and found Maxie's earlier call to him. He had her card somewhere, but this seemed the easiest way to reach her. He pressed redial and let it ring.

"Maxie, it's Devin," he said when she answered. "Sorry to

bother you, but I just got home—my place has been turned upside-down. It seems the vandalism is contagious."

"Don't touch anything. We'll be right over," she said, and abruptly ended the call.

"Okay," he said aloud, after the call had already ended, slipping the phone back into his pocket. While he waited, his eyes dropped to the pool area. Again, the area was crowded. He could see some women alone, lying on the pool recliners, enjoying the sunshine.

I should go down there and just get away from here, he thought. Then talked himself out of it again. The thought of having to start a conversation with a stranger seemed daunting. Conversations leading to potential dating were the worst. These were filled with fake sentiments and over-extended enthusiasm. *One heck of a lot of work*, he reminded himself, and this was why he had not dated in what seemed like forever. It wasn't for lack of wanting—his heart was not into the amount of effort it would take. Besides, most of his friends seemed to burn through relationships like they changed clothes. The happily-ever-after scenario seemed to be elusive. It would have been just another complication in his already complicated life.

A HALF-HOUR LATER, Maxie arrived with Jameson and two uniformed cops. The officers went through his place, making sure that no one was there—a redundancy as far as Devin was concerned. Jameson took a few photographs, checked for prints, and then jotted some notes that he kept to himself. Once done, he dismissed one of the two officers, while the other was assigned to watch the apartment for the next day, just as a precaution. Jameson started to help Devin pick up the mess.

"They did not kick your door in," Jameson noted. "They picked the lock—professional job." Devin had not thought of that. Nothing surprised him at the moment.

"Beer?" Devin offered them both.

Maxie looked at her watch. "Sure," she said, glancing at Jameson. He also nodded. Devin fetched them each a bottle, then pulled one of the dinette chairs outside, so they all had a place to sit.

"This is not a coincidence," he said.

"No," Jameson said.

"There are no...," she started to say. He finished the sentence for her.

"...no coincidences."

She nodded at him. "Which begs the question of what they are looking for, because they're obviously looking for something. Or you're suddenly extremely popular."

"What was taken?" Jameson asked.

"My laptop is gone. Not much there. Most of the work stuff is cloud-based, so it is all backed up."

"Anything else?"

Devin shook his head no.

"Tell me more about you and Curtis," Maxie asked. "You're cousins? There's a connection I must be missing."

Devin took a mouthful of beer and swallowed hard. "Technically...no," he said. "We're not cousins. Biologically, we're not even related. That's how we used to explain it. It made it easy for people to accept. Curtis and I went to the same private school on the East Coast. We were best friends, grew up as neighbors."

Maxie was studying him, and he knew it.

"Look, we both lost our parents on the same day. Curtis's

biological grandparents, Reid and Doris Stanton, raised us after that. We were ten years old at the time, and all we had was each other."

"Wow," Maxie said. "How did your parents both come to die at the same time?"

"Plane crash," Devin said, taking a large sip of the beer. "They were all passengers on Flight 93. September 11th, 2001."

Maxie's hand rose to her mouth. She had not expected that piece of information and was suddenly caught off guard. "Oh my gosh.... I am so very sorry. How terrible."

Devin nodded. "Yes. It was. We were in school at the time. The principal called us into his office and sat us down. There was just no easy way to tell us. Reid and Doris had phoned as soon as they knew. Even though they were devastated, their first thought was for Curtis and me. They rushed to the school. All we knew at that time was that the passengers had fought back against the terrorists and forced the plane to crash in a field in Pennsylvania rather than their target. The White House, I believe. I can't imagine how much bravery it took."

"Your parents are heroes," Jameson said. "You should be proud of their sacrifice."

Devin nodded. "I am. We were. It bonded Curtis and I. Thankfully, we had Pops and Gram—the Reids—to lean on. Curtis's mother was their daughter. Because I had no one, they took me in, and they legally raised me."

"Where are your ... grandparents now?"

"They both passed away last year. First, Pops died after a battle with cancer. Gram passed away a few days later, with a broken heart. We were glad they passed together. They had so much love for each other, and for us. Now, Curtis...murder." He stopped to regain his composure. "I just came from the crematorium, to this...."

Maxie was silent. Words wouldn't express what was flowing through her mind. One of the aspects of her job was the sheer intensity of emotions brought out from all the levels of complexity that life presented. This was no exception. No matter how long she had worked through homicides, no two were alike in the devastation left behind. She felt overwhelmingly saddened for Devin. She also felt a deep need to help him.

"I understand why you want to be in on the investigation," she finally said. He could tell by the silence and her expression that she was holding back her emotions deliberately. *She did not need to*, he thought. Emotions were a good thing.

Devin nodded. "Maxie, I am a reporter by trade—the *Tribune*. Apparently, you know my editor, Hank Remsted?"

Maxie nodded. "I know him well."

"He wanted me to reach out to you to help with the investigation. I'm not sure if that works for you, but I promise not to get in your way. I know it can be sensitive. "

Maxie nodded. "It's okay, hun. If Hank wants you to be involved, you can be."

"Thanks. I'm hoping my investigative background might be useful."

"I'm sure it will be," she said, taking a larger sip of her beer, casting a quick look at Jameson, who was already studying her demeanor. "You understand in this business, nothing moves quickly. Patience and observation are the best tools. This case is not just about your...Curtis."

"It's the same for journalists, although we often have a deadline. But most stories have to be kneaded. Are you suggesting that Curtis and the other murders are connected?"

"Well, first we should use your skill to figure out what

someone wanted from your place. Whatever *it* is, I suspect we will need to learn what it is to help move this case forward. And yes, I believe, in some way I have yet to figure out, Curtis's death is connected. "

"If Curtis had something important, he would need to get it safely into someone else's hands, so it could be an insurance policy for him. So why kill him if they did not find it?"

"Also, why toss the office and your place if they had found it?"

"Unless they killed him thinking they had, only to find out they did not."

Maxie finished her beer and turned to Jameson. "You're a detective. Any thoughts?"

"Only a question," Jameson answered. "What will they do next? If they searched and found nothing, what would they be willing to escalate to?"

Maxie nodded. "Excellent question, Detective Jameson."

"I'm not sure who else Curtis would have sent anything to. I certainly didn't get anything in the mail. I have not found anything to suggest what *it* might be."

"Patience," she said. "Sooner or later, the truth will emerge. Once that happens, we will know what we need to do."

"Hank did imply that he thought this might be bigger than just a bunch of murders."

"How so?"

"He said his gut made him suspect organized crime. Is it possible?"

"Anything is possible," Jameson said. "These murders have been going on for too long."

"We haven't found any proof that it is more than just local crime, though," Maxie said. "Did Hank have anything to go on?"

"Just his—how did he put it—newspaper man's instinct."

"He has good instincts, but was that before or after his Jack Daniels? We'll keep that as a pocket idea to explain this and see where it can go. Right now, though, I'm beat—one helluva long day for us all. You should try to get some rest. Let's touch base tomorrow to figure out the next steps."

"Thank you," Devin said. "I appreciate you coming over."

Maxi leaned over and pulled him in for a hug. It seemed the right thing to do. "Sure thing, hun. Call if you need anything."

IN THE CAR on their way out, Jameson turned to Maxie. "You seem quite taken with this one?"

"Do I?" She sighed, adjusting her rear-view mirror. "I have a feeling this case is only just starting to get complicated."

"What do you mean?"

"Like Hank said, there are forces at work here, Kobe. We do not have the whole picture yet. Not just this murder, but the others. They are all connected, and we need to find out how and why. I worry about what we will find out. Drop you on the way?"

"Thanks."

10

TIA DEWILLA

Devin tossed fitfully for most of the night. His mind was ablaze with thoughts of Curtis getting killed, of the office and his house getting ransacked, and images of Maxie accusing him of the murder. That's when he woke up each time—in reality, she had not accused him of anything, and the realization within his dreams snapped him awake.

Why would he dream it? Dreams have a way of taking pieces of reality and blending them with fantasy, using angst, guilt, fear, as well as other negative emotions as glue, somehow allowing it to make some kind of sense—a feeling of reality despite the craziness.

He sat upright and looked around his bedroom. Things had not yet been put back; pictures were still on the floor, as were his books.

Getting out of bed, he gazed out the window toward the water. The moon was out, and the light danced across the slight current. It was peaceful, and Devin wished he could just wade into the water and sink beneath the surface to enjoy some peace.

Instead, he walked to the kitchen, turned on the coffee maker, and watched as it brewed. A few minutes later, he poured a cup, went back to the bedroom, and sat in the chair by the window.

Curtis could not have been involved, he thought. *Curtis would have never been involved in anything criminal. So what had he discovered? And why was my place ransacked? What do I have that someone would want? How would it be related to Curtis? He must have sent me something.*

The questions kept piling up like cars in a traffic accident, each slamming into the next without reason. Devin found no pattern. The only thing making any sense was the timing of the events he knew to be facts: the murder, both places ransacked. This meant there *was* a connection; Devin just had to find it.

He sipped on the hot coffee, watching the steam rising from the top of the cup. *Rob seemed equally shocked*, Devin thought. He doubted Rob was involved; the two had been best friends for years. From the moment they had met in Hawaii—both attempting to surf and failing badly—they had become close.

Devin remembered that meeting. He had been traveling with Curtis at the time—Curtis was attending an investor conference, and Devin was his guest. After the work day, Devin would watch Curtis surf with the locals. Devin would not be caught dead on a board; it was not his skillset, and Curtis knew it.

Rob was also surfing, a fish out of water, and clearly so. Six feet tall and completely out of shape, sporting what many women would call a "Dad bod," the lingo of the day. Rob had made the mistake of declaring, "How hard can it be?"

And Curtis, while not an amateur, was not particularly good at it. Unlike Rob, Curtis was slim and toned, and weighing just under one-fifty-five, at least looked the part of the 'California surfer dude.' On the board, Rob was an unmitigated disaster.

After both getting thrown from their boards in under five seconds and landing in the water close to each other, they dragged themselves to shore, egos in tatters, parked on two beach chairs, each with a cold Corona in hand, laughing at their defeats.

A few hours later, Curtis knew he'd found his new partner, someone with, at least, a bit of savvy investment know-how, and from there the friendship developed.

"You're not jealous?" Curtis had asked Devin, who was speechless after watching the whole surfing fiasco unfold. Devin shook his head, raised his beer, and toasted them. "To the Dad-bod team!"

Devin smiled at the memory. *No way Rob could be involved,* he thought, *although Rob could also be a victim.* It was a thought worth consideration, given that Curtis and Rob were very close.

That said, there was a shortage of possible other suspects. *Unless it was simply a random event,* he pondered. *What if my association with Curtis was the reason for my place getting tossed, and what if Curtis was just in the wrong place at the wrong time?* It was worth considering given the recent uptick in gang-related crime in Corpus Christi over the past two months. Maxie had expected it would subside once arrests were made, he knew, still, he wondered whether she had discounted a random event dragging in Curtis and Devin?

He glanced at the time—4:00 am—and grunted. The coffee did nothing to alleviate the sleepiness he felt. Begrudgingly, he climbed back into bed and pulled the covers up. His mind was still active despite the sleepiness, and he worried he might not fall asleep again. He tried controlled breathing, counting down, thinking of three things in a row to distract his mind—he had seen that online somewhere, but now dismissed it as stupid.

After a few more restless moments, however, he did fall asleep, unaware of the transition until he awoke when his phone rang.

It was two hours later, and there was no caller ID. Cautiously, he answered it.

"Is this Devin Parker?" A melodic female voice asked. She had a slight accent he could not place.

"Speaking," he said. "Who's this?"

"Sorry, my name is Tia Dewilla. I'm Rob Meeker's girl-friend. I need to speak to you privately. It's really urgent."

"Is Rob okay?" Devin asked.

"Oh...yes, he's fine. Can you meet me? I have to tell you something important."

"Where?"

"Coffee Waves. It's on Alameda."

"Um...okay. You can't tell me on the phone?"

"Please. It's very important I tell you in person."

"Fine," Devin said. "When?"

"Ten O'Clock," Tia replied.

Devin relented. "Okay. I can do that. Are you okay? You sound scared?"

"I'll explain when I see you. Be careful," Tia begged of him.

"I will. See you then." *How odd*, he told himself. He'd never met Rob's girlfriend before—didn't know he had one. *Obviously, it had something to do with Rob*, he thought. *But what?*

He took a quick shower, shaved, and changed his clothes. He felt better. Walking out to the living room, he dismissed the idea of picking the rest of his furnishings from the floor

—he'd do it later. For some reason, leaving everything alone meant that it could not get worse. He knew that made no sense, but somehow it was comforting.

He still had plenty of time to get downtown—it would take him ten minutes on his bike, so he poured some cereal and milk, sat down to eat, and flicked on the TV.

Local news was recapping the murder. He muted the sound, didn't need to relive it again, but Maxie popped on. She was being interviewed. Devin watched, captivated by the way—even in silence—she had a presence. Her expressions and hand gestures all revealed a dynamic personality. He studied her face, her hair—something about her was very compelling. He watched her whole interview in silence. *Even in the midst of a terrible murder*, he thought, *she manages to come across as a positive light.* Although he was not ready to concede to the fact, he liked being around her. *Be honest*, he chastised himself. *I like her.* Not that he would date her, or even that she would want to date him, because he had already established his dislike of dating and the awkward conversations that invariably made one cringe after the fact. *And she's a cop. Wake up, Parker. You're being delusional from a lack of sleep.*

The interview ended—he turned off the TV and finished his breakfast. Maxie needed to know about the phone call. Then he sent Maxie a text informing her where he'd be. There was no immediate reply, so he assumed she was either asleep or busy. Either was fine; he didn't need her for this part, certain that whatever it was Tia wanted to share, he could just recount later. *How important can it be?* he wondered.

11

THE DEADLY CHASE

Coffee Waves, a cute, student-friendly coffee shop close to Texas A&M University off Flour Bluff, was semi-packed. Its outer facade peaked in a pale-blue ocean wave, the company name, and tagline: *Sit, Sip, Surf....*

Devin parked his bike off to one side, glanced around at his surroundings—as any good reporter would—and walked inside.

The interior was all wood, floors, doors, tables.... A large brick arch at the rear led to an area with sitting tables, while large leather couches were placed randomly throughout the front section. A refrigerated display case and order counter allowed the barista to monitor who entered.

To one side, Devin spotted a young woman seated, early twenties, slim, copper skin, straight dark hair, and cobalt eyes that glowed. She was watching him and waved as their eyes met. He moved closer to her.

"I'm Tia," she said, shaking his hand. She was nursing a coffee. Devin sat down. "Thank you for coming. I'm sorry if I scared you calling so early."

"Your call intrigued me," Devin said. "How come you couldn't tell me on the phone?"

"It's dangerous," she said. "I'm really scared. I think they're watching me." Her eyes darted around the room as though somehow, someone might have sneaked in.

"Who's watching you, Tia?" he asked.

"I don't know," she said, shaking her head. "I know I have been followed."

"Do you know why?"

"I know things," she said, leaning closer, her eyes opened wide. "They don't want me talking to anyone."

"So what did you want to tell me?"

She fidgeted with her hair. Devin studied her face. She was a pretty young woman, likely in her early twenties. Her skin was smooth, with no blemishes. Her eyebrows were thin, curved around her eyes. Her eyelashes were long, and Devin noted that between her eye color and lashes, they made her eyes stand out.

"You're in danger. You have something they want. Curtis found out."

"You know Curtis?"

She shook her head. "Only in passing."

"What did Curtis find out?"

"Everything," she said. "He was killed because of it. And Rob...."

"Is Rob in danger?"

Tia looked like she was trying to get the words out, but wasn't successful. Flustered, she blurted out: "Yes...I mean, no. You're in danger. It's not safe for you—*ein kheili khasteh konandeh ast*—this is so frustrating."

"Tia, what is that? Farsi? Why is it frustrating? You have to calm down. Take a deep breath. It's okay."

"Sorry. When I get stressed, I revert to my first language."

Tia looked down at the table and tried to gather her thoughts. From the dingy motel she stayed in last night, she had rehearsed what she wanted to say after calling Devin, knowing she would not have much time. She had paced the floors in her undergarments, lost to any thought but getting here and finally revealing the secret that she was carrying. It was bursting out of her, and yet now, faced with him, the words would not come as she had wanted. Now that she was in front of him, the words were lost to her.

Glancing out the window, she spotted something outside. Her eyes widened, and without warning, Tia stood and grabbed her purse. "I'm sorry. I can't stay. I have to go...it's not safe anymore." She started for the door.

"Wait!" Devin called out after her, but she was already outside, getting into her car—a small red Kia, and deftly zipped out of the parking lot and onto the main road just as Devin was stepping outside.

His eyes tracked where she was heading as he put on his helmet, then climbed on his bike and fired up the ignition, peeling off after her without thinking. He failed to spot the silver utility van parked off to one side, or the two men inside watching them. The van also started up and quickly followed.

Tia was speeding up now, heading toward downtown, then turned sharply on Airline Road, ignoring the traffic lights that had just turned red. Devin followed, weaving between cars to get closer. He had to catch up to her—she had answers that he needed. She could not get away like this.

Moments later, Tia merged onto the freeway—S. Padre Island Drive—heading north. Devin followed closely, unaware that the silver van was also closing in behind him.

His attention was fixed on her car—it stood out against the traffic. He scanned the roadway, looked at possible exits that she might take, but she remained steadfast to her course.

They traveled north for ten minutes, then Tia suddenly exited at Agnes Street, Highway 44 off-ramp, towards Corpus Christi Airport, a two-lane road that ran for a few miles before abruptly becoming a single-lane road in the countryside once you passed the airport.

After passing Oso Creek, she turned left onto a small dirt road that led toward a cemetery a few hundred yards ahead.

Devin followed, banking his motorcycle sharply and in close pursuit. The silver van was just behind him now. It sped up, and Devin finally caught sight of it in his mirror. Uncertain what to make of it, he sped up, hoping to outrun it. His attention was on Tia and nothing else.

The van abruptly accelerated to pass him, came alongside, and strategically turned directly toward him, forcing him to lose control and sending his bike into a ditch. The bike rolled, Devin holding on as best he could, and landed on top of him as it came to a sudden stop, crushing him beneath it.

Smoke started billowing from the engine. Devin was still conscious despite the searing pain that was shooting through his lower body, and a moment later, he watched in horror as the bike burst into flames.

The van did not stop; instead, it maintained its pursuit of Tia's car, quickly disappearing from view. Devin struggled to move, but couldn't. The pain in his legs faded into a sensation of heat, and he tried to squirm out of the wreckage. He was stuck. Fear gripped him, and the prospect of burning alive consumed him. First, Curtis had died, and now he was facing a similar fate.

He struggled as hard as he could to no avail. The flames grew larger until he could feel the heat against his face, searing into his skin. And then, as he closed his eyes, preparing to burn to death, he felt hands pulling under his arms, gripping him and pulling him away from the flames. It was an older man pulling him away, struggling to drag Devin a safe distance in case the motorcycle exploded—his last thought before blackness surrounded him.

1 2

RECOVERY BLUES

He awoke in a hospital bed. It was dark outside. At first, he was disoriented, uncertain where he was. Flames—he remembered flames and a fear that he was going to burn to death. He looked at his arms, and they seemed fine. He touched his face. It too felt fine aside from some cuts that were tender to the touch.

He looked up and spotted Maxie sitting in the guest chair, reading a magazine. She glanced up and saw him staring at her.

"Oh, thank goodness," she said, jumping up and moving toward his bed. "You scared us."

"How long?" he muttered. His throat was dry and sore.

"You've been unconscious for almost a day. Do you remember anything?"

"Silver van. Ran me off. Chasing Tia." The fog was clearing a bit. "My bike?"

"Totaled, I'm afraid," she said. "You're lucky you weren't killed."

"Tia?"

Maxie shrugged. "Vanished. No signs of an accident. What did she tell you?"

"Danger...," Devin answered, recounting the parts he clearly remembered. "Something I have? Chased her—life in danger. She was scared."

"We have an APB—all points bulletin—on her. We'll find her," Maxie assured him. "Get some rest. Let me tell the nurse you're awake."

Maxie left the room for the nurses' station. Devin tried to move. His body hurt, his ribs throbbed. He was bandaged around his chest. His wrist also. He had a large bandage on his head. It stung. His legs seemed okay, though. But when he attempted to move them, all he felt was a searing pain in his lower back. His legs didn't move.

He pulled back the covers and stared at them. The right leg had a bandage wrapped around it. He saw the blood that had seeped through to the top. *How come I can't feel it?* he wondered. He tried moving them again but was unable. He touched his left leg with his hand, then smacked it—nothing. Now he was starting to panic. *My legs...my God....*

The nurse, whose name tag identified her as Helen, came in with Maxie. Both saw what he was doing.

"Sir, you need to be calm," the nurse told him. "Please, lie back. Doctor's on his way." She started to push him back toward the bed.

"My legs...," he cried out, staring at them both in horror. "I can't feel them. I can't feel anything there."

Maxie moved closer to him. She was visibly upset for him. She leaned down to hold him, and he wrapped his arms around her and started to sob. "I'm paralyzed, Maxie," he said. "Oh God, tell me I'm not paralyzed for good?"

"I don't know, hun. The doctor has more answers than me." She didn't want to give him any conflicting information.

It was terrible enough everything he had gone through. This was too much, and it tore at her to see him like this. She knew he deserved none of what had happened to him.

For the few minutes before the doctor arrived, she just held him, rocking slightly, back and forth.

"Mr. Parker, Harold Rainier. You need to calm yourself. Let me tell you where we're at."

Maxie let go and moved away from the bed. Devin wiped his face, took a deep breath, and tried to calm himself.

"Sorry," he told her.

"Mr. Parker. Your lower vertebrae sustained a massive impact in the accident," Rainier explained. We operated and repaired what we could. Everything there is inflamed right now. It's too early to tell the extent of the paralysis. Once the swelling goes down, we will have a better idea."

"There's a chance I will be able to use my legs?"

The doctor gave no indication by his facial expression. "We have to wait to see. I don't like to make promises until we understand the full extent of the damage. There are also some therapies we'd like to try, but I will discuss them with you in the morning. Mr. Parker, you're fortunate to be alive. Frankly, I'm surprised it's not worse. The fact you had your helmet on likely stopped your neck from snapping."

Devin absorbed the news. "Fire?" he asked.

"Someone at the cemetery where you crashed called it in. He pulled the bike off and put out the fire before it reached you. Again, given the circumstances, you are extremely lucky."

He looked at Maxie. "Silver van?" She shrugged.

"I'll be back later to check on you," the doctor told him. "Please rest, allow your injuries time to heal. I've prescribed a painkiller for back pain. Just ask the nurse if it becomes too bad. We'll talk more later, okay?"

Devin nodded numbly and watched as he left the room.

"Can I bring you some juice? Something to eat?" Nurse Helen asked.

Devin shook his head—no.

"Yes, please," Maxie interrupted. "He would like that. Wouldn't you, Devin?"

Devin stared at her. He didn't feel up to arguing.

"Be right back," the nurse said.

Devin looked at Maxie. "Not...my...mother," he said feebly.

Maxie smiled at him. "Hun, don't act like a baby. You need to keep your strength up. It'll help your recovery. You've been out a long time. You need to eat."

Devin frowned. Of course, she was right. He knew it, but was just too stubborn to admit it.

"I have to run. Still working. I assigned a policeman to guard your door. You're safe. I want to keep it that way. We'll talk more in the morning when I come back."

"Thank you," he muttered.

"You betcha. I also filled Hank in, so I'm sure he'll be by tomorrow, as well. Rest up, okay?"

He nodded, watched as she left the room. Outside, the blue and black cap of the officer guarding him was reflected in the window. He closed his eyes. He felt overwhelmingly exhausted. It was all too much. Sleep overtook him, and his body went limp. He didn't even notice the nurse return with a tray of food and some juice.

13

DEATH IS EVERYWHERE

In any given year, Corpus Christi would have around five or six murders. Most of these are domestic in nature—husbands or wives killing each other, neighbors settling a long-standing dispute. And in that mix, gang killings, drug deals gone bad, the usual for most American cities.

This year, the murder total in Corpus Christi was already at fifteen, and summer wasn't even here yet. That was when the tourist influx added to the problems. Tourists made for easy prey for professionals. You name it, they'd tried it. Scams kept renewing each year. The police chief hated it. The city council hated it. Maxie hated it.

The spate of deaths had started months earlier. Aside from the deaths considered domestic in nature, the rest had the markings of gangs. But worse. They had the markings of targeted hits: gunshots to the back of the head, often at close range. Bodies dumped as a message. And the message was clear—someone was establishing territory, leaving no doubt that they meant business. It was a message that local thugs and gang members noticed. They understood the 'if you can't beat them, join them' mentality, fostered by the expectation of allegiance and loyalty, with the punishment of death.

And yet no one knew who was behind it. Maxie had read the signs, knew that a huge power play was in motion, but there was insufficient evidence to point to one boss, one location. Just the gunshot wounds to the back of the head.

Except for the Curtis Delaney killing, which had been a blunt force trauma to the back of the head instead of a gunshot. Nonetheless, Maxie, who always trusted her instincts, believed this one, too, was related. She had to figure out how and why.

And once she had the information, she would also discover who was behind it.

Murder number sixteen had been discovered after she left the hospital. This victim, a forty-year-old Hispanic man, had the same injury to quickly tag it as a related killing. The body had been dumped by the recycling center.

Because it was evening, Maxie had happily beaten the media to the scene. Jameson was already there, along with the medical examiner.

"Fingerprints identify him as José Moranga, a ..."

"...a retired CCPD cop rumored to have had associations with gang members," Maxie said, cutting him off. "Shit. This is getting bad. I was afraid this was where we were headed."

"Explain," Kobe asked.

"All these killings. Curtis, with Devin almost killed. Now Moranga. This is bigger than most gangs. Hank was right. This is organized crime working into the territory, getting rid of local-level guys, making way for their own militia." She paced around the body as it was getting bagged.

"If that is true," Sammy replied, "this is only the start."

"If we don't end this, we'll have more brazen attacks as they cement power. It won't be isolated to gang members."

Jameson watched her. When Maxie paced, it meant she was worried. "We need a break in the case. We need to find the person behind it all."

"But now we understand what we are dealing with, we just need to find out who is pulling the strings."

Jameson held out his hand to stop her pacing. It wasn't only this killing that rattled her.

"How is Devin?" Jameson asked as she stopped.

"Paralyzed," she said nonchalantly, then caught herself. "Dammit Kobe, they tried to kill him. I don't know what's worse: being dead or paralyzed. He's been through hell."

"So it seems they wanted him dead."

"Whoever *they* are. Yes. I have police at the hospital door. I hope it's enough."

The medical examiner watched as his assistant loaded the body into the van to take to the morgue.

"It would be a lot easier with more surveillance cameras," Sammy said to her, trying to be helpful. It wasn't the right thing to say to Maxie, a strong conservative voice for keeping what freedoms existed, free from governmental overreach.

"And make it a police state where they follow our every move?" Maxie shook her head. "I'm not ready for that. But yes, Sammy, I guess it would make identifying the crooks a lot faster. "

"What is the next step with Devin? He needs ongoing protection?" Jameson asked.

"He needs protection. For now, he's safe. I have to make sure."

"And after the hospital? Do they have a guess how long he will be there?"

"It'll be a while. They have to assume the paralysis is permanent before they release him, which means he will need to undergo therapy to assist him in his daily life."

Jameson smiled slightly, looked down at the ground, but it was too late. Maxie caught the slight smile.

"What?"

"Nothing."

"Out with it Kobe."

Jameson took a deep breath. "You cannot save everybody, Maxie."

She looked away and thought about what he had said. "Are you suggesting I am a fool?"

Jameson shook his head. "You are a good person. Part of what makes you good at your job is that you have a huge heart."

"Well, can you blame me? I want to make sure he is not killed before we have a chance to solve this case. These cases."

"Is that all?"

She turned away from him and watched as Sammy closed up the van and got in.

The coroner van drove off, leaving Maxie, Jameson, and a uniformed officer standing there. The light was fading fast.

"Thank you, you can go," she told the cop, who nodded and left.

"And I want to solve them as well as you. Just be careful."

She smiled and patted him on the shoulder. "Awww, I'm always careful, Kobe."

"Except when you are not."

She nodded. "Except when I am not." She sighed. "Let's get out of here. I'm beat. Tomorrow we go talk to Meeker about Tia. Let's see what we can dig up. See if we can rattle him. I'll meet you there at nine. I'm going to swing by the hospital first. Afterwards, I have a golf appointment with the chief. Busy day. You?"

"Not as busy as you," Jameson said. "I'm going to help at the gym before school starts, then meet you at Meeker's office."

"You do good work with those kids, you know? I'd love to come help sometime."

He smiled at her, knowing she was being genuine. "Do you box?" he asked.

"Do I box? Come on, Kobe, you know the answer to that."

"I do. You do not box," he replied, stifling a laugh.

"You're mean. There are other things I can do."

"It was a kind offer. If something comes up, I will let you know."

"Good," she answered. "I might not know how to box, but I do know how to kick some...."

"Ask again," he said, taking her words and turning them.

"Good one," she said.

The light was almost gone as they reached their cars. She opened her door and, as she was about to get in, winked at him. "I still think you killed him," she said cheerily.

"Of course you do," he answered. He shook his head. Her lightness lifted the gloom of the crime scenes. He watched as her car started, her headlight staining the sand as she pulled off onto the paved road. He could not imagine working with someone more serious, or less egocentric. Despite her looks and charm, Maxie was not ego-driven in the least.

Jameson got into his car and started it up.

14

THE BALL IS IN HIS COURT

At eight the next morning, Maxie was at the hospital. Devin was already awake, restless, and yet, as she walked through the door, his face brightened and he smiled.

"Hey there," she said. She had brought a small vase with some flowers she had picked up the night before. "Something to brighten the room."

"Thanks," he mumbled. "I'm glad you came—I'm climbing the walls."

"Did you sleep?"

He shook his head—no, then patted his legs. "My new desk ornaments," he remarked, trying to joke, but realizing that it fell flat.

"Be patient," she told him.

"How about you? Any new developments?"

"Some leads. Nothing solid yet," she answered, trying to decide whether to mention the murder from last night. She had promised he could help in the investigation, but that was before he was almost killed. Maxie thought about it, deciding it would be better for Devin to have something to focus on rather than whatever disability he might face for the rest of his life.

She pulled the chair closer to the bed. "This is all confidential, right?" He nodded. "Well, we had another murder last night. This one was a biggie, a former cop that we believe had mob connections."

"No shit!"

"I'm trying to focus on the connection between him and what's been happening."

"So, how would that be tied into Curtis. Or me?"

Maxie scrunched her face. "Honestly, I do not know. Yet. Do you ever have those feelings when you chase a story and you know that you're not quite there yet, that the answer is just over the next hill?"

Devin nodded. "That's almost always the case."

"That's where I believe we are at. There are too many loose bits to pull it all together, but...we are getting there. Wish I had better news for you."

"Anything on Tia?"

"We're going to meet with Rob after I leave here. I just wanted to pop in and tell you we haven't forgotten you, or anything."

"I appreciate that. More than I can say. I keep thinking about my legs and..."

"I won't say something stupid like 'don't think about it,' because I know it doesn't work that way, but try to keep your mind busy."

"I will try. Keep me updated. I want to feel useful. If you need me to research anything, I still have lots of contacts."

"Thank you. I will." She stood up, pushed the chair back

then offered a small wave as she left. He watched her go, then realized he was smiling. He liked her; they seemed to connect…, but then he remembered his condition…his legs. *I'm a cripple. How could anyone love a cripple?"*

THE STRANGER WATCHED Maxie leave from the stairwell on the third floor, where Devin was housed. He was now dressed in an orderly's outfit that he had lifted from the laundry cart downstairs, along with a large potted bouquet from the still-locked gift shop. He had no identification badge, but hoped that he would be able to get past the cop on duty and reach Devin. As he walked along the corridor, he held the potted flowers high to obscure his face, not that he stood out; it was more in insecurity on his part that he might get recognized.

The cop at the door held his hand out and stopped him. "Sorry, you can't go in there."

"I work here," the man replied. "I was told to deliver these to this room." He glanced over at Devin, who was not paying attention. The cop examined the flowers, then shook his head.

"Strict orders. No unauthorized entries. Tell you what, though," he suggested, taking the bouquet, "I will bring them in to him. Best I can do for you."

Defeated, the stranger nodded. "Thank you. I know you're doing your job."

He turned and left. At the stairwell, he watched as the cop took the potted flowers inside. The two men were having a conversation, which he saw through the window, but the stranger could not hear what was being said. *No matter*, he thought. He had planted a listening device in the pot. His equipment was downstairs in his car. He would have to replay it later.

A HALF-HOUR after leaving the hospital, Maxie met Jameson at Rob Meeker's office.

"How was the gym?"

"Fine. Thank you."

"Who's that little boy you're close to. Tyler...?"

"Tyson," Jameson answered. "He is making excellent progress."

"Is he the kind of kid that would like to get an ice cream sundae, sometime?"

Jameson smiled at her. He nodded. "I'm sure he would enjoy that."

"Let's plan on it soon," she said. "It will be better than me boxing." Tyson was important to Jameson, and Maxie wanted to be sure to make him important to her, as well. Jameson was one of the good ones, an honest man trying to make a difference. The least she could do was support him where possible. "Now, let's see what Mister Meeker has to say about Tia."

Inside, Rob kept them waiting in the lobby while he was on the phone. When he was done, he waved them in. His demeanor was different from their last meeting, more confident and assertive, and Maxie made a note of it and decided to be abrupt with him to see his reaction.

"You really need to come clean with me," she told him. Striking assertively, she hoped, would rattle him enough to give up a sign of his involvement—she believed he was involved, even if she was not sure to what extent.

"Really," Rob sneered, annoyed by the intrusion. "What did I do to piss *you* off?"

"You're not being very cooperative."

"I believe I have been very cooperative. But you can't just waltz in here and demand to interrogate me. "

"Really? I actually can. Either now or downtown," Maxie answered, her eyes glaring at him. "Of course, I would have to arrest you first!"

"Fine," Rob said, standing. "I don't know what I've done to make you react this way. We are on the same side."

Maxie sat down on one of the chairs. She didn't believe they were on the same side at all. She studied the room, the walls. Everything had been straightened up.

"You've cleaned up, I see."

"Of course. Can't have clients coming into a messed-up office."

"Tia," Maxie said. "I want to talk about Tia."

Rob raised his eyebrows and sat down again. He had decided he did not like Maxie. "What about...Tia?"

She half-expected him to say *'Tia, who?'* but he did not. "She contacted Devin two days ago. Did you know that?"

Rob shook his head nonchalantly. "How would I know that?"

"She is your girlfriend, isn't she?"

"My girlfriend?" He let off a forced laugh. "Not for several months, and even then, I would never use that word. We went out a few times," Rob replied. "That one is a loon." He made a swirling motion with his finger against his head. "Certifiable. Why was she bugging Devin? Hitting him up for cash?"

Maxie adjusted herself. "Apparently, she had some information for him. About Curtis. Is there something you're not telling me?"

"Am I a suspect? You're acting as though I am. Should I get my attorney to join this conversation?"

"Only if you feel you might incriminate yourself answering my questions, Mr. Meeker," she said calmly. The threat of lawyers never bothered her.

Rob took a deep breath, stared up at the pencil still stuck in the ceiling tile, then back at Maxie. "As I said, Tia's nuts. She started meddling in our business, wanting to learn everything. It was not her business. She started bothering Curtis, asking him all sorts of strange questions. I saw him get annoyed. Anyway, I broke it off with her after a few dates. Curtis wasn't sorry to see her go away."

"So, just to be clear," Maxie said, leaning forward, closer to Rob. "You have no idea why Tia would want to talk to Devin?"

Rob shook his head. "Is that why you came here? You're focused on Devin. I have no clue why she would be bothering him. Why don't you just ask Devin?"

Maxie stood, took a deep breath. "I will. In a few days after he is stronger."

"Stronger?" Rob seemed perplexed. "Stronger from what? He seemed fine when you were both here."

"Devin is in the hospital. He was following Tia after she came to see him, when he was run off the road by a silver van that tried to kill him and left him for dead."

"Oh my...," Rob muttered. "That's terrible."

"It seems *terrible* is following him—and you—everywhere these days. He's paralyzed from the waist down. Doesn't know if he will ever walk again."

Rob seemed genuinely shocked, staggered back, and found a chair to sit in. Maxie noted all this, although she knew firsthand that liars were often very convincing—a derivative of where the word *con* came from.

"Poor Devin. I should go visit him. Can I do that?"

"You might wait a bit," Maxie advised. "He's...adjusting to what happened. It's a major shock for him."

"What about Tia? Did you find her?"

Maxie shook her head. "I was hopeful that you would have some answers. Sadly, I suspect we may be too late."

"You never know when she'll turn up again," Rob said. "That one is like a bad penny."

Maxie thought she detected a smirk, but he quickly turned serious.

"If I hear anything from her, I'll contact you," he added.

"Will you?" Maxie asked, then, before he replied, she got up. "Thank you for your time. See, it wasn't that difficult."

She walked out of the office. Her tolerance level for Rob and everything that had happened had vanished. Whether Rob was involved or Tia was involved, someone on the loose was directly responsible for what had happened to Curtis, and especially to Devin. And there was no shortage of lies. *Shakespeare would have been proud of the intricacies of this play,* she thought.

Outside, Jameson was waiting in her car.

"How'd it go?" he asked when she got in.

"He's hiding something. He said they'd broken up months ago, and he had no idea. Claimed she was certifiable."

"Could he be right?" Jameson asked.

"I could be the Queen of England," Maxie replied curtly. "But who knows? Let's get out of here. I'm expected at the golf course at eleven."

"Cochran?"

"Official update on the case. Besides, our chief thinks he can improve on his last game. What do you think?"

"I think it is good that the police chief wants to play golf with you. Still."

Maxie laughed. "What do you mean, still?"

"Well, after the last time, you put him to shame," Jameson explained.

"True story. What can I say—the man's a sucker for punishment."

MAXIE PARKED at the Oso Beach Golf Course, downtown Corpus Christi. Against a backdrop of open space and palm trees, the course was greener than most front lawns in the city. Chief Bryan Cochran was waiting off to the side, having a conversation with his caddy. He was dressed in golf pants, white shoes, and a blue Polo shirt. His hair was combed back, his handlebar mustache trimmed. Maxie waved at him, and he waved back. "He seems happy," she noted. "Hopefully, his mood will stay that way. I know he's pushing for an update with some progress. Kobe, take my car and see what you can find on Tia. I have to believe something bad happened, so check the area hospitals. I'll give you a holler when we're done here, and we can go check on Devin."

"Try to enjoy yourself," Jameson told her.

She popped the trunk. "I will." She pulled out a golf bag, then closed it, placing the bag to the side by the green. She waved at Jameson, who carefully backed out and left, before she moved closer to Cochran.

"Good morning, Bryan," she said, offering her cheeks, in turn, for him to kiss, European style—a slight air smack of the lips on each side.

"You look lovely," he said. "Ready for a loss today?"

"Ha," she laughed. "Hopefully, *you* will have a lucky day, for a change. Shall we?"

Her club caddy approached and grabbed her bag, walking with the chief's caddy behind them both.

"How's the Delaney case going? Something good I should know, I hope."

"His cousin, Devin Parker, is recovering from being run off the road. Paralyzed from the waist down. He was following a lead. It seems they wanted to keep him quiet."

"That's not good," the chief replied. "Any leads? Arrests?"

"Working them. I hope to have something soon. This isn't a pleasant one, Bryan. It has organized crime all over it."

"Ties into our recent spate of killings?" He pulled out a quarter. "Your call?"

"Heads," she said, watching as the coin spun in the air before landing in his palm. "I believe there is a connection. Curtis's killing was not the same; however, the markings of a mob hit are not there, although all the others could fall into that category. Does the name José Moranga ring a bell?"

Cochran's face frowned. "Former cop, dishonorable discharge? Mob connections? Is he involved?"

"Found dead last night. Single GSW back of the head."

"Poetic justice, I suppose. You start," he said, looking at the coin.

Maxie pulled the driver club from her bag, placed the ball on a small wooden tee, and adjusted her grip on the handle. She glanced up at Cochran and winked at him, then, with a swift power stroke, launched the ball high into the air. Both stood watching it for its six-second flight. It landed well into the green of the first hole and came to a stop.

"Nice," he told her, slightly envious of the ease with which she executed the shot. "So what's next?"

She stared at him. "Now that we have a connection, we

need to start linking anyone else involved. If this is organized crime, Bryan, we run the risk that some of our people will be compromised. That would be a terrible thing to happen. I'm working as fast as I can on this."

"Fair enough. I trust you, Maxie." He placed his ball down, got into position, practiced his swing to the side of the ball, then settled into position. Pulling back on the club, he brought it down hard against the ball. *Thwack!* The ball launched high, traveling the same path as Maxie's had done. They both watched as it descended the fairway, landing a foot away from Maxie's ball.

"Very nice, Bryan," Maxie told him, patting him on the back. "It's looking promising."

The chief handed his club back to the caddy, and they began their trek toward the balls.

"You know, Maxie," he said. "I always enjoy our time here."

Maxie smiled. "As do I, Bryan. As do I. It's peaceful, and for a short time, I can forget the work."

"But the world is changing, Maxie. And we have to change as well."

"How do you suggest we do that? New technology only goes so far."

"That's why I am counting on you, Maxie. Get these cases wrapped up, and I'd like to have a brainstorming session with you as to how we take our department to the next level. We have to set the lead for the future, and you're the person I want on point."

Maxie stopped. That was quite the endorsement. She waved her hair back and took a deep breath, then stared directly into his eyes. "And if you lose the game?"

Cochran let off a deep belly laugh. "Well, maybe then, I

will need to find someone else," he teased. "Only you would say that!"

"I still won't let you win," she answered coyly.

"Good," Cochran told her. "Nor would I want you to. I've got enough kiss-asses in the department. And that's why I still want your input in bringing us forward."

Maxie smiled. "Thanks."

15

JACKSON POLLAK

Devin, now alone in his room, contemplated his future. What kind of life would he have? Simple, everyday tasks, things ordinary people don't think about, had suddenly become enormous challenges for him. Certainly, he couldn't be a reporter anymore. He couldn't see how it would be possible to get around chasing stories, especially the people wishing to avoid his questions.

His mood had progressively worsened since the day before, and he now found himself fluctuating between feelings of depression and anger. He declined breakfast, although he did drink the coffee. He wanted to punch someone, especially the men in the van who had forced him off the road, leaving him to almost die in the fire of his motorcycle. *And what of Tia?* he wondered. *Was she still alive? What was so important in the information she wanted to share? Certainly, it scared her enough to fear for her own life.*

He studied the patterns on the ceiling tiles, focused on smears on the small hospital room window across from him.

He listened for the footsteps of people passing and imagined what they looked like. He hated being locked in.

Eventually, he dozed off, waking only when Doctor Rainier entered the room.

"How are you today?" Devin noted the cheer in his voice and wondered if it was for his benefit.

"Still no feeling in the legs."

"Let's see the surgical incision on your back," Rainier said, helping Devin lean forward and lifting the back of his gown to expose the bandages across his lower spine. He peeled them off. "Looks good," he told him, flatly. He repeated this with bandages on the side. "We needed access to help secure your vertebrae," he explained.

Reaching for a tray Nurse Helen had earlier left on the bedside table, he grabbed a gauze pad and antiseptic and wiped the areas. He took smaller bandages and applied them to all three spots. "There." When he was done, he pulled down the gown and helped Devin back. "It looks good. A few more days and the incisions will be fully healed."

"How long will I be here?" Devin asked.

"For a while. Tomorrow you can start physical therapy— we secured the damage done to your spine, and it should be stable enough, but you'll need to take it easy for a few days to allow the inflammation to subside. PT will teach you how to be mobile using your arms and body. Our specialist will show you what you need to be able to take care of yourself. He's amazing. You can live a full life. But it's going to depend entirely on your state of mind, and only you have control over that. You're very lucky to be alive."

"You keep telling me that, Doc. Right now, it doesn't feel that way."

Rainier nodded. "Maybe not right now, but once you get

some mobility, you'll be surprised by how much you can do and how it changes your state of mind."

"Is there anything I can do to try to get feeling back in my legs? Any exercises...?"

Rainier patted Devin on the shoulder. "Get some rest. That's the best medicine right now. And you need it. Your body's been through a major shock. It takes time. There's no rushing. There is a new therapy I would like to try. It requires an injection into the damaged area. Long story short, the injection delivers a high number of special stem cells into the pial membrane and the spinal cord's superficial layers. These neural precursor cells can reduce the risk of further injury and also boost the propagation of cells to repair the damage."

"Is that what you recommend?"

"It can't hurt. I was going to schedule you for this afternoon if you're interested."

"Interested? Of course, I'm interested," Devin answered enthusiastically. "I'd make an animal sacrifice if there was even a remote chance it would help. Sign me up."

"Okay. I'll check in on you later before the procedure. Remember, it is not a guarantee—more of a long shot."

"But, it is a shot, right?"

"It is. Let your nurse know if you need anything to make you more comfortable. I'll be back later."

Devin nodded. "Thank you. Guess I'll work on my patience skills."

Rainier left the room, and Devin watched him stop at the nurses' station. While he had no idea what words were spoken, the two nurses looked up and back in Devin's direction.

As if it wasn't bad enough to have lost mobility, Devin quickly realized it also meant a loss of bladder control. He had noticed a catheter had been inserted through his penis, and the tube extended to a bag by the side of the bed. At first, he thought little of it; it was merely to keep him in bed as he recovered from the surgery. It was only when the nurse changed the collection bag for a new one that the realization of permanence sneaked in.

"If it is too uncomfortable for you, we also have adult leak guards," Nurse Helen informed him.

"Diapers?" he responded.

"I know this is difficult," she replied, reassuringly. "It will take you some time to figure out the best method that works for you. We have some patients who handle their own catheters—we can teach you how— and there are also different kinds of catheters to minimize chafing and infections. Other patients prefer the...diapers for the convenience factor."

Devin's head was spinning with information overload. *What next?* he wondered. *This is all a nightmare, and maybe I can wake up?* "What do you suggest?" he finally asked.

"Since you'll soon be out of bed for physical therapy," she advised, "I would suggest that we remove the catheter and have you practice changing yourself. That way, you won't have the collection bag getting in your way."

"Fine," he said. "Let's do that."

Nurse Helen reached down into the bedside table and pulled out a package of adult-size diapers. She peeled off the plastic wrapping and placed the contents atop the table, within arm's reach of Devin. She handed him one.

"Open it flat. What I'm going to do is remove the catheter —it will feel strange, but shouldn't cause any pain. Then you can slide the pad under you and secure it. Be warned, it sounds easy, but when you're paralyzed, you have to find new ways to do the simplest of things. In your case, you will need to use your arms against the bed bars to pull yourself to each side so you can maneuver."

Devin nodded. She put on some surgical latex gloves, lifted his gown, and gently withdrew the tubing. The sensation was odd, a tugging, but no pain. She lowered his gown again and removed the collection bag, bringing everything to the red medical waste container by the door and dropping it inside.

Devin opened the diaper flat, tried turning his body to lift his right side off the bed, but couldn't. He remembered her advice and reached for the left side-rail with his right hand and pulled himself to one side, exposing his buttocks. He tried to maneuver the diaper into place but only succeeded in scrunching it up beneath his butt. He tried again, this time using his left arm hooked around the left bed rail once he was in position. To hold himself in place, he used his—now free—right hand to adjust the diaper. After a few attempts adjusting it, he reversed the process and rotated onto his right side, using his left hand to pull the diaper more in that direction. He lay back, panting. *It was a lot of work,* he thought. Now he pulled the diaper from beneath his legs and secured the tabs. *Done!*

Nurse Helen returned and noted his progress. "Well done. It will get easier, I promise. You'll find these tricks help."

"Thank you."

"A word of advice," she added. "Since you have no feeling there, you won't know when you need a change. I suggest periodically just checking. I placed extras over here." She pointed to the side table.

He thanked her, his ingrained manners forcing him to be polite when in reality he wanted to scream. It wasn't her fault. She was doing her job, and she wondered whether inside she might also wish to scream. This was just another indignation forced upon him. He hated it.

A half-hour later, he rechecked, trying to get used to doing so regularly. He found the diaper in need of changing. *I'm like a* baby, he thought. *Next, I'll need a* bib.

Grabbing a fresh one, as well as a wet wipe, he managed to change himself faster this time. After he was done, he realized he wasn't as tired; it had taken less effort. Holding the now full diaper, he closed the tabs and used the adhesive strips to keep it closed.

He spotted the trash can by the door and studied the weight of the diaper in his hand. *I can do this,* he thought. Deftly, he aimed and tossed the diaper into the air toward the direction of the can. The diaper rolled through the air and came unstuck mid-flight, landing open-faced on the floor, short of the can, with a loud *THWACK*.

Damn. Not much I can do about it. Four points for effort, he told himself, then lay back down again.

He stared at the patterns in the ceiling plaster again—shapes blended until he made out imaginary faces before fading into some other form. This amused him for a while before it became boring and cheerless. He wondered how long he would be stuck in the hospital, and what he could do to keep busy.

By the time Nurse Helen came in with lunch, he was famished, having passed on breakfast. She spotted the diaper on the floor and cast him a mischievous look. "Nice try," she told him, bending and picking it up and dropping it where he had aimed, and then washing her hands at the sink. "I'm glad to see you trying to do things yourself. It will make it much easier for you to adapt."

"Adapt?" He frowned. "Not much to adapt. Diapers for life?"

She moved his food closer and lifted the metal lids off the plate.

"You could think about it that way, like it is a hindrance," she advised. "Or you could look at it like any of the many other routine things we have to do every day. Like brushing our teeth. Bathing. Seeing a dentist, etcetera. We do these things because we have to, not because we want to. The same is true for your new procedures. The sooner you change your perception of them and accept them, the less you will hate them and the happier you will be."

Devin had no response; she was right. This was his new reality, and there was nothing he could do to change it. Hating it wouldn't change it, neither would liking it, and he knew the latter might make it bearable, but he was a very, very long way away from accepting it, let alone liking it.

Lunch was a club sandwich with a pickle on top, held in place by a long toothpick, and he relished every bite. A single-serve container of chocolate ice cream completed this meal. *Even the hospital coffee tasted okay,* he thought. He was too stubborn to admit to himself that this meal was the first bit of joy he had experienced since regaining consciousness.

A male orderly, Bobby, came in to bathe him—another indignity to face and get used to. But Bobby explained Devin would soon be able to do it by himself. This was more of a "show you" exercise.

"More tips and tricks?" Devin asked. Bobby just shrugged.

"Whatever makes your life more whole, bro."

Bobby was in his early twenties, and this was likely a part-time job because of his body-building training that required a funding source. Moving and lifting patients came easily for him.

Devin tried his best to relax as Bobby handed him the soap and told him to lather up. He stood there waiting.

"You mean you're going to watch me?"

"Either I watch you, or they told me I have to bathe you. I'm sure you'd rather have your own hands between your legs?"

"I do know how to bathe myself," Devin said. "And yes, my own hands would be better than yours, no offense."

Bobby grinned. "None taken, bro. Let me put a towel under you so the bed doesn't get wet." He slipped his hands under Devin's butt and easily lifted him off the bed, sliding a towel there and straightening it out before lowering Devin again.

Reluctantly, Devin removed the diaper, which was still dry, and placed it to one side. He grabbed the soap from Bobby and dipped it into the small container of water that Bobby had brought and quickly lathered it up against his body, between his legs, his back, and arms. He tried to avoid looking at Bobby, not caring if the man was staring at him, but finally looked up and realized that Bobby was watching the television imagery, even with the sound off.

Once he was done, Bobby handed him a towel to dry off with. Then, he gave him a new gown, which Devin quickly tied into place after replacing the diaper. Finally, Bobby held out a razor, shaving cream, and a comb while holding up a mirror, so Devin could see what he was doing.

"Thank you," Devin said.

"Does that mean we're now friends, or are we officially dating?" Bobby was laughing, and Devin found himself caught up in the moment and recognizing the humor.

"Funny guy," Devin said. "But, just because you've seen my man junk doesn't mean we're dating!"

Bobby enjoyed the quick comeback and told him so.

"Stay cool, bro," Bobby said, gathering up his supplies and leaving the room.

Now dressed, hair neatly combed, face shaved, he felt more like himself and ready for visitors.

His first outside visitor of the day was Hank. Entering the room quietly, as though he might be caught doing something he wasn't supposed to, he cast a quick glance at Devin, who was watching him, then stopped in his tracks and smiled sheepishly.

"Sorry, didn't know if you were sleeping. How are you?"

"What you see is what you get," Devin replied.

"Maxie called me," Hank said. "My God, Devin, I don't know what to say."

"There's not much to say, Hank. Except you're gonna need a new reporter now."

Hank frowned. "What do you mean?"

"I'm a gimp, Hank. There's no comeback from this; it could be for life."

"Don't say it. You're still you."

Devin shrugged.

Hank pulled a chair closer to the bed and sat. "The paper's got your medical bills—it's covered under our policies. And you're still on salary. I don't want you to worry about that, or anything but recovery."

"Thanks," Devin said flatly. "But you and I know I can't be a reporter in a wheelchair."

"If it comes to that, we'll figure it out."

"The last thing I need is pity, Hank."

Hank shook his head. "No pity, Devin. Let's talk about all of it after you're back on your...er...out of here. Maxie's working the leads. She's good at this, Devin. She'll get to the truth. You focus on recovery."

"Doing my best. What's new out there?"

"Not a lot. The public is getting annoyed by the lack of progress in the recent murders. People don't like crime in their back yards, especially more affluent areas—it screws with their property values. Maxie seems to think it will come to a head soon—she's determined."

"I hope so. This is the most helpless I've ever felt. I don't like being out of control."

"Life is about letting go of control and trusting your instincts. You know that. Give yourself time."

"Time is one thing I seem to have plenty of."

He stood and pushed the chair back. "You're supposed to rest, so I won't stay. Call me if you need anything—reading material, crosswords, decent food—I know what hospital food is like. I can have someone sneak in some Chinese?"

Devin nodded. "Thanks, Hank. Maybe some papers, crosswords, and a notebook would be good. I'm tired of just lying here. Thanks for coming."

"Of course. I'm not only your boss—we're friends. Don't forget that."

Hank left, and Devin reflected on their conversation. There had to be answers, he knew. There had to be something he could do. He hated feeling dependent on others. At least with a notebook, he could get his thoughts down on paper. Maybe it would help him put some of the pieces together. The nagging feeling that he was missing something obvious was still with him. *And what was so important to Tia to scare her like that?"*

Devin settled back to pondering what else to do while stuck here. He couldn't bring himself to watch daytime television. Even with the sound off, whenever he glanced up, all he saw were game shows and soap operas.

America is one big game show, he thought. All the entertainment seemed to be focused on exposing the shortcomings of the individual rather than their strengths. Of course, not everyone had strengths. Too many people coasted by with the least amount of effort. He dreaded the way society was headed, accommodating all the needs of those too afraid, or too challenged, to try to become something. This was always at the expense of the people actually busting their rear-ends, whose taxes actually paid for the things everyone else wanted for free.

It made him angry to think about it, so he tried to think about other things. *Perhaps I should move somewhere else when I get out*, he thought. A change of scenery might be what he needed for a fresh outlook.

His musings were interrupted when he was greeted by a surprise visitor. A man in his mid-thirties, with a military buzz-cut hairstyle, large upper body musculature, and confined to a wheelchair, rolled into his room. Devin stared at him in shock.

"You're Devin Parker? Jackson Pollak," the man said, rolling closer and reaching up, extending his hand. Devin shook it.

"Do I know you?"

"No. But you will. I'm your physical therapist."

Devin perked up. "What? You're kidding me, right?"

Jackson shook his head. "Because I'm in a wheelchair doesn't mean I can't be your PT. Don't be so narrow-minded."

"I'm sorry. It's just...."

Jackson smiled. "Perceptions, my friend, will ruin your life. Every time you think you cannot do something, you will fail. My job is to show you what you can do and help you to do it. Afterwards, the only limitation you will face will be yourself."

"You sound quite sure of that," Devin told him.

"I've lived it. I was like you a few years ago. My military career was over. I was useless. A gimp. A burden. I was angry, felt sorry for myself. Pushed away the people who loved me. We all go through those phases. It's a normal part of healing."

As Jackson talked, Devin noted he was rubbing his hands over the top of the wheels, light strokes that made the chair move slightly, just enough to notice.

Devin squirmed a bit. "I might walk again," he said. "I don't want to do anything that might make me stop believing."

Jackson wheeled back a bit, then, using his body weight, shifted the wheelchair so one wheel was off the ground, using his hands to push the other wheel back and forth to maintain the balance. Gently, he allowed the airborne wheel to touch down.

"I understand what you're saying, Devin. I don't want you to lose hope, either. But, I do want you to be a realist. I've seen your scans. If you ask me, you should prepare for the worst. Just in case. Worst case, you won't be disappointed, and will be ready to handle things. Best case, you're right, and you get to walk. Either way, you win."

Devin listened, somewhat in awe of the optimism he saw before him. "How did you get to be in the chair?"

"Roadside IED in Afghanistan." Jackson flashed all fingers in the air, an explosion followed by a *BOOM* sound. "Fast, dramatic. Shrapnel sliced me apart. One day I ran marathons and the next day I was a cripple for life."

"I'm sorry. Sounds rough."

"After I passed through the pity phase, I got angry and determined. It took a lot of work, but there's very little I can't do anymore. I can take down soldiers who have use of their legs. I can go where I want. I can drive. I have my body in top shape, so I feel good about myself, and I am content with where I am and how my life is. That's why they have me doing PT. If I can do it, you can, too."

Devin was encouraged. "You make me want to get up and do something right now."

Jackson laughed. "Whoa...you're not ready yet. First, you recover a bit, then we train. Let me be your guide. And hopefully your friend. I *know* what you're going through, so feel free to call me anytime." He wheeled in closer, pulled out a business card from his shirt pocket, and handed it to Devin. It read: **Jackson Pollak, Recovery Engineer,** along with his phone number.

"Recovery Engineer," Devin repeated. "I like the title."

"Hell, if a janitor is a sanitation engineer, then the title works fine for me. I'll be back tomorrow. We can work out a training plan. Meantime...rest up. You're gonna need it."

"I will."

He smiled, waved, then wheeled to the door. Using one hand to push it open, he spun around once and wheeled out before the door closed. He was filled with confidence. It poured from him like a flood unleashed. Devin watched as Jackson vanished down the hallway. His mind was reeling with what he had seen. Jackson had more energy than Devin remembered having before the injury. *Recovery Engineer!* Devin began to laugh.

If he could achieve even half of what Jackson could do, being paralyzed would not be as much of a curse as he believed. And if he were to regain use of his legs, he would be way ahead of the game. *Jackson was right*, he noted. *"I win either way."*

He was feeling much better.

16

THE TRUTH ABOUT TIA

The body was found face down in the water, bobbing with the gentle currents of Whitecap Beach. By the time Maxie arrived, Sammy Yatsuki had already removed it onto a stretcher, examined it, and showed her the fingerprint scanner results.

"Tia Dewilla," he said. Maxie wasn't surprised. After the news of the chase and what had happened to Devin, she hardly expected that Tia would be found alive. What did surprise her, however, was where she was found, a good thirty miles from where Devin had been run off the road chasing after her.

"Any sign of the car?" she asked, pointing at the water. "It could have been dumped?"

Sammy didn't know—not his area of expertise. He waved over one of the uniformed officers so Maxie could speak with him.

"Search the water. It's not deep. Her car might be just below the surface. Devin said it was a red Kia."

The officer nodded and left to get some additional help.

"How'd she die, Sammy?"

"Drowning would be my guess. Bruising at the back of the neck suggests her head was forced under the water. We'll do scrapings under fingernails as well to see if we can ID her assailant."

"Lemme know what you find."

"I will," he told her. "By the way, how was golf? Did he redeem himself?"

Maxie smiled. "He did just fine," she said, heading back to her car.

"And you didn't just let him win?"

"Not my style, Sammy," she said.

"Tia?" Jameson asked as she got in.

"Drowned."

"Not good."

Maxie shook her head. "Not at all. Things are looking worse. I think the car's in the water."

"Devin?"

"He's still in danger. Maybe more so now."

"So what will you do?" Jameson asked the question, although he already knew the answer—he knew her that well.

"Ask me tomorrow."

A uniformed cop tapped on the window, and Jameson rolled it down. "Car's in the water, alright. A few inches down. Tow is on the way."

"Lemme know if you find anything once it's pulled."

The cop nodded, then left.

"You are not waiting for it?" Jameson asked.

"There won't be anything to find. They just needed to shut her up."

THAT EVENING, Maxie and Jameson arrived at the hospital just before visiting hours ended. One of the perks of being a detective, she told Jameson, was that they could stay as long as they wished.

Devin was awake, using the arm bars of the bed to push himself up and down. Maxie watched from the door, admiring the effort, before entering.

"Are you supposed to be doing that?" she asked as they walked in.

"Good evening to you, too," he said.

Maxie grinned. "Someone is in a good mood, Kobe."

Devin nodded. "I've had a chance to think things through. This can't defeat me."

"No, it can't," Maxie said, pulling up a chair and sitting. "But, I do have some bad news to share. Tia was found dead."

"Dead?" He wasn't surprised. "Guess we'll never know what she wanted to share."

"Perhaps," Maxie said. "Kobe and I are following some leads. But I did speak with Rob about her. He claims they broke up months ago and that she was probably stalking you for money. Did you get that impression?"

"No. She seemed genuinely scared," Devin said. "So much so that she bolted from the coffee shop. It must have been the silver van. I didn't see it until later when it ran me off the road, but it must have been there all along. Tia recognized it."

"And you said there were two men in it?"

"I couldn't see them clearly—wasn't paying attention—but they were men."

Maxie looked at Kobe. "We'll check traffic cams and see if

we can get a plate. Whoever got to her took the time to finish her off in a different place. We found her at the beach, quite a distance from your crash."

"Poor girl. I'm surprised Rob made her sound like a scam artist. I did not get that sense from her at all, and I'm a pretty good judge of character. I also didn't know he had a girl-friend. You'd think I would have known about that, right?"

"That is a puzzle, isn't it?" she said. Then changing the subject: "So anything new on your end?"

"I'm getting an injection of some kind of cells into my spine. The doc says it may help in the healing. I'm hoping it might make the difference in me being able to walk again."

"I see." Maxie didn't sound convinced. "Well, that's good. Right?"

He nodded. "And I met my physical therapist—he's also paralyzed, but he can do some interesting things." Devin explained Jackson's visit earlier and how impressed he was with what Jackson was able to do.

Maxie spotted the potted floral arrangement by the sink. She got up and stuck her finger into the soil. It was dry. She turned on the faucet and placed the pot under the water. "Need to keep these things alive," she joked. Then, turning off the water, she put her finger back into the pot to test it again, and felt a small hard object. She looked closer, then pulled it out. A listening device. A small cup was by the sink. She filled it with water and then dropped the device inside. *So much for that*, she thought. But she chose to say nothing about it. It did, however, make her consider that Devin was still a target. Even more so now.

"Listen, something for you to think about when you get released. Just mull it over. And for the record, I don't usually make this suggestion."

"Okay...."

"Your apartment is on the third floor. Granted, there's an elevator, but it's not conducive to wheelchairs. That and the fact that someone is out to silence you, and has already committed two murders...." She took a deep breath. Jameson was smirking. He already knew where this was going. "I just think you should stay with me on the island until things blow over, or we find the killers."

"Stay with you," Devin repeated. "The island? Padre Island?"

Maxie was nodding. "I have a two-story house on the water. The ground level is self-sufficient. You can stay there. It will make protecting you a whole lot easier. Besides, you wanted to be involved with the investigation, and we can go over what I find."

"Wow," Devin said. "That's incredibly generous of you."

Jameson was grinning. "And she has *never* offered that to anyone before now," he said to Devin. Maxie flashed him a dirty look. Jameson shrugged.

"Anyway," she continued. "Don't make a big deal about it, okay?"

Devin nodded, not sure what to say. "Okay. I'll keep it quiet."

"Good. Now tell me about the therapist. Do you think he'll be able to help?"

"Yes. He's a former military, injured in Afghanistan. He's built like a tank. His whole philosophy is to train your mind to train your body...something like that."

"Interesting." Maxie got up and fluffed his pillow. Jameson watched her scurry about like a mother hen. Devin said nothing; he was enjoying the attention. "What about the information Curtis had. Do you still think he would have made sure it got out? Either to you or someone else?"

Devin thought about the question. It made sense. Had Curtis truly found some damming information to get him killed, he would have found a way to share it. *What about Rob? Perhaps he gave it to Rob? Surely Rob would have said something had that been the case. Rob seemed baffled about it all.* "There has to be something," he finally answered. "I just have no idea what."

"Perhaps Tia had something she was going to give you?"

He shook his head. "I honestly think she would have just given it to me right off the bat. What she wanted was to share information."

"Well, keep thinking about it. Hopefully, by the time you're released, you may have some added thoughts. Meantime, Kobe and I will go run some video footage and see if we can get a plate on your silver van."

"Take care," Jameson told him, pointing at Maxie. "If you are going to live with her, you will need all your strength just to keep up." He was laughing, and Devin couldn't help but break into a grin.

"Oh, shush," she told them both and left the room. Jameson followed her, giving Devin a thumbs-up sign.

THE STRANGER HAD BEEN LISTENING to the hospital room conversation. While not particularly enthralling, he had overheard details about Devin's condition, including the conversation about using a catheter. That made him cringe. *If I were paralyzed*, he thought, *I would rather die than submit to such humiliation.*

He also heard what they knew about Tia's death. It wasn't news to him. He was the one who had killed her. After the van had pushed Devin off the road, it had pursued Tia, eventually catching up to her a mile later. The two men inside—associates with whom he worked—had brought Tia to him, along with her car.

Tia had been hysterical, he recalled. He had to strike her to silence her, then offered her a tissue and told her he wanted to talk on the beach. She had become docile at that point, and he drove with her in her car, down Whitecap Blvd, to where the paved road ended and the sandy beach merged, turning left, away from the pier further down. The tide was out, which was convenient. He parked her car facing the water and then told her to get out, so they could walk along the edge of the water and talk. Tia had reluctantly obliged.

As they walked, he told her things to calm her down, lies to make her feel better.

"Once you relax, you will no longer feel afraid. Think of your sister, Dournia. Come look at the shells here. You can bring her some."

It was a lie, Tia knew. The man still had Dournia captive; only she had managed to escape. He was evil, she knew. He had bought them from their parents in Iran a year earlier, promising to protect them from harm. Almost immediately he had raped them both, threatening to kill the other if their obedience was ever questioned.

When Tia formulated an escape plan, she had begged Dournia to go with her, but Dournia, the more passive of the two, had declined. That and the boy she was attracted to, part of the evil one's group, possibly even family.

After she had escaped, she knew nothing of the aftermath or what had happened to Dournia. And then she had met Rob, and everything seemed better. He was kind, stable, and financially secure. At least until things changed.

The man, realizing she had no interest in seashells, grabbed her arm and roughly marched her into the water, pointing at some nonexistent point, until they were midway up to their knees. Only then did he stop, turn her to face him. The beach was deserted. Any cries for help would go unheard.

"Such a pretty girl," he told her, his hands now rising to grip her neck and push her down into the water. She tried to scream but was unable even to breathe, such was his grip.

He pushed her further down until her head was beneath the small waves, her arms struggling to grab onto him, gripping his shirt and trying to pull herself up. He tightened his grip and held her until seconds later she stopped resisting, her arms dropping into the water. He could see a cloud of bubbles from where her lungs had just replaced air with salt water.

He held her there for a few moments more before releasing his grip and allowing her body to drift on its own, the water tugging her further away.

Returning to the car, he released the brake and allowed it to roll straight into the water until the engine compartment flooded and the motor stopped, the water brimming over the open windows. The tide was coming in, and soon it would be mostly submerged, pulled out further by the water.

He turned and after a glance at Tia's body bobbing with the small waves, he walked back along the path until he was on paved road and waited for his associates in the silver van to pick him up. He glanced back again long enough to see the red of the car roof slip beneath the water line.

His thoughts ended abruptly as the sound from the device in the flower pot ended. He had heard the running water and assumed that somehow it had been shorted out as a result.

No matter. He had heard all he needed to hear for now. Once he ascertained where the information Delaney had copied could be found, his employer would, no doubt, have him finish off Devin Parker. At least *he* would do the job right. After that, he could forget this city and move on with his real plan, the one that he hoped would bring down America in a fiery reign of terror.

AN HOUR LATER, Doctor Rainier and Bobby, the orderly who had overseen Devin's sponge bath earlier, arrived with a wheelchair. "We'll bring you down to radiology and perform the procedure there."

Bobby pulled back Devin's covers and lowered the bed a bit. Wrapping his arms around Devin's back and under his legs, he lifted Devin into the wheelchair. They then walked him to the elevator and down to the first floor. Large wall signs indicated the Radiology Department.

A long corridor that smelled of antiseptic cleaner led to the lab. Inside, Bobby again lifted Devin and placed him on the side of an elaborate examination table, the same one used for X-rays and even radiation treatments.

A pillow had been placed midway so that Devin's back would be curved once he was on his stomach. Bobby guided him into position while Rainier pulled a fluoroscope closer. A nurse came in with a tray of tools and two hypodermic syringes.

"I'm going to give you an anesthetic first. It also has a dye in it to help me trace where I am. You'll feel a pinch, but it shouldn't be worse than that."

"Okay," Devin said.

The nurse lifted Devin's gown, exposing his entire back, then used a cotton swab and rubbing alcohol to clean the area. After Rainier had put on a mask and gloves, she handed him the first syringe. It had a reddish hue. Rainier located the site within the surgery's incision and injected the anesthetic slowly, pushing the needle in deeper. All the while, he was looking at the fluoroscope to guide him further. The dye spread around the area he was aiming for. He withdrew the empty syringe.

"I'm going to wait a moment and give the shot a chance to numb everything. If you feel anything, let me know. It shouldn't take long."

"Okay," Devin said. He felt strangely comfortable on his stomach, not a position he usually slept in—he was a side-sleeper. He felt the pillow pressing against him, and then, slowly, he felt a warmth extending slightly up his spine.

"It feels warm," he said.

"Your nerves under the sedative," Rainier told him.

"Feels good."

Rainier extended his hand for the second syringe. This one had an indigo dye in it. "Hold still," he instructed. Carefully, he placed the needle where he wanted and then gently inserted it. This one had to go further, into the spinal area itself. He watched as the scope showed the needle position relative to the nearest vertebra. He guided the needle further into the cavity where he had performed the surgery after the crash. Then, carefully, he released the contents of the syringe until it was empty before withdrawing it. A small droplet of blood formed where the needle had been, and the nurse wiped it with a sterile gauze pad. She opened a suitable-sized bandage and applied it over the wound. Then she pulled Devin's gown back down and motioned for the orderly to return him to the wheelchair.

"That's all there is," Rainier told him. "If this works, it will happen on its own, but there's no way for us to know short of sensations. So my advice is to act as though you feel nothing, use the physical therapy—which you will need anyway—and do your best to acclimate to having a wheelchair. Okay?"

"Thanks, Doc," Devin said. "If it does work, how soon would I know?"

"Anytime from now on. If you feel nothing in a week, you should prepare yourself that it might not have worked. It is experimental."

"At least it's something. When can I start therapy?"

"In a few days. And, I'll have Jackson go easy for a while. Don't overdo it."

"How will I know if I am overdoing it?"

"If it hurts," Rainier told him, "you are overdoing it."

ON THE WAY back to his room, Devin asked if he could push the chair himself. Bobby agreed and stood back, allowing Devin to feel for the motion and the strength he would need. At the corner, just before entering the room, Devin decided to try Jackson's maneuver, leaning to one side and trying to lift the other wheel off the ground. Bobby watched in amusement.

"You're already trying to copy Jackson," he said. "It took him a year to learn that move."

"Oh!" Devin felt deflated. Jackson made it look so easy, seamless, as though he'd been doing it all his life. Devin wondered how long it would take him to master even the basics.

Bobby lifted him back into the bed, then pushed the wheelchair to the side of the bed. "It's yours to use."

"Thanks, Bobby," Devin said. He adjusted himself and then remembered it was time to check down below. He reached down to feel the diaper. It was time. He grunted in disgust and reached for a new one.

17

TRUTHS BE LEARNED

Days blended together. Each day, Maxie and Jameson would visit, once in the morning and once in the evening. Maxie reminded him that he would stay at her house upon his release, and they would discuss every aspect of the ongoing case.

Hank also visited, mostly to make sure his prize reporter was not falling into the depths of depression. Once he saw that Devin was active, engaged in the case, and eager for therapy, he worried less about visiting, often just sending over books, more notebooks when he noticed Devin was running out of room, and once, a Chinese takeout meal that Nurse Helen pretended not to notice, especially after Devin offered her a spring roll. The next day, a courier delivered a new laptop with a note that read: *Write something. Hank.*

Devin found he was excited and looking forward to his therapy session with his 'Recovery Engineer', Jackson. On the fifth day of his recovery, Nurse Helen advised him that Jackson had requested Devin meet him in the therapy room on the third floor.

"He said you needed to get your...um...rear, out of bed and come alone," she recounted. "I'm afraid that means I cannot assist you getting out of bed."

"Oh," Devin mouthed.

"Not that you need my help. However," she went on, "Were I to help you, I would advise you what to do. And I can move your chair to within arm's reach."

"That's something," Devin said. "Thank you."

"You're welcome. But don't thank me yet." She placed a set of sweats on the bed next to him. "You'll need to change into these. If I may suggest, for the pants, start by positioning them around your buttocks. Then, using your hands, bend one leg all the way. Slide on that leg and pull it up as high as you are able. Then put that leg down and repeat on the other side."

"Sounds simple enough," Devin said.

"Easier said than done, Mr. Parker. And also, you have something to tend to first. I need to grab a chart from my workstation, so I'll be back in a few minutes." She smiled, turned, and left the room.

Something to take care of? He pondered. *Oh. That!* He reached for a clean diaper, deftly swapped it out with the one he had on, and folded the old one. He noted that the trash can was now by the side of the bed, so he dropped it in. *Done!* It was getting more comfortable to perform, even if it was still uncomfortable to think about.

He followed Helen's instructions to get the sweatpants on. With his right leg bent, he tried getting them around his foot. It was awkward. The first few times, he missed, and then he considered opening the sweat pants so when he pulled his leg up, it would already be *inside* the pant leg. *Bingo!* He repeated it with the other leg, then wiggled his body to pull them up all the way.

Nurse Helen walked back in. "Very good. Now for the chair. The first thing you need to learn is to lower your bed closer to wheelchair height. The controls are on your right side."

Devin fumbled with his right hand and felt a group of controls.

"Which is the one I should use?"

"Up and down are the ones closest to the wall behind you."

He pressed one of the switches one way, and the bed began to rise.

"Oops, wrong way." He pressed the same switches the other way, and the bed quickly descended. When he felt it was at the right height, he stopped.

"That's good," the nurse said. "I'll be right back, once again." She left.

Devin realized this was her way of pushing him to perform the tasks alone. He decided to tackle this problem as he would any other problem—logically.

To get into the chair, he would need to ensure the brakes were applied. The hand lever to lock the brakes was just beneath each armrest. He reached the one closest to him, but the other would be too far away.

Think, Parker, he told himself. He lowered the bed rail on his right side. He leaned over and pulled the wheelchair closer to him so that the leg supports were aligned with where his legs would be. *Be careful,* he thought, *or you'll wind up flat on your face on the floor.* Then he locked both sides in place. Using the lowered bed rails as grips, he pushed the right side of his body as close as possible. Then he could reach for the chair handle and arm handles.

He leaned his upper body weight over the wheelchair arms, his left hand still holding the bed bar. Then, when he felt he had a firm grip on the right armrest handle, he pushed down and allowed his body to slide over more. It took a few adjustments to get his butt into the seat, but he managed, even though his legs were still across the left arm rest. At least now he could use his hands to reposition his legs where they needed to be, without falling out.

Finally, he had it, unlocked the brakes, and started to roll toward the door. He had been so busy focusing on the task at hand that he failed to see Nurse Helen standing there. She was beaming.

"Well done, Mr. Parker. Your first big step." She moved closer, straightening out his bedding, and replaced his old gown with a freshly laundered one. "When you return to the bed, put your chair right against the bed. With your dominant arm as far onto the bed as you can, use the other arm to push yourself from the chair. This will get your posterior onto the bed. From there, you can make the adjustments needed."

"Thank you," he said.

"Don't thank me," Helen said. "You did all the work. Mr. Pollak's therapy room is on the third floor. Ignore the signs for rehabilitation—he doesn't use that one—he has his own. When you get out of the elevator, turn right and go down the hallway. Look for the room labeled *engineering*." She smiled. "Mr. Pollak's idea."

Devin was excited. He nodded at her and wheeled quickly out of the room toward the elevator. People were getting off, so he waited and then rolled inside, leaning over to press the button for the third floor. The doors closed. He swiveled around to face the doors. He was feeling an element of freedom that caught him by surprise. It had only been a week since he was in the accident, and until today, he had felt confined. Jackson had managed to fire him up.

The doors opened, and he wheeled out to the right, as instructed, and down the hallway. Finally, he caught sight of the door. It had a 'Star Trek' insignia, and below it a sign that read: Engineering. Authorized Engineers Only.

Devin chuckled, pushed against the door to open it, and entered the room.

It was large, a former storage room, some six hundred square feet in size. On one side, there was a free-weights tray with assorted barbells. The room had a modified treadmill with an overhead bar and support lines. *Did people really use that?* Devin wondered.

Jackson was at the other end, behind a set of parallel bars that gymnasts use. "Come on over," he shouted out. "Glad you made it."

Devin wheeled past the resistance machines—the same that you would see at any gym, only these had no seats; instead, they had a slot where a wheelchair could fit and lock in place.

"Do you like engineering?" he asked as Devin approached.

"Classic," Devin said. "Or should I say *Aye, Captain?*"

Jackson laughed. "You have to enjoy what you do, Devin, or what's the point?"

"You do look like you enjoy your work."

"I try. I spoke with your doc. Your wounds are healing nicely. Your spine is strong enough that you can put some exertion on it, so I don't have to worry about killing you today."

"That's good news."

Jackson moved closer until their knees were almost touching, then locked his own wheels. "Today, we'll start with something simple. See those bars?" He pointed at the parallel bars.

"Yeah?"

"You ever worked those?"

"You serious?"

"Absolutely."

"You're nuts," Devin said.

"I hear that a lot," he said with a grin. "Wait until you see what's coming after." He leaned forward, locked Devin's wheels, then, wrapping his left hand behind Devin's back, gently pushed him forward, despite Devin's resistance, and out of the chair, onto the floor. He reached over, unlocked the brakes on Devin's chair, and pushed it back out of his reach.

"You asshole," Devin shouted. Caught off guard, he was fuming, struggling to move his body toward Jackson, floundering on the floor like a fish out of water. "This is crazy!"

"Isn't it?" Jackson happily said. Then he leaned forward and allowed himself to fall out of his own chair, onto the floor next to Devin. He pushed his own chair, rolling out of reach.

Devin twisted and tried grabbing him, but had no leverage.

"Whoa, boy, don't hurt yourself," the man teased. "Now, shut up, watch, and learn."

Jackson used his arms to drag himself across the distance from the chair to the bars, then, reaching one hand up, lifted his body off the ground enough to use the other hand to grip even higher up the vertical strut. With some effort, he hoisted himself even higher, grunting hard with the effort. He stopped for a moment to catch his breath, then resumed, one hand gripping above the other, using sheer arm strength to reach the horizontal bars, his legs now hanging below him.

Holding onto one of the bars, he reached over and grabbed the one furthest from him, then pulled himself up and over the top of the first bar until he was lying across the two. He caught his breath again. Then he used both arms to force his limp legs over the first bar and into the space between, where they just dangled. His body was being held up by arm strength alone.

Now in the position—and looking like a professional gymnast—he looked down at Devin, a strained look on his face, and forced a smile. He began to swing his legs using his upper body as leverage, back and forth, back and forth, higher and higher until his legs were perpendicular to his torso. And then, with one giant swing, he released his grip on the bars, twisted his torso around hard, forcing his legs to follow, and grabbed the bars once again.

Now he was facing the opposite direction, his legs still swinging back and forth. After a few more swings, he allowed them to come to rest across the top of the two bars and looked at Devin.

"Your turn, champ."

Devin, throughout the demonstration, couldn't remove his stare. *How the hell did he manage that?* "You're joking, right?"

"Man, it's all in your head. You decide what you can and can't do. Not your legs. Not anyone else. You. So make a choice. Be a helpless, depressed cripple plodding through life, or live and enjoy life. Your call."

Devin listened in silence. His earlier elation had turned to anger. *If this crazy SOB can do it, so can I.* He started to drag himself to the bars.

Jackson watched.

Devin copied what he had seen Jackson doing. He grabbed a vertical bar and pulled himself up. It was excruciatingly painful, but he pushed past the pain and yanked his body off the ground enough to use his other arm. On the first try, his right hand slipped, and he collapsed on the floor, panting.

He looked up at Jackson, who said nothing.

He tried it again, this time able to reach the first horizontal bar. But he was unable to get across. Looking at Jackson, he shouted, "What do I do?"

"Grab the second bar and use that."

Devin did so and managed to pull himself across the bars on his belly. He was out of breath, panting as if he'd just run a marathon. His body hurt.

For a moment, he remained there, balancing. Finally, he managed to adjust his position, dragging his legs to the space between the bars and allowing them to drop into that space, his arms bearing the weight. Holding that pose for a moment, he started to swing his legs back and forth a few times, ending with both legs matching Jackson's.

Jackson dragged himself closer to Devin, leaned over, and extended his hand. "Lesson one—your brain runs the show. Your body goes along for the ride."

"Right," Devin said, panting. He was feeling elated again—he'd managed to do something he had, only a few minutes earlier, considered impossible. *If I can do this*, he thought, *I can do...anything.*

"I've found there's very little that people like us can't do if we choose to do it. The word they use is *disability*, meaning a lack of ability. I like to call this *reAbility*. What do you think?"

Devin nodded. "I like it. I am reAbled. I have just one question, though. How the heck do we get down?" He was laughing now, as was Jackson. And for the briefest of moments, Devin Parker believed that he could fly.

18

REABILITY

Every day, for the next two weeks, Devin and Jackson trained twice a day. Devin's upper body strength rapidly increased, and muscles developed that had not existed before. Each session was tougher than the previous one.

At the same time, Jackson had him work out his legs, as well. The treadmill was a little tricky and required some practice. The overhead bar was motorized, and the controls were on the treadmill handle, both above and below. First, you had to position yourself beneath the bar, just at the back of the treadmill. Using the motor to drop the bar, you had to put your arms over the bar so that it was resting under your armpits. A Velcro strap was then tied behind your back so the bar would not slip.

A small box on the treadmill leg held electrodes. These you placed on your legs at set locations. The electrodes would generate a tiny current, causing leg muscles to spasm in a set rhythm that simulated a walking motion.

The first time Devin tried it, Jackson had to help him.

Once in position, Jackson told Devin to use the switch to have the motor hoist his body up. Now he was hanging over the treadmill, his arms over the padded bar. A second switch moved him forward—and later backward—into position on the treadmill. He reached the controls. Jackson told him to start at 2.5 mph. As the belt moved, his legs dangled awkwardly.

"Now comes the hard part," Jackson said. "Turn on the electrodes. They're programmed to send the right pulses. Once your legs start moving, you'll have to use your upper body to make sure the legs are square on the belt. Got it?"

Devin shook his head. "Here goes, anyway." He activated the electrodes, and his legs started to move as though he were walking. Only his feet were not on the belt; instead, they were still hanging behind.

"Pull up with your body," Jackson told him. "More...."

Devin obliged, forcing his upper body to curl upwards, bringing his feet onto the treadmill. All of a sudden, his shoes made contact, and he was walking. Devin started to laugh. "Amazing...I'm walking."

"And you thought it was crazy," Jackson reminded him.

Devin's feet were perfectly timed to the movement of the belt. "Did you invent this?"

"Nah. I just put these ideas together as one. With practice, you'll be able to do it by yourself."

Every day of the two weeks, Maxie continued to come visit twice a day, often without Jameson. She enjoyed spending time with Devin. She enjoyed discussing cases with his reporter's slant, small things that she may have overlooked. But most of all, she enjoyed watching his progress, developing from a paraplegic back into an enabled person, no longer allowing physical impediments to slow him down.

By the time he got to his room, Maxie was already there.

She had brought him a Danish pastry and a newspaper. "I hope Jameson did not get shortchanged on his pastry," Devin said.

Maxie laughed. "Don't you worry, Kobe got his own, so there is no jealousy between you."

Dr. Rainier arrived and gave him more news. "You're going home. You've done remarkably well."

"When?"

"Today. Now. Unless you want to stay for our fine luncheon?"

Devin feigned a look of horror. "It's not that bad, but I think I will pass on lunch. I feel good. Everything except for my legs."

"Give it time. Your body is still healing. If you have no progress by this time next month, let's talk more. But you've done very well. Jackson says you're good to return as an outpatient. At least twice a week. More if you can squeeze it in."

"More?"

"If you want," Rainier told him. "And I want to see you next week for a follow-up. The nurse will set up an appointment."

"Thank you," Devin said.

Rainier shook his hand. "You're very welcome. I do hope that things improve here on out."

After he had left, Nurse Helen came in with some papers for him to sign. "Your ride is on the way. Your boss said he was coming to get you, but I told him you had a ride already." She turned and smiled at Maxie. She handed him a bag. "These are discharge instructions—just a formality. I've also put some extra *items* and a few catheters in a bag. If you decide you'd like to try them, just let us know. We can send a visiting nurse to assist you."

"I appreciate all your help, Nurse Helen," he said. "I'll miss seeing you."

"Thank you, Mr. Parker. It's been a pleasure," she said. "And you're always welcome to visit." She moved to the closet and returned with his street clothes, placing them on the bed for him. These were not the clothes he had on—*the accident must have ruined those*, he considered. "Your boss brought these for you," she said. She then pulled the privacy curtain closed so he could get changed.

Having already managed to change into and out of sweats, getting his street clothes on would be easy—or certainly not as challenging as it would have been a week earlier. *Just a few more pieces*, he told himself.

Ten minutes later, he was done. There were no shoes, but he had the hospital slippers. He hoisted himself into his wheelchair and then slid open the privacy curtain.

Maxie was talking on her phone. She waved and gestured that she'd just be a minute longer. Then the call ended. "Ready to get out of here?"

Devin nodded. "I need to swing by my apartment first, if that's okay?"

"Sure. Pick up enough things for a week. We can always go back and get more, but the less often we are there, the better. At least until this mess is cleared up."

"Any more leads?" Devin asked.

Maxie shook her head. "Something will pop up. It always does."

Bobby the orderly arrived. Devin was already in a wheel-chair—the hospital would provide it until he had purchased one of his own. Bobby insisted he would push him—hospital regulations—to avoid any liability from injuries that happened on the way out.

Maxie walked ahead of him. "I'll bring the car around," she said. "Meet you out front."

He nodded, watching as she quickly left. He found his eyes tracking after her, and felt reassured when she was around. *I like her*, he thought. It was a good thing to feel that way, although he reminded himself not to get too attached; she was being friendly. Besides, he was wheelchair bound and despite Jackson's affirmation of *reAbility*, the fact remained that he was wheelchair bound.

Moments later, her Audi was out front. She had popped the trunk and got out to open the passenger door.

"Let me," Devin said to the orderly, who was about to lift him into the car. Devin wheeled alongside the seat and deftly hoisted himself into his seat, careful not to bash his head on the top of the door frame. "Ta-da!" he proclaimed proudly.

Maxie was smiling. "Well done. You've learned a lot." Then to Bobby, "You can just put it in the trunk, thanks."

Bobby folded the chair and placed it flat in the trunk, closing the lid. "Good luck, bro," he said.

"Thanks, Bobby. I appreciate what you've done."

Devin reached out and closed the passenger door as Maxie went around to get in the driver's side.

"Thank you again for this," he told her. "Are you sure it's not an imposition?"

Maxie laughed. "Of course it is, hun, but I'd rather keep you alive than worry about a little bother. Don't worry about it, okay?"

Devin nodded.

THEIR FIRST STOP was at his apartment. She pulled the chair out of the trunk and unfolded it, but Devin did the rest, getting himself into the chair, closing the car door, and leading the way to the elevator.

Outside his apartment, he handed Maxie the keys. With her gun drawn—she had it concealed in her waistband behind her back- she unlocked the door, pushed it open, making sure that the apartment was empty before putting her gun away and allowing Devin to enter.

The place was still in disarray, and he had to maneuver around items still on the floor. In his bedroom, he grabbed a duffel bag from the closet and filled it with shirts, underwear, pants, socks, and shoes, before wheeling to the bathroom for other toiletries he might need.

In the living room, he spotted the photograph he had taken from Curtis's office and added that to the bag. Beyond that, he could not think of anything else he would need. Hank had replaced the laptop stolen during the break-in.

Maxie was looking out his deck. "Nice view you have," she said.

"One of the few joys of the place," he said.

"Do you like sailing?"

"Never been."

Maxie stared at him in disbelief. "Well, we'll have to fix that."

"Have you ever saved a paraplegic from drowning?" he joked.

Maxie cast him an indignant look. "Are you saying that I'm a lousy sailor?"

Devin laughed, then shook his head. "But I'm sure I'm a lousy swimmer."

"Maybe," she said. "Now let's get out of here."

In her car, she took a few moments to check the area. She

was looking for anything suspicious. The last thing she needed was someone following them home.

Maxie lived on Padre Island—what the locals simply called *The Island.* To get there, you crossed the bridge from Flour Bluff, a short five-minute drive that was flat until the deepest part of the harbor, when the bridge went up, over fifty feet, to allow boats to pass beneath, before descending again.

The Island had different names, depending on which way you turned. Turning left toward Port Aransas, it was called Mustang Island, complete with a State Park leading to where the beach was. Port Aransas also had a car ferry to take residents across the short bay to Aransas Pass on the mainland side. From Port Aransas, you could take cruises for Dolphin watching, fishing charters, restaurants, and much more.

The right side was Padre Island, a long, thin inlet that ran down south all the way to the Mexican border, although broken up, eliminating a continuous drive.

Down there, it was named South Padre Island, but the setup was similar. It was close enough to Elon Musk's SpaceX launch facility in Boca Chica. The launch pad was just off the main road. It was close enough for tourists to stop for a photo op with at least one of the rockets sitting on the launch pad. Whenever a launch was to take place, the area was placed on lockdown. The nearest place the public could watch the launch was Port Isabel, on the land side of South Padre Island.

Spring breakers, flocking to Padre Island, were often disappointed to learn South Padre Island was three hours south. It didn't stop them, however, from filling the beaches, causing massive traffic jams, and allowing the local police to issue endless citations. During spring break, there was a patrol car to be found everywhere you looked. And during that period, they were absolutely unforgiving.

Locals like Maxie were happy with the added police presence.

Maxie lived in the main area of the island, down Whitecap Boulevard, on Yardarm Court, a short spit of land where houses on both sides enjoyed canal access. Each home had private boat docks and, of course, a wide variety of boats, sailboats, fishing boats, and even paddle boats that were parked there.

Her house was at the end of the street, a two-story house that, outside, resembled her neighbors—a whitewashed, sun-bleached exterior, gravel front lawn, and two palm trees—everyone had palms.

Maxie opened the trunk and pulled out Devin's wheel-chair, unfolding it and moving it toward him. Devin already had the door open, pulled the chair closer, and lifted himself into it. He reached for his duffel bag and put it on his lap. Maxie put the hospital bag over the back of the chair handles, then moved toward the front door.

"Hi Maxie," Maxie's neighbor, Jan, called out from her front yard. Maxie waved.

"Hi Jan," she said, then pointing at Devin, added, "This is Devin. He'll be staying with me awhile."

"Hi Devin," Jan said. "Welcome to the neighborhood." Devin waved.

Maxie unlocked her front door, shut off the alarm system, and motioned Devin in. "This is the ground floor," she said. The interior was warm, with wood paneling and paintings of marine life. Potted plants flooded the floors, but she had pushed most of these against the walls to clear a path for Devin. Maxie adored her plants. The coffee table held a few books, a framed photo of two older people who looked somewhat like her—Devin surmised these were her parents. Large, puffy cushions sat atop the soft couches. The room was colorful.

"You have a bedroom to the right, an office study, a bathroom with a shower and tub, and a kitchen. And the living room is here. Upstairs is my bedroom and another room that's mostly a storage room." She pointed out to the deck. "There are two levels to the deck. This level has a boat slip. So you see, we have a measure of privacy."

"It's very nice," Devin said. "Beats my view."

"Well, let's not compare. Get settled and let's have a bite to eat on the deck, okay? I've moved anything that might get in your way, but if I missed anything, tell me."

Devin nodded. "Sounds terrific." He rolled to where the bedroom was and placed his duffel bag and moved the bag from the handles onto the bed. He was now in the habit of checking himself and realized that a change was in order. Quickly, he handled that, unpacked the duffel bag, and placed the photo frame next to his bed.

By the time he rolled out, Maxie had made a ham and cheese sandwich for them both and had also poured a glass of chilled rosé. She was at the table on the deck, enjoying the view, when he showed up. He noticed that she had moved the other chair aside so he could fit. "Thanks for that," he said.

"I took the liberty...," she said, pointing at the glasses. "If you would prefer something else...?"

"This is fine," he said, reaching for a glass and raising it. "Thank you again, Maxie."

She smiled. "You're quite welcome. Hank said he'll be stopping by later to check on you. I can invite him to dinner if you'd like."

"Maxie, please don't add more work for yourself. I appreciate the offer, though."

He took a bite of the sandwich, washed it down with the rosé, and breathed in the salt air. "It's incredibly peaceful," he said. "I'd never leave."

Maxie nodded. "There are days, let me tell ya. But it is home, and after work I surely need it." She refilled his glass.

"Thanks."

"I gotta tell you, Devin. When you told me about your parents and how you and Curtis were raised, I was just amazed when I look at you how you've taken it all in stride. Just half of that would crush me."

He took another sip. "What else can I do, Maxie? I mean, you either deal with what life gives you or you don't. It's not like I have many choices."

"I suppose."

"So what about you? You know all about me. I don't know much about you at all."

"What would you like to know?"

Devin thought about the question. "For one thing, you are not what most people would call a regular detective."

Maxie threw her head back and laughed. "I guess I'm not."

"Not married? Family? What makes you tick?"

"Long stories, all." She grabbed her wine and took a large gulp. "Okay. Fair enough. I guess I am so used to being the one asking the questions...."

"You don't have to answer if I've made you uncomfortable," he told her. Her face softened into a smile.

"Hun, you don't make me uncomfortable at all. In fact, quite the opposite. But here goes.... I was married, really young, a lifetime ago, it seems, right out of college. He swept me off my feet. Good looking guy, tall, thick, dark hair, and blue eyes like the water. He had style. Kind of guy that walks into a room and everyone looks."

Devin was listening intently and nodded. "Sounds like true love?"

Maxie laughed. "Yes, it was. He was truly in love with himself, that's for sure. He was an up-and-coming actor. Went to school in Los Angeles, and I followed him. I believed that we had a future. But once we got there, he discovered what most of Hollywood discovers when they begin to make it...they are the center of the universe. Everyone tells them how wonderful they are. How beautiful they are. How big a star they will become. Fans adore them, crazy little women with no life that line up for hours to catch a glimpse."

"Wow," Devin said. "So I'm guessing that did not end well?"

"You could say that. He found success in film and in quite a few bedrooms of other women. It wasn't personal, he would say. It was just how business was done. Only that was a lot of bull. It was a choice he made, and I was just a small trinket that he had to show for his success."

"I'm sorry," Devin said. Maxie stopped, realizing that she was getting angry, then took a breath.

"Don't be. I'm not sorry anymore. I learned a lot because of him. I discovered my own strengths. So I left. Never looked back. Thank God I never had kids with him—can you imagine how messed up they would be?"

"I think you'd be a great mother. You have a lot of heart."

"You're sweet. Thank you."

"Do I know who this guy is? You said he was successful?"

"Probably," she said, sipping at her wine. "But you ain't gonna hear it from me. I took a vow to never mention his name again. I also vowed to never see his movies—no way I am supporting that ego."

Devin laughed. "Okay. Enough said, then." He raised his glass. "To being tough and surviving," he said.

"Now that I can drink to." She pushed the bottle closer to him. "Please help yourself—anything in the house. Don't wait to be asked, okay?"

He nodded.

"So what about you? No special person?"

"Funny, I was thinking that after Curtis died. All I do is run around getting stories. It seems that time just passes so fast, and the world is one story after another. And then one day you realize how much time you've lost. So no." He was staring at his glass, caught up in the thought.

"Well, hun, I would say that's a shame, but who am I to give romance advice?" She raised her glass in a toast. "To us." He leaned over and they clinked glasses.

"To us, Maxie. And brighter days."

"I like that."

19

ANSWERS TO FIND

Maxie was annoyed at herself for taking so long to get back to Marjorie. As she and Jameson approached the alleyway, she hoped that the woman had not changed her mind and bolted—they needed her as a witness.

She had left Devin with a police guard out front, told him she wouldn't be too long, but then felt guilty when she left, as though she was leaving him undefended.

The alleyway leading to the encampment was wet from the humidity of the night before. Texas was swamp-humid, and even though other areas of the south endured the harshest of humidity, Texas, in general, and here, in particular, the feeling of wetness pressed in around you. It was an acquired flavor. The stone walls were dripping wet. Between the darkness of the stone, the lousy lighting of this overcast day, and the mood that both Maxie and Jameson were feeling, the overall sensation was one of hopelessness and gloom.

Maxie was feeling helpless; there was no denying it. Countless murders and a narrow band of leads, witnesses that led nowhere, and more recently, Devin—Devin who had burst into her life, first as a next of kin, then as a witness, then as a victim. Now he was a house guest, because she knew that alone, he would be a target. But was it more than that? She liked him. There was a decency about him that permeated whatever he did. She liked that. The only other person she knew like that was Jameson, not that she had ever entertained any romantic feelings toward him. Jameson was like a brother to her, a partner as attuned to her as she was to him. She trusted him with her life, and she knew that he felt the same way.

Decency is hard to find, she contemplated as they pushed in further. The encampment was before them, and she scanned for Marjorie, hoping that she would be standing in the open. But she was not.

Maxie approached another woman pushing a cart. "Darlin, I'm looking for Marjorie?"

The woman stopped, pointed back with her thumb to a tent at the corner, then continued, uninterested in anything more to do with Maxie. Maxie and Jameson moved closer.

"Marjorie, it's Maxie. You home, dear?" She hoped that Marjorie would not be scared and come out. "Marjorie," she called out again. "Remember me, we spoke ?"

"I remember," a voice said from behind them, and Maxie spun around to face Marjorie. Maxie placed her hand across her chest.

"Lord, you scared me," she said.

"Sorry, didn't mean to. But you were talking to the tent."

"Indeed," Maxie said with a smile. "Weren't we Kobe?"

Jameson shrugged. "I was looking elsewhere," he said.

"I thought you were coming the next day? It's been many days."

"I know," Maxie said. "We had a big problem that we needed to focus on. But we're here now."

Maxie pulled out a sachet of photographs. "I promised all I wanted was for you to see if you saw the man who dumped the body. You do not have to testify. Remember?"

Marjorie nodded. "I remember. I trust you. You're very pretty. I know you mean well."

Maxie blushed. "Well, thank you, sweetheart. That means a lot to me." She handed her the photos. "Now I need you to look carefully and take your time. It's okay if you do not recognize anyone. I don't want you to tell me unless you are sure, okay?"

Marjorie nodded, taking the pictures and looking through them. She studied each face, moving the photographs closer, then further back, then flipping to the next, placing the old one at the back of the stack.

"Not these," she said. "Too small. Beady eyes. Bald."

Jameson cast a look Maxie's way. He had wondered why it had taken her so long to get the photos to Marjorie. All she would tell him was that she wanted to add some other photos. Suddenly, Marjorie began to laugh, her solitary front tooth standing out amidst the blackness of the rest of her mouth.

"You're trying to trick me," she said, holding up one photograph. It was Jameson who saw it and looked shocked.

"You didn't?"

Maxie was giggling. "Sorry, Kobe. I did." Maxie took the photo back. "Keep looking."

Marjorie swapped photos. On the fourth photo, she stopped, stared at it hard. She looked up at Maxie, then back at the photo again. Finally, after she had scrutinized it further, she took it and handed it to Maxie.

"You're sure?"

Marjorie nodded, her eyes dropping to the ground. "Can't forget it."

"Thank you, Marjorie," Maxie said, reaching for the other photos and adding them to make a single pile.

"Well?" Jameson asked, exasperated.

Maxie gave him the pile to hold as she reached into her purse for her wallet. Finding it she retrieved two twenty-dollar bills and handed them to Marjorie. "You did good today, Marjorie," she said. Marjorie took the bills. "The Corpus Christi Police Department would like to thank you for helping us solve a crime."

Marjorie beamed.

Jameson scanned the photos. Then stopped. He looked up at Maxie, who gave him the look he knew so well. This was the break in the case that they needed.

"Take care of yourself, Marjorie," Maxie told her. "We won't bother you anymore." She steered Jameson back toward where they had parked.

Once they were out of earshot, Jameson turned to her. "Is that why you delayed showing her photographs?"

"Something just did not sit right with me," she explained. "And since the attempt on Devin's life, it's been eating at me more and more."

"Did you discuss it with Devin?"

Maxie shook her head. "It would only devastate him further."

"You will have to tell him now."

"That I will."

As they walked, Maxie was too busy studying the alley walls as they exited onto the street that she failed to notice the small vehicle there. Inside, the stranger watched her and Jameson as they approached. When they were close enough, he opened his car door and got out, making sure to stand staring at her so she could not miss him.

"Detective Maxie. I must speak with you."

Maxie and Jameson stopped and turned toward the man. Neither recognized him, but moved closer, anyway. Jameson had his hand silently on his gun in case it would be needed.

"Do I know you?" Maxie asked.

"We have not met, but I know who you are and the case that you are following."

"And how is that? Are you somehow related?"

The man shook his head. "I have been following this investigation for some time, and believe that I have information that will be of use to you."

"Go on," Maxie said.

"My sister was Tia Dewilla." He lied, but considered it an excellent way to disarm any suspicion on their part.

Maxie's face fell, believing that the man had a valid reason to contact her. "Then you know...?"

The man nodded.

"I am very sorry for your loss," she said sympathetically. The man offered no response.

He walked around the front of the car until he was standing next to them both. Maxie, studying his face, saw that the realization of what had happened to Tia had been fresh news to him, at least that was how he wished it to appear. "How did you learn of her passing?"

"I cannot reveal that," he said. He had a slight Middle Eastern accent, the pronunciation of his R and L letter sounds was more accentuated. "Forgive me for this secrecy. It is essential for now."

"Go on," she said.

"My sister had come to me several weeks ago fearful of information she had acquired. It became a matter of urgency for her only after Mr. Curtis was killed. She became fearful for her own life."

"What information?"

"I do not know. She would not tell me. She was planning to tell Mr. Devin Parker, and had asked me to ensure that he was trustworthy. Sadly, my efforts were not enough. While I had learned that Mr. Devin was trustworthy, and my sister arranged to meet with him, she was discovered and chased, leading up to the attempt on Mr. Devin's life."

"You know a lot," Maxie said, unsure whether to believe him. This was overly convenient and she debated whether a better course of action would be to arrest him; he obviously had information. "So why come to me?"

"I wish to avenge my sister's death. I have been watching you and have concluded that you are trustworthy. And, I wish to give you information that I have obtained."

"That's good," she said. "I need all the information I can get."

"What information?" Jameson asked.

The man stopped to consider his answer before speaking. "I have a small problem, however...."

Maxie cast Jameson a look. "And what might that be?"

"The information I am about to share with you was not obtained in a legal manner."

"I see."

"While I wish for you to use this information to make arrests, you need to know this fact."

"I appreciate that warning," Maxie said. "What's your name?"

The stranger stopped. "Name?"

"You have one, right?"

"Of course. I am afraid that I must withhold that information from you."

"Or I could arrest you for meddling in a police matter," she said calmly.

"I wish to not be involved legally in this matter. You have enough people involved. Would it not be possible for me to remain anonymous?"

"Anonymous is hell for the paperwork trail we have," Maxie said.

"Ah," the man said. "Then we are at an impasse."

They stood silent for a moment, neither sure what the next move should be, and then the man turned back to his car.

"Wait. How certain are you that your information is good?" Maxie finally asked.

"I have copies of emails, telephone communications, and video feeds," the man said.

"That you obtained?"

The man nodded.

"Illegally?"

The man paused, then nodded. "Sometimes the legal way is the least efficient way."

Maxie sighed. "Tell me about it. And the information will allow me to move this investigation along to arrests?"

"Yes. It is my wish that I could incite revenge upon those responsible myself; however, my investigation has concluded that there is more than one player, and that the ultimate truth would be too much for me to handle alone."

Maxie considered what he had told her. She looked at Jameson. "Kobe, your thoughts?"

"You already know my thoughts," he said. "We need to have a break in this case. If this will help us to move forward...."

Maxie nodded. "And I can always arrest this gentleman if he turns out to be wasting my time."

"Exactly," Jameson said.

Maxie turned back to the man. "Let's give you a name," she told him. "You are my confidential informant, my CI. Your name is Jones"

The man looked puzzled. "Jones?"

"It's for the paperwork," Maxie explained. "Since you will not give us your real name.

"What is it you wish to share with us?" Jameson asked.

"I have surveillance equipment that I left in the offices of Rob Meeker. This included a surveillance camera, wire taps on his telephone, and a digital interface allowing me to access his office computer." Jones said all this plainly and with a straight face, although Maxie hardly believed what she was hearing."

"You're a one-man CIA," she quipped. "No wonder you needed to qualify how illegal it was."

"I did warn you," Jones said.

"And what did you learn?"

"While I could not obtain direct evidence that linked Meeker to the death of his office partner, I did obtain information of another individual with whom he had been dealing. Encrypted emails that led back to other individuals with criminal backgrounds, financial records that were partially erased—I believe in the rush of cleaning up prior to your arrival. I have all of these for you." Jones held out a plain, unmarked USB thumb drive for Maxie.

Maxie gingerly took it from him, holding it between two fingers before allowing it to settle into her palm.

"Even if the information is inadmissible in court, it should help with our investigation?"

Jones nodded. "That is my hope. There is much to be gleaned from the information."

"And what do you get from this?" Jameson asked.

"Justice," Jones said. "I heard your conversation with Meeker at his office. I heard what he had said about my sister. It is not true. They did not have a breakup, although he frightened her greatly." He looked around to be sure that he had not attracted any unwanted attention.

"You believe that he is responsible for your sister's death?" Maxie asked.

Jones nodded. "I also believe that he is the most likely suspect in the death of Curtis Delaney. That evidence is not in the files I have given you."

"He could be innocent?" Maxie asked. "He was reportedly the closest of friends with Curtis Delaney."

"This may be true," Jones answered. "I do not believe that his involvement would have been of his choosing."

"Someone else ordered him to kill Curtis?"

As much as Maxie believed what she was hearing, a part of her remained suspicious. Certainly, the pieces to the puzzle fit. Rob may well have had the means; however, the motive was still a mystery.

"You will have to come to your own conclusions," Jones said. "I can tell you that the other people involved have strong criminal connections. You may discover more than you wish to know."

Maxie carefully pocketed the thumb drive. "Nothing will surprise me, Mr. Jones. I thank you for coming forward."

Jones smiled. "It has been an unfortunate series of events. With luck, God willing, you will make it whole again."

"How can I contact you?" Maxie asked.

Jones walked to his car and opened the driver's door. "Hopefully, I will be close by," he told her.

Maxie stared at him, unsure how to react. He got in the

car and pulled out. Jameson began to jot the plate number down. He would check it later.

After he had driven off, Maxie asked Jameson for a pair of latex gloves.

"They're in the car."

"Just give me the used one you stuff in your pockets."

"I try not to litter," he said, handing her one. "But why?

Slipping her thumb and forefinger into the glove, she retrieved the thumb drive from her pocket, then slipped it inside the glove as she removed her fingers. She handed it to Jameson. "Dust it for prints before we see what's on it," she said. "I do not trust that man."

JONES PULLED to the side of the road several blocks up and waited until he saw that Maxie and Jameson had driven off in the other direction. The flash drive he had given them served only one purpose; it contained information they already knew, and would offer no other clues other than the alibi he had just established.

Of course, it was all a lie. Tia was neither his sister nor a friend. He had killed her. His employer had decided to tie up some loose ends, and the information on Meeker was part of that. Jones had swept the office, found nothing at all that Delaney had left behind. This meant that whatever form the copy had taken, it was out there, most likely with Devin Parker, the only logical choice.

The flash drive's other purpose was the tracker embedded in it. Jones would be able to determine where Maxie lived, as well as where she went. No doubt, since Parker had left the hospital and had not gone home, she had placed him in protective custody. He would determine where that was by the repeat visit locations. Then, when his employer approved, he could finish the job.

FINALLY A DECENT LEAD

By the time she arrived at her house, Jameson noted that she was furious. The meeting with Jones and the information from Marjorie was damning for Rob. She knew it would only hurt Devin more than he had already been hurt.

She slammed the car door as she got out. Jameson noted her anger. The police officer she had assigned to guard her house just stared at her.

"What? You never saw a lady slam a car door before?"

"Not you," Jameson said calmly. "In all our time together, I have not seen you so angry."

"Well, I am," she said, stamping her feet. "But not at you, you know that?"

"I do," Jameson said. "For now, we should focus on the positive—you have information that can move us forward."

"Finally," she said. "Anything to report?" she asked the officer.

"No ma'am," he replied.

"Well, that's something, at least." Now they could check for prints and examine the thumb drive contents.

She unlocked the front door, and they went inside. From the door, she saw Devin sitting on the deck, his chair locked to the table. His laptop was open. She hoped that he was writing, but he wasn't.

"We have good leads," she said, stepping onto the deck. She showed him the thumb drive. "Want to plug this in after we check for prints. It's supposed to have a lot of information."

Jameson took the drive and placed it on the table. Using a portable dusting kit, he removed it and checked the thumb drive. There was a print, and he used his phone to scan it before sending it to his assistant to run through CODIS. He then handed it to Devin.

Devin plugged it into the open port on the side of his laptop. "It seems to have a lot of files."

"Browse through and see if anything stands out."

"These look like encoded files," Devin said. "I see phone logs. Also, some video files." He selected one, and it opened up, showing a view from Rob's office from above—perhaps a ceiling camera. "Nothing much to see. Where did this come from?"

"We were approached by a man claiming to be Tia's brother. He has been surveilling Rob. He believes he is involved."

"In Curtis's death?" Devin asked.

Maxie nodded. "He's correct. Kobe and I just found a witness who identified the person dumping Curtis's body in the alley. It was Rob."

Devin's face fell. He felt numb. "He was Curtis's best friend. Curtis trusted him."

"I know, hun. I am so sorry." Maxie went to the fridge, took out a bottle of Viognier and three glasses, and brought them to the table. She poured some for each of them. "According to the informant, there is a level of organized crime taking shape. If this is true, we need to get the names of everyone involved before this escalates into a full-on mafia-style gangland."

"So Hank was right about his conspiracy theory."

"I hope you like this wine," she said, handing him a glass. "I'm still stuck on finding out what it was that Curtis had found that they wanted so badly."

"This isn't it. I can't open the files." Devin took a sip of the wine. "It tastes good." He continued checking the drive, although now his mind was on Rob's involvement in Curtis's death. *Why would you do it, Rob?* "If you were Curtis, and you wanted to ensure that someone would find the information in the event of your death, who would that person be and how would he get it to that person?"

Maxie was following the process to a natural conclusion. "We all agree that Curtis was smart enough to protect himself."

Devin stopped, pulled out the drive, and placed it on the table. "This is useless." He pushed it toward Jameson. "I would like to believe that Curtis would try to get it to me. As for what and how, I have been constantly thinking about that. He did not send anything. No calls, texts, or emails. I did not see anything in his office, and it would not have been there since the place had already been ransacked."

Devin took another sip of wine, rehashing the question in his mind. He remembered being in Curtis's office, sitting at his desk. The place was a mess. *If I were Curtis and had to keep something safe, so it would get to me, Devin, what would I do? Let's say I have no time... I would need to be sure that Devin would find it.*

He sat up straight. It suddenly dawned on him what it could be. "In Curtis's office, I had been sitting at his desk. The office was a mess. I picked up some things from the floor, Maxie. Remember?"

"The photo frame?" Maxie chimed in.

"In plain sight," Devin said. "No one would suspect." He wheeled to his room to retrieve it. Jameson and Maxie exchanged looks. *Could it have been so simple?*

A few moments later, Devin returned with the photo frame on his lap. He parked and placed it on the table.

"If I were Curtis and had no way to get information out, I might expect that the one thing I, Devin, would want, would be this photograph because it meant a lot to us both. And I did."

He flipped it over. The back had been taped shut, in addition to the clasps. He peeled the tape and pushed the clasps aside, then popped the photograph from the frame. A small micro-SD card, no larger than a half-thumbnail, was taped between the photo and the backing paper. Devin peeled it loose and held it between his fingers. "And there it is."

They all stared at it for a moment. This small piece of plastic could hold all the answers. It may have cost Curtis his life.

"Will it fit in one of your computer ports?" Maxie asked. "If not, I have a reader that will work."

Devin's new laptop had ports for both standard SD cards and micro-SD. He slipped it in and lifted the lid, powering up the laptop. Using the file explorer app, he selected the small drive. A multitude of files popped up, including a video file. He selected it.

Curtis's face filled the screen. He looked tired, nervous. "Dev, I hope it's you seeing this. I don't have much time, and if you see this then...I'm a dead man, already dead. On this

SD, you have all the files you need to make sure that the criminals can be brought down. It's the mafia, man. Long story—Rob got himself involved. The data was delivered to me by mistake. Once I saw what it was, I copied it. This is the copy. It's bad, man. Everything I've built is going to be ruined. These are horrible people—killers. Trust no one. They're everywhere." Curtis paused for a moment, glanced around the office. "Sorry, I can't tell you this in person. I know this is going to hurt you, after all we have both been through. Just promise me you will stay safe, nail these bastards. And live a good life. For me. Love you, man. Couldn't have asked for a better brother." The video ended, Curtis's face frozen on the screen.

Tears were flowing freely down Devin's face. Maxie walked behind him and wrapped her arms around him and held him tightly. "I'm so sorry, hun," she said softly. Devin wiped at his face, trying to gain composure. Then he opened up the other documents on the card, Maxie watching from behind him.

"Financials. Bank records. Payoffs." He clicked that file open. The file opened a spreadsheet program on the computer, revealing a long list of names, dates, and amounts paid.

"Sweet Jesus," Maxie hissed. "Kobe, look at this... I know these cops... Barrett, Domingo, Johnson, Lopes, Sanderson, Valdez...Judge Harmon, Judge Lopez, Council members Patron and Dixon, Congressman Flinders, Senator Bordana...unbelievable." Maxie took a step back—she was reeling from the extent of the names. The list went on. All told, nearly a hundred names on the payroll of this organization.

Jameson turned the laptop to see, scanned the names, and then looked at Maxie. "The chief is not on the list."

"Thank goodness," Maxie replied. "Can you imagine...?" She checked for the names of the officers assigned to guard her house. Also, not on the list.

Devin scanned the other files, opened them, and checked their contents. Businesses that were covers for the mob—a list of ten. Names of residents working as the eyes of the group—thirty of those.

Maxie sat down, put her head in her hands, and tried to digest what she had just learned. "We have a lot to go on. But who is behind this?"

Devin held up the thumb drive that Jones had given them. "Most of this is useless to us. Are you sure about Jones?"

"I'm totally unsure about Jones," she said. "Kobe, any word?"

Jameson checked his phone for any word on the prints. He had a message that had slipped by. He pressed it to expand the report and read it.

"Ahmad Hassan," he said to them both. "Known terror operative, assassin, involved in bombings in the Middle East and Asia."

"An unsavory character," Maxie noted. "Why am I not surprised?"

"But then why approach us?"

"Distraction?"

"I am not so sure," Jameson told her. "Either way, we must take care to avoid the names on the list."

Maxie looked up. "No, we need to arrest them. But carefully. And we need help. This is out of our league." She pulled her cellphone from her purse and dialed a pre-programmed number. "Bryan. Maxie. It's late and I'm sorry, but I need you to come to my place right now. It's of the utmost urgency and can't wait."

On the other end of the call, Chief Cochran, already in

pajamas and finishing off an evening cognac, listened carefully. He put down the glass, stroked his mustache with one finger, and tried to understand the scope of what was happening. "Bordana? Flinders? Unbelievable. Yes, I'm on my way."

He ended the call. Cochran's wife, Betty, was knitting in a chair by the television, their old chocolate Labrador curled up at her feet. She glanced at her husband over her reading glasses. "Bad news?"

Cochran turned to her. "The worst, I'm afraid. You remember the case I've had Maxie on? It's about to break and in a big way. Lots of people are going to go down. But for right now, I need to get to her place and put a plan together with them."

She smiled at him. It had been a long time since she had seen him fired up about something. Back in his younger days, he had brought down a local triad, and he glowed for weeks. *He looks so handsome when he's on a roll*, she thought. "Be careful, dear," she told him.

"I will." He moved closer to kiss her on the forehead. "Don't wait up, okay?"

"I won't. But before you rush off, you might want to change?"

Cochran looked at his pajamas, smiled, and nodded at Betty. "Getting old," he muttered, moving quickly to the bedroom.

COCHRAN LIVED IN PORT ARANSAS, a twenty-minute drive from Maxie's house. Luckily, the road was straight with little traffic, and with his beacon light atop the car, no eager cops would delay him with questions.

He parked behind Maxie's Audi, greeted the officer on duty, then let himself into her house. She waved him to the deck. "Chief Bryan Cochran, meet Devin Parker."

Devin extended a hand, which Cochran leaned over and shook. "Call me Bryan," he told Devin. "I've heard a lot of good things about you. Evening Kobe. It sounds like you've all made a huge breakthrough." Maxie pulled out a seat for him.

"Whiskey?"

"Better make it a double."

She went to the kitchen. Jameson began to fill Cochran in on the events that had transpired. By the time Maxie returned, Cochran had the gist of the discoveries.

"Thanks," he said, taking the glass and taking a large sip. "So we have a mafia-style crime syndicate infiltrating our people. I assume the murders were eliminating opposition?"

"Aside from Curtis Delaney," Jameson noted.

"Curtis discovered his friend and business partner had been handling the finances. He intercepted a file intended for Rob, the partner," Devin explained. He tried to speak objectively, as a journalist. This was not an easy feat. Allowing his emotions to cloud the facts would serve no purpose. "Luckily, Curtis made a copy of the information, in case he was killed, and left it for...me to find."

"I am sorry for your loss," Cochran said. "I know he was close family."

"Thank you, Commiss...Bryan," Devin replied. "He was one of the good guys. You'd have liked him."

"Because of Curtis, we may have the chance to clean up this city." Maxie sat down. She had brought glasses for the rest of them and the bottle of Jack Daniels and placed it on the table after pouring herself one. "This is huge, Bryan. I wanted to make sure we were well coordinated before the next steps."

"Crooked cops...."

"Crooked council members, judges, and politicians, as well," Jameson added.

"We have to bring them all down," Cochran said. "This cannot be tolerated."

"Bryan, tomorrow we'll arrest Rob Meeker for murder," Maxie explained. "But we need to make sure that what we do is not revealed to the person behind it all. We still have to determine who that person is."

"Can you?"

"We hope that Rob will confess," Devin said.

"Will he?"

"I think I can make that happen," Devin said.

"We don't want any of this blowing up in our faces."

"I'm concerned that our plans might reach the top before we can execute them."

"So what do you need me to do?"

"We'll arrest Meeker with a handful of trusted cops, keep it off the books, and delay the paperwork. Take him to a safe location for interrogation. Once we learn who is the head of the organization, we can move forward, place Meeker in holding, while we go after the big boss. At that point, hopefully tomorrow afternoon, or at the latest, the following morning, we can have you arrest everyone on the list while we take down the head guy. That's the simple version."

Cochran considered what he had heard. "Lots of room for mistakes," he advised. "We don't even have a name for the leader." He stroked his mustache. "Today is Monday, I would suggest that you arrest Meeker tomorrow, put him in holding —for legal reasons—and interrogate him there, as you would any other suspect. I'll make sure the officers on the list are nowhere to be found. It will also give us a chance to see if any other rats are in the nest. I'll call for a department head meeting for first thing Wednesday morning. The cops on the list will be arrested at that time by their supervisors. I'll use people I trust. At the meeting, I'll get all the remaining department heads up to speed on our plan and have them ready for a mass raid. They won't be able to share details until it's underway. Just in case. Once you have the name and location of the big boss, we'll do a city-wide sweep and arrest everyone on the list, including those on the council, judges, politicians—everyone. Let's cut the head off this snake before it can strike."

Maxie smiled. "Now that's what I call affirmative action!" Jameson cast her a look. "It's a play on words, Kobe. Don't be so sensitive."

"I am not being sensitive," he replied. "But I like action over words."

"Agreed," Cochran said. "I like this plan. It tells everyone that justice will be done—good old-fashioned American justice—Texas justice, the way it used to be done before everything became so damned politically correct. This will send a strong message to criminals—we will get you! You cannot hide behind lawyers or politicians."

He finished the last of his whiskey. "Well done, people. This makes me feel young again. Maxie, get me a copy of that list tonight on my personal email. Let's talk again in the morning." Cochran stood, shook everyone's hand, and started for the door. He turned back for a moment. "I doubt I will get much sleep tonight. Haven't had this much excitement for a long time. G'nite all."

Devin pulled up the list of names and drafted it into an email. In the subject line, he wrote: FROM MAXIE. He pushed the laptop toward Maxie for her to enter the chief's email, which she did. She pressed SEND, then pushed the laptop back to him.

"The way I see it is that we need to let the chief handle the meeting and the arrests. Our focus is to go through the material and isolate who is behind this. If we can't, then let's hope Meeker will be forthcoming."

As Devin was combing through the files from Curtis, Kobe used the thumb drive from Jones and started to go through it, in case it was an oversight that it appeared inoperative.

Maxie leaned back. She liked what she saw; these two men were getting along and working together. Devin caught her watching him and smiled at her before resuming his search. *Funny,* she thought, *but the idea of liking a guy in a wheelchair is not a turnoff.*

"You guys must be starving. Why don't I make us something to eat and get some coffee on? It's going to be a long night.

She went to the kitchen and rummaged through the choices for food. She had butter lettuce, tomatoes, olives, peppers, onions, cheese, sliced roast beef, and a can of tuna. *Easy enough,* she thought. *Tuna salad and a roast beef sandwich.* She started to prepare everything. She turned on the electric kettle to boil water and readied her French Press for the coffee once that was ready. Glancing up again at Devin, she smiled. She liked having him around.

Devin discovered a file with a list of businesses that were paying money. *Protection money,* he wondered? He copied the list to a new file. Most of the documents were financial transactions, deposits, payoffs, purchases, and receipts. He started looking at the receipts, then looked up at Maxie. "I may have a location of their base. Quite a few receipts have the same delivery address. Off Crosstown at Dillon Lane."

"Good," she said. You have the chief's email now—send it to him. Any names on the delivery receipts?"

He checked. "Leo Toscana is a name that keeps coming up."

"Kobe, can you discreetly find out about Mr. Toscana? Be careful not to involve any traitors."

Jameson nodded. First, he did an Internet search. "Leo Toscana is a name that is tied to New York crime. Likely, the FBI has information on him, as well."

"Bingo," Maxie said. "And there is our game piece. How did we not know he was here?"

"Likely because of the crooked people associated with him," Devin suggested.

Jameson called the bureau and spoke to a colleague, Gary Resnick. "Gary, Kobe. I need a favor, but it must be strictly off the books. No one must know." He listened for a response. "No, not even Maxie. Totally quiet." He glanced at Maxie with a huge grin! "What do we have on Leo Toscana? No, don't call—message me. Thank you." He ended the call. "Now we wait," he announced. Not long after, he got a text from Resnick. Jameson read it aloud: "Mob associations in New York and Chicago. Brother of Frankie Toscana, Italian mob, currently serving life in prison. Sounds like our guy. They want our intel."

"Sounds like junior is making a name for himself," Maxie added. "As for our intel, they can wait until we have something more. Better give the chief a heads up that he may be hearing from them."

It was midnight when they had finished compiling all the data from Curtis's copy. Jones's drive was a false lead, not the material he had promised. She wondered why he even bothered giving it to them. It nagged at her. The whole thing was suspicious. She had a few ideas, especially since she trusted nothing to chance.

"Kobe, examine Jones's flash drive. Something's not right."

Jameson pulled the device from the computer and looked at it closely. It appeared slightly larger than other thumb drives he had seen. This one had an edge. He placed his thumbnail against it and pushed in hard. The drive shell split open. He separated the two parts. Now one part looked like a thumb drive. The other part had been added. Inside it held some circuitry.

"Very strange," Jameson said. "This part does not go with the other part."

"Could it be a tracking device?" Maxie asked.

"Why would...." Jameson stopped. "He was tracking us. Now he knows where you live. I should stay here tonight."

Maxie considered the options. *Did Jones/Ahmad know that Devin was staying here?* She wondered. Certainly, the police presence outside her house would be a clue. "We should be fine, Kobe. I also have an officer on duty. Go home, get some rest. We'll talk in the morning."

"Are you certain?"

Maxie nodded. "Don't forget that I am well armed and I won't hesitate to shoot the SOB."

"Goodnight, then," Jameson said to them both, and then left.

Devin, using his lap as a tray, collected the dishes and wheeled them into the kitchen. He could not reach the sink, so he left them there for Maxie to load in the dishwasher.

"You've done so well," she told him, finishing the load and starting the machine. "I can't tell you how impressed I've been."

"You're just being kind. I feel like all I do is react to events. It's like walking into a movie that's already started."

"And hopefully will be ending very soon," she reminded him. "It will be good to have closure and put it all behind us."

"I hope it's that easy." He wheeled out to the deck and parked, so he could see the underwater floodlights illuminating the fish swimming. *She has a lovely house*, he thought. *How can you not feel at peace here?"*

After she was done, she came out onto the deck and stood behind him, her hands across his shoulders. "I forget how spoiled I am having this view."

"I don't think you're spoiled. You work hard for what you have. And you are so decent about it—humble."

She smiled. "Humble. Why, Mr. Parker, you sure can make a girl's head spin!"

"I'm sorry," he started to say, but she stopped him.

"Shh, don't say anything. Just listen. We're always told what we should think, what we should say, and how we should be. And if we choose otherwise, then we offend somebody, and God only knows in this culture of ours, everyone gets offended."

She moved to the bench and sat next to him, her hands holding his. "The problem is that everyone gets so offended they never stop to just look at the world and all the wonderful things in it. It isn't perfect. It's filled with problems, but you can have moments like this where it's just two people who watch some fish swimming in the water. It's real. It's simple. I miss the days when things were simple."

Devin listened to her talking. His eyes fell to their hands. Hers felt warm, and he felt comforted—reassured by the touch. He also enjoyed hearing her voice when she was calm, relaxed. It was soothing. But, too, he felt a need to protect her; that despite her strength, ability, experience, she was just a person wanting to be liked...loved. Not to mention that his presence now put her in danger. He glanced up, and their eyes met.

"Sometimes the world makes me feel very insignificant," he said softly. "Like if I were not here, it would all go on and make no difference whatsoever. Does that make sense?"

Her eyes glistened. The corners of her mouth curled into a slight, nervous smile. "I feel that way, too. Sometimes. It might sound silly, but in this job I feel like Batman with all the gadgets and armor, and then I get home and take off the costume and it's just me, and no one really knows that person."

"The Japanese say we have three faces," Devin said. "One the world sees. One that people close to us see. And one that only we see."

She smiled. "They are very smart, those Japanese. Not so smart in the last world war, but generally insightful. I'd like to think that when we meet someone who breaks through all the walls, they see all the faces, that there is nothing left hidden. Wouldn't it lessen a relationship to still have a secret face you could not show even to the one who loves you?"

"I don't know," he confessed. "I've never had a relationship *that* exposed."

"Even now?" Her eyes held a gaze into his. *What was she saying,* he wondered? *Was she feeling what he was?* He held his gaze, then, after a moment more, looked away.

"You've seen me at my worst," he said. "I don't think I've felt more exposed."

She reached up and stroked the side of his face with one hand. "I know, hun. And I think you've seen a lot of me, as well. I can no longer imagine a time when you were not a part of my life. That sounds silly, I know, since we've not known each other for long."

"Not silly. I feel it, too. But I also feel like I'm…damaged goods, Maxie. Look at me. Stuck in this chair. Half the man I was."

"Stop," she said, her voice firm. "Do you think that defines you? I don't. When I look at you, that's not what I see. I see a strong man, a smart man, a fighter who has endured a lot of pain and come out strong. It's admirable. You're not damaged at all, Devin."

He smiled, trying to push thoughts of the two of them out of his mind. *Bad timing,* he thought. "And what happens after this case? There won't be this thing pushing us together."

"You reporters always think of the future. There is the now and the here. What happens later happens because we choose it. Unless, of course, you get tired of me?"

Devin laughed.

"You're laughing at me?"

"No. I'm laughing because I could not imagine getting tired of you, Maxie. You are so filled with life, and you bring joy into everything you do, even the bad things."

"Remember that, Mr. Parker," she said softly, leaning in closer, their noses touching, lips close, brushing against the other before fully locking and kissing. Maxie reached around his neck and pulled him closer, and Devin reached for her. For minutes, they remained like that, silent, locked in this embrace that was only broken by the sound of a fish jumping from the water and loudly splashing back. The two of them sat back, still staring into each other's eyes.

"I think I know your faces now," she said coyly with a smile.

"And this chair?"

She leaned in and kissed him again, lightly this time. "What chair?" she whispered. Then she straightened up. "But

I do imagine we need to keep this quiet for now. It can't interfere with finishing this case, nailing the bad guys."

"I don't want anything to ruin bringing Curtis's killer to justice."

"Well then," she said, getting up and turning off the deck lights. "We need to get some sleep. And, when this is done, I want to take you out on a fantastic dinner date, with dancing."

"Dancing?"

"You have wheels," she teased. "We can make it work. Trust me."

"I do," he told her. "You're crazy, but I trust you completely."

The underwater lights still illuminated the canal. As they moved back into the house, Devin turned for one last look. The fish were playing now.

21

TIME TO SAY GOODBYE, MR. PARKER

Hassan had been watching the house for the past two hours. Parked on the lateral street to the canal, he saw Maxie's house clearly. He had seen them on the deck, and watched as the lights turned off.

He knew he could not enter the house from the street side, having seen the officer on duty, so he had driven further down until he found a house with a small rowboat attached to the dock. *It is amazing how these wealthy people care so little for their property*, he thought, as he untied the boat and hopped in. If he was quiet, the theft should pass undetected, even with the water illuminated from beneath.

Quietly, he rowed to the end of the canal from which he had stolen the boat, then across two more canals, before rowing back into the one where Maxie lived.

He took his time, imagining himself in some foreign film, perhaps in Paris, taking a leisurely row with a beautiful woman at the front. He would be smoking a Gitane while she had a glass of wine. Quite Parisian. But not his style—just a good momentary distraction to kill time. His background would forbid such things. The way of the Western world was so corrupt that the only cure was the total destruction of their culture.

It was a plan he held as a closely guarded secret, something for the future. Already, he knew the targets and had formulated a rough idea of what would be needed to execute it. That was beyond the scope of his current employer, a man he considered to be a blunt instrument, and a means to a financial end for his own cause.

He stopped, made sure that he was at the right house, then tied his boat to the empty slot in Maxie's two-boat dock. He stopped, watching for any signs that his presence had been detected. There were none. He quietly stepped out of the boat, then up the wooden steps to the glass door leading to the lower deck. It was locked. That was no problem for him. He had made a custom shank—a piece of thin metal an inch wide that he slid into the gap between the sliding door and pushed further in until he felt the latch lock. He slid it up and down as quietly as possible until it finally released the lock. With one swift upward motion, he forced the latch up, unlocking the door. He pocketed the tool, waited to be sure he had not disturbed anyone. *Foolish Americans*, he thought. *All those deadbolts and alarm systems, and the sliding door is the weakest part.*

Sliding the door open, he stepped inside, closing it behind him. For a moment, he stood still, surveilling the interior. There was an upstairs which he knew had at least one bedroom. Since the tracker had not shown her going to any other location, Hassan assumed that Devin Parker was here as well. That Parker was in a wheelchair meant he had to be confined to a downstairs room. It was only logical.

He moved to the nearest room and slowly opened it. Through the illumination provided by the moon outside, he saw it was an office. No one was there.

He closed the door. That left only one room slightly further down. He reached for the knife on his belt. *This will be the quietest way in which to dispatch Devin Parker to the next life,* he thought. *After that, I can search his room for whatever had been left to him. No one will know of his demise until morning, by which time Hassan would be long gone.*

With knife in hand he slowly turned the door knob and opened the door. The bed was across the room, and to the right of it was the wheelchair. He was in the right room. Emboldened, he stepped inside so he could see the bed more clearly. A body was tucked in, but it was too dark to tell who it was. Given the wheelchair, he just assumed it was his intended target.

He edged closer to the bed. From there, he could see Devin's head. It was facing away from him. *This will be swift,* he thought. *One slice, cover the mouth until the struggle stops, then back out the way I came after I search.*

He adjusted his position, readied his left hand to grab and turn the head so the blade would find its target easily, and raised the knife. He took a breath, choosing to hold it until after the rapid motion that would end Parker, and silently counted down.

At two he heard the **click** of a gun now cocked, pressed against his head.

"I would consider your next move very carefully, Mr. Hassan," Maxie said, her Glock pressed against the back of his head. "I would hate to make a mess and ruin my curtains."

Devin, now roused, turned and opened his eyes, horrified to see the knife-wielding figure over him. "It's fine, hun," she said to him. "Mr. Hassan is about to drop the knife before I put a bullet in his brain. I'll count to two." She took a deep breath. "One...."

The knife fell to the floor. Hassan raised his hands high and slowly turned around.

"You are a very resourceful woman," he said.

"And you are under arrest," she said. "Get down on the floor with your hands behind your back." He did as instructed. Maxie moved around him and handed the gun to Devin. "Shoot his ass if he moves."

Devin held the gun, still confused as to what had happened. Maxie leaned over and cuffed Hassan before dragging him to his feet. She took the gun back.

"Sorry, Devin," she said. "I just had a feeling this was coming."

"You've been awake the whole time?"

"You'd be surprised what I can see from my bedroom window, like this fool rowing a boat to my dock. I'll bet it's stolen. We can add that charge to all the others."

"It will not help you," Hassan said. "My employer has everything he needs."

"Not everything," she said. "He's underestimating us."

"We shall see. I have nothing further to say."

She placed him on a stool by the kitchen counter, then walked to the front door and called for the officer to come inside. When he saw Hassan in handcuffs, he was bewildered and began to apologize. "Ma'am, I have no idea how...."

"Relax," Maxie told him. "This scum came by sea. I need you to take him downtown and have him booked. He gets no visitors. Understand? No one!"

The officer nodded, then used the radio Velcro-tied to his shoulder to call for backup. Devin rolled out of his room toward the front door.

"I had no idea...."

"I know, hun," she said. "I didn't want to worry you. I knew there was no way he could do anything, but I needed to handle it."

Devin smiled. "I trust you, Maxie. Looks like you handled him well."

Maxie looked at Hassan. "Three in the morning. You had to screw up my sleep." Hassan shrugged. "And since we already know your real name and background, your future does not look so bright."

"You know what you know," Hassan replied smugly.

"Why does everything with you people always have to sound like a riddle. What I know is that your sorry ass will be rotting in a jail cell for a long time."

From the smirk on Hassan's face, Maxie knew that he may have expected this outcome. She wasn't sure which worried her more: capturing him or discovering his endgame. Time would tell.

AFTER THE OFFICER had taken Hassan away, Maxie went to the kitchen and put on the water for some coffee. "Can you go back to sleep?"

Devin shook his head. "I'm quite sure the image of him over my bed would prevent that. What tipped you off?"

"The thumb drive was a tracker. He wanted to find out where I lived, but also to see where I went. I'm sure they realize you are not at your place. Since I came home, the thumb drive has not left this house. I just didn't know if they would try to get past the guard or the back door. One of the downsides to living on the water is that anyone with a boat can come and berth at your dock."

"You should install an alarm."

"I think I will, now. And maybe a sign announcing that I shoot first."

Devin smiled at Maxie as she was pouring a cup of coffee for them both. Despite the revelations of their feelings from the night before, there was no awkwardness and, Devin considered, no regrets. In fact, quite the opposite; it felt extremely natural, as though this was how it was meant to be, and Devin found himself excited at the possibility of where this relationship would go once the case was closed.

"Let's try this again," she said, her voice soft and melodic. "Good morning."

"Hi," he stammered, feeling more like a teenager unsure of what to say than a grown man. She didn't kiss him, but she did run her hand across the back of his neck as she passed and handed him a coffee. "I guessed how you took your coffee—black?"

"It's perfect."

At five in the morning, her cell phone rang—Cochran. "Good morning, Bryan."

She put him on speaker. "You didn't call me about the intruder."

"Were you enjoying a good sleep?"

"Yes."

"Thank me later. It's not like he was going anywhere."

"Everyone is okay?"

"Yes. Just fine. Enjoying our second cup of coffee."

"Couldn't go back to sleep?" He chuckled. "I remember those days. The adrenaline rush."

"Bryan, make sure that they don't have Hassan near any of the dirty cops. We need him alive."

"I'll call down there to make sure, but most of those have been assigned to a special recon today."

"What recon?"

"Exactly," Cochran replied. "You totally understand."

Maxie laughed. "Good plan."

"You arrest Meeker, and then let's see what we get from him. Talk later." He ended the call.

"Recon?" Devin asked.

"He's keeping them busy on a fake call. They'll be busy until he calls it off."

"Ah. He seems like a good chief?"

"He's a good guy. I trust him. He's the reason I came to Corpus Christi."

"Then I trust him, too."

"Are we ready to do this?"

Devin nodded.

"Me, too," she said. "After we eat something, and after Kobe gets here, we'll head down to grab Meeker."

JAMESON ARRIVED SHORTLY AFTER SEVEN. Maxie had a coffee ready for him, which he took to the deck, sitting and watching the interaction between Maxie and Devin as they recounted the night's events. It didn't take a genius to understand something was different. Of course, he had picked up on it early in the investigation. He had known Maxie long enough to understand her reactions, her methodology, and the things that affected her. This case—from the moment she met Devin—had been different.

Maxie caught him looking at her. "What?"

He just smiled and returned to his coffee. She knew that he knew was the theme here. It was enough for now.

"I wish you had called me," he finally said to her.

"If I had felt there was any danger, I would have called you immediately. Somehow, this just made sense. Are you angry with me?"

"No," Jameson said, a slight smile on his face. "I would like not to have to come to your funeral."

Maxie stared at him, then broke into a grin. "Who said you were invited?"

"Maxie," Devin said. "That's mean."

"It is a joke," Jameson told him. "You better get used to them."

"Really?"

Maxie smiled and shrugged.

"Okay, getting serious now. We take my car. We have two patrol cars outside. They go in full SWAT—I want the crap scared out of Meeker. They will arrest him, and then we come in. Devin stays out. Kobe and I will do our thing, and then if we need an extra push, we can have Devin come in at the station."

"Do you think Meeker will give up information?" Jameson asked Devin.

"The Rob I used to know seemed to be a decent guy. But if this Rob killed Curtis, I'm not even sure who we are dealing with. It's too difficult to make sense of this."

Maxie put her hand on his neck. "In the academy, one of my instructors told me something I will always remember. He said, after your first kill, you're never the same."

"He was talking about cops shooting and killing the criminal," Jameson said.

"Was he? I suspect that decent people, when something like this happens and someone dies, change. How could they not? The most sacred thing is the life of a person, especially an innocent person. How could you just kill someone and not be changed by it?"

"Were you changed after you first killed a bad guy?"

"I went home and cried my eyes out, hun. It seemed very surreal, but I felt like I had offended God or something. They send you to a shrink to talk about it. You can't let it fester. But that did not help. When my chief, at the time, sat me down and showed me the history of the perp I had killed, the list of everything from juvenile offenses, burglary, assault, rape, kidnap, murder of a mother and child...well all I thought about was what would have happened if I had not killed him. He was an animal."

"Did that make it easier?"

"Not easier. It took my guilt away. I swore an oath to serve and protect the people of this city, and I do that every day. I don't ask to kill anyone. In fact, I don't kill anyone. Unless they are shooting at me and I am defending myself. Do I like it? No. Have I made peace with it? No. I don't ever want to feel okay with taking a life, but I will if that is what my job entails."

"You cannot overthink it," Jameson told Devin. "You are no good to anyone and can not do your job if you overthink everything."

"That's true," Maxie added.

"When I learned that Curtis had been killed, I just wanted to find out who had done it. I would have happily killed them myself. But I realize that just feeds the hatred. I want to believe that there's justice out there. I just hope that it's enough."

Maxie squeezed his hand. "Me, too."

AT NINE, after eating some breakfast, they closed up the laptops and got ready.

"I backed up a copy of the card to my computer," Devin told her. "In case. The last thing we need is to lose the evidence."

"Good. Kobe—ready?"

"I am. It will be an interesting day."

Jameson looked at Devin. "If I may offer some advice?"

Devin nodded. "Of course."

"Allow us to lead, even if you feel you must get involved. Trust us."

Devin thought about what was said. Jameson was right. The worst thing would be to jeopardize the validity of the arrest, to give some lawyer a way to get Rob out of a conviction. "Good advice," he replied. "And you're right. Once he is processed, however, I want him to see my face. If we can get anything out of him, that guilt will, I hope, do it."

"Guilt is a very powerful force," Jameson replied. "I am sure you will know what to do."

"Who will be with us, Kobe?"

"Officers Laske, Ferrera, and Mindy Hobbs are waiting for our instruction."

"Remind them. I want it to be dramatic," she said. "Guns drawn. I want the fear of God in him."

"I will tell them when we are in position."

She looked over at Devin. "Ready for this?"

Devin nodded. "Let's do it."

AT TEN-THIRTY EXACTLY, the three officers stormed the offices of Stanton Investments, guns drawn on Rob Meeker.

"On the ground, hands where I can see them," one of the officers shouted to a shocked Meeker, who quickly complied. "Lock your hands over your head." He was quickly handcuffed and hoisted onto a chair, all guns still aimed at him.

Maxie and Jameson entered the building. "Robert Meeker, you *are* under arrest for the murder of Curtis Delaney. Anything you say can and will be used against you in a court of law. You have a right to an attorney. One will be provided if you cannot afford it. Do you understand what I have just said?"

Rob nodded.

"Go through the place and log what we discussed," she instructed the officers. Then, to Rob, she moved closer. "What I do not understand, for the life of me...Curtis was your best friend. I have heard this from so many people. I just do not understand how a best friend commits such a heinous crime."

"I...," Rob started to say, but Maxie raised a finger.

"Don't waste my time with some bullshit excuse. We know you did it." Rob bowed his head. "We know you dumped the body. We have a witness. Where did you kill him?"

Tears were welling in Rob's eyes, as if he was fighting against himself to keep the truth concealed as he had done for so long. Finally, he grunted. "Roof."

Maxie motioned for the officers to hold him. She and Jameson headed for the stairs. Two flights up, there was an unlocked door to the roof. Guns drawn, in case of an ambush, Jameson pushed open the door and strode out, swiveling in both directions.

"Clear," he called back, and Maxie walked out.

The roof area was exposed. Off the sides, it offered a clear view of the surrounding buildings, and beyond that, open sky. To one side, piping had been stacked, some tools, and drop cloths. One of the central air units had a panel opened. It appeared that work had been interrupted.

"Over here," Jameson called. By the edge, there was a bloodstain on the ground. Maxie looked around. Sammy had identified the weapon as a tool, such as a wrench, and an imprint that was made confirmed it. Behind the bag of tools, Maxie found the pipe wrench that had been used. Blood coated the top. She pointed it out to Jameson.

"I'm betting Rob's fingerprints will be on it." She took a deep breath and tried to clear the image of Curtis Delaney getting hit by Rob from her mind. "Just savages," she muttered, then turned to return to the office below. Jameson called for the forensics team to gather the evidence and process the crime scene, but first, he snapped some photographs as backup. Given the scope of the people involved, he wanted to be sure no evidence could be destroyed through intent or incompetence.

When Maxie stood before Rob again, he was still staring at the ground. He looked up at her, his eyes reddened. He was about to speak, but Maxie had heard enough.

"Save it for the station. You get to explain it to Devin, as well." She said that part purposefully, wanting to see the reaction. Rob's face fell, and she knew that she had hit a nerve. She hoped that the impact of what he felt would translate into a solid confession, and added information that they had not yet uncovered, but more importantly, direct them to their final task—arresting the leader of this new crime organization and ending the murders once and for all.

"Just so you know," she added for good measure, "we found the SD card that Curtis made for Devin." She had grabbed Rob's attention. Despite everything, he still managed to ask where Curtis had hidden it. "You actually had it in your hand when I was here with Devin. You gave it to him."

"The photograph?" Rob muttered. "I was so stuck on how much he loved that photo...."

"It's all over. When we get to the station, I hope you will do the smart thing and get it all out. This needs to end not just for Curtis, but for Devin. Do you have any idea what this has cost him? He's paralyzed. For what?"

She turned and walked out to her car as the officers led Rob to their patrol car. As he was placed inside, he glanced after her and saw Devin sitting in her car. He had no idea what he could say to Devin, not now, not after all this. Maxie was right—Devin had suffered the most.

Maxie slammed her car door shut. "Sorry," she muttered. "It just pisses me off."

Devin placed a hand on hers, held it there for a moment, and then removed it. From the back seat, Kobe watched. *I was right*, he thought, not that he harbored any ill feelings; he wanted Maxie to be happy. She deserved it. He just hoped that Devin's condition would not hurt her more.

"You got him," Devin said.

"They'll process him and put him in holding. We'll let him stew for a time before we arrive."

"You have a mean streak," Jameson teased.

"Don't forget it, Kobe," she said. "Now, I am hungry. Anyone want a Whataburger? A Monterey Melt sounds awfully good."

Devin scrunched up his face. "Seriously?"

"She is serious," Jameson told him.

"Pass," Devin said.

"Me, too," Jameson said. "Too early. But a coffee sounds good."

"That I can do," Devin added.

"Weaklings," she teased as she started the car and drove off.

ROB WAS SEATED, handcuffed to the chair in the center of the holding cell, a drab, ten-foot square room with a single window that allowed observers outside to view in, but not the other way around. The room was void of any distractions; the only light was from the overhead fluorescent light that cast a harsh, bright glare, somewhat blinding to look at.

He sat there for a half hour waiting for someone to come in. Maxie, Jameson, and Devin watched from outside after arriving from her food run. Cochran arrived moments later and joined them.

"He looks nervous," Cochran said from their side of the window.

"He should be," Devin said. His voice was flat, and Maxie knew he was seething.

"Don't let him get to you," she whispered, reaching for his hand and squeezing it once. "I'll go in first. Kobe, come in after we get him talking a bit. Devin, come in to finish him off—squeeze the last drop of guilt out of him."

She went inside. Rob looked up at her, uncertain what to expect.

"I'll cut to the chase," she said. "You killed Curtis. I want to know why?"

"You have the SD. You know why?"

"That tells me *what* this is about. Not *why* you had to end the life of a man who was your best friend, as well as your business partner."

Rob thought about what she said, but did not reply.

"Why did you kill him?"

Rob looked away. He was sweating now, droplets gathering on his face. His cheeks had turned a ruddy color, as though he had too much to drink, but that was not the case. It was the stress of the moment bringing out the changes that Maxie saw.

"You hit him with a pipe wrench. Why?" she asked again, this time louder.

Rob took a deep breath. "I had to do it. I didn't want to do it. I had no choice. It couldn't be in the office, so I got him to the roof."

Jameson entered the room, moved to Rob, and jerked the chair hard, shifting it slightly, but enough to startle Rob.

"Mr. Meeker, for what reason would you kill your best friend?" Jameson asked, his voice clear, punctuating each syllable. Rob looked up at him, saw a look of indignant determination on his face.

"I had no choice. You don't understand how hard it was." Rob began to sob, his body heaving with ever-increasing waves of sorrow. "I didn't want to...."

Outside, Cochran saw Devin tensing up with pent-up rage. He put a hand on his shoulder.

"Easy, son," he said softly. "Let them do what they do best."

"You're a piece of work, Meeker," Maxie said. "Do you realize how pathetic that is for an excuse—you *had to*? He was your best friend. He was Devin's family. Because of Curtis, you had a fantastic business. You had a bright future. Why on God's green Earth would you bring that all crashing down?"

"Because I screwed up," Rob shouted, fighting against the cuffs and the chair. "I screwed up. I got involved with the wrong people, and next thing I knew, they OWNED me. Don't you get it? You can't escape those people."

"What people?" Jameson asked.

Rob thought for a moment. It was too late. He had already passed the point of no return and knew that his fate was sealed, no matter what happened. "A guy from New York. Big shot crime guy. Name is Toscana. Leo Toscana. They needed someone to handle their financials, take care of money."

"Why you?"

"Because I made a bad investment. I never consulted Curtis; I wanted to show him that I had the gift. Curtis had the gift. I was so sure. I banked the entire company in a single investment. It was a sure thing. It was supposed to turn around within a few days. I just wanted to be able to show him that I pulled my weight. He was everything to me...and I screwed up, lost it all."

"What happened then?"

"When I realized how badly I had made things, I didn't know what to do. I reached out to a buddy of mine online and begged him to keep it quiet. He said he knew a way to handle it—knew someone who knew someone. Next thing, I get a call from a local guy wanting to set up a meet with this bigwig money guy from New York—Toscana. So we meet. He lays it out. Tells me it isn't pretty, but he can handle the loss, but it's a life debt. I ask him what that means, and he says that for the amount of money I would need, it could never be repaid in a lifetime. He gets me a drink. Tells me that all he needs from me is to do what I normally do. The only thing is that no one knows. Especially Curtis. What I do is off the books. But he says that I will always do this for him, no questions asked. Only at the end of my life will the debt be paid. So I think that is okay, that I can live with that. I can do it so long as Curtis never finds out. Curtis's business will be safe, no one will know, and I will forget my mistake. Stupid, I know."

"Go on," Maxie said. "More...."

"They courier an SD card to me to process each month. I always intercept it outside the building, sign for it, and done. Curtis asked about it once, and I told him it was my uncle's business stuff that I was doing *gratis*. Curtis was fine with it and said nothing more. Then last month I was out sick—stomach bug. Never made it to the office until the next day. But by then, Curtis had received the SD card—the courier came inside when I was not there. Curtis wanted to help since I was sick, figured he would do my uncle's financials for me. He was always like that, always putting everyone else above himself. So he sees what's on the card, sees the names and the money and...my God...it's so clear when you look at it what's going on."

"Was he angry?" Jameson asked. "Is that why you killed him?"

Rob shifted in the seat, his movements limited to a few inches. He was sweating profusely, tears staining his face, eyes bloodshot. "When I came to work the next day, he was waiting for me. He wasn't angry, just wanted to know what it was about, why I was doing this? So I told him. It crushed him. I saw it in his face. It was like the whole world had been ripped out from under him."

"Go on," Jameson urged.

"The problem was that when he signed for the courier, it was clear that it was not me, and Toscana found out. He also knew that Curtis was as straight an arrow as you would find, that he was not corruptible. He asked me what Curtis knew. I lied and said he only signed for it and never saw it. He then told me that he had phoned Curtis and asked him what he saw on the card. Curtis had no idea who he was talking to. He didn't answer, but the way the conversation went, Toscana knew that Curtis had seen it. So, next thing Toscana is telling me that Curtis has to go, that he is a liability. They would make him disappear. With Curtis out of the way, it would be easier for me to keep working their stuff. I begged him not to. I told him that I could make sure that Curtis would leave it be. Toscana did not care about Curtis. He told me he had too much riding on not having some do-gooder messing up his plans. I begged him, asked him what I could do to not have that happen."

Rob stopped, looked away to the side. "Toscana told me that nothing would stop it, but if he had to come handle it, then Curtis would die in a painful way as payback for my mistakes. He said the only difference I could make was to do it myself. Make it quick and painless, otherwise he would have to clean up my mess. He gave me twenty-four hours to decide otherwise, he would handle it."

The door opened, and Devin wheeled in, moving right to Rob's face. He leaned over and smacked him across the face. "You bastard. You selfish bastard." Devin was in a rage; the veins of his forehead were bulging with his anger, his face contorted into a look that Maxie had not seen before.

"Dev...," Rob sputtered. "I'm so sorry. I didn't want to...I loved Curtis like a brother...."

"You're so full of shit. You screwed up and you kept screwing up, and to cover your ass you killed Curtis, you killed the nicest person I'd ever known."

Rob was bawling. "I know...."

"You should have called the cops. You could have warned Curtis. You should have sacrificed your life for his...."

Devin raised a fist, his face tensed with the hatred that was flowing through him. Jameson moved between them, wrapped his hand over Devin's fist, and gently brought it down. "Do not allow his evil to become your evil," he said firmly. "You are a much better man than this."

Devin's eyes were flushed with tears. He glanced up at Jameson, their eyes meeting. Through the anger, he saw Jameson's steadfast look, his strength, and calm. Devin knew he was right. No matter what, he did not want to do anything that would give Rob a legal way out. He lowered his hand and wheeled back away from Rob.

"I want to know how you did it," he said flatly. "I want to know everything that was Curtis's final minutes. Do you understand me? I need to know."

Through his tears, Rob looked at Devin and nodded. "I knew I had no choice. Better me than Toscana. I wanted it to be quick."

"Go back. What happened after Curtis knew?"

"Oh, Devin, he told me he was disappointed that I did not just come to him. I told him that I had lost millions of dollars and ruined the company he built, and he said...it was *only* money. He could make more. Can you imagine that? He just wished that I had come to him and told him. I wish I had, none of this would have happened, and Curtis would still be here."

"Yet you still killed him," Jameson interjected.

"How could I tell him that Toscana left me no choice, that he was going to die one way or another, that nothing could stop it. That night, I went through all the options I had. There was no time to save Curtis—I could not protect him. We had been having work done on the roof. The air conditioning was acting up, and they needed to replace pipes and ducts. All the materials were up there. Some tools had also been left. The next morning, I asked Curtis if we could talk on the roof, as I believed the offices might be bugged. So we went up. He was staring at the view. I picked up a large pipe wrench that was still there and...."

Rob looked to the ground, shaking his head, his body

limp, defeated. "He fell to the ground. I felt for a pulse, but there wasn't one. I remember staring at the wrench—blood on the top where I had hit him, and then walking around the roof looking for a place to put it—I wanted to get it away from me."

Jameson and Maxie looked at each other. Maxie looked up to where she knew Cochran was watching.

"He wanted to own you for the murder," Maxie told him. "You're a fool."

"What about the body?" Jameson asked.

"There were plastic tarps covering open vents. There was an unopened package. I used it to put Curtis in. Then I had to wait until dark to move his body. I went to the office and washed the blood off my hands, then closed the office and went to Bullit's Bar and had quite a few drinks, watched the news, and waited for the day to end. When it was dark, I parked in the back, dragged the body from the roof, and then into the car. I drove around for an hour trying to figure out where to leave him. I didn't want anything to happen to his body. I found an alley, pulled over, dragged him out, leaving the plastic in the car, then left. I found a dumpster a few miles away and dumped the plastic under garbage bags. Then I went home and threw up until I had nothing left inside me."

They all remained silent for a moment, their energy expended by the horrific details. Maxie moved closer to Devin and put her hand against his neck. She could not imagine what he was feeling at that moment. She knew that she was feeling an empty sadness, anger, loss, even though it was not her loss to feel. *When you love someone, you feel their pain*, she thought. *How will he recover from this?*

After a few moments, Rob looked up. "You do know Toscana is everywhere? He has cops and important officials in his pocket. And he doesn't care about killing anyone who gets in his way. You know that, right? You know you are all in danger?"

"You let us worry about that," Maxie said. "Let's go," she added to Jameson and Devin.

Outside, Cochran was waiting.

"I changed my mind and had the cops on the list arrested. I didn't want any surprises out of my control. They're temporarily off-site until we get done. They'll be charged soon enough. I'm meeting with department heads in an hour if you want to come."

"You handle that," she said. "We have more work to do."

"Well done in there," Cochran said. "I realize that was extremely difficult."

"I wanted to kill him," Devin said, rolling past the chief.

Cochran looked at him from behind. "We've all felt that rage at one time or another. Don't beat yourself up on that. In life, you choose to be the good guy or the bad guy. There's not much wiggle room on that." He grabbed Devin's arm. "You're one of the good guys. Hold that close."

"Good advice," Maxie said, but Devin was already gone.

When Maxie, Jameson, and Cochran caught up to him, he parked his wheelchair and asked them to sit down. He had made a decision.

"Now we know who is behind this, and why, we need to end this," he began. "The only way I can imagine is a two-prong attack. First, the chief needs to arrange to round up everyone on the list. But before that, we need to find out where Toscana is located, and arrange a meeting with him. That way, we can arrest him before he can act."

"And just how do you plan to get him to meet with you?" Maxie asked. All eyes were on him now. No matter how he said it, he knew that it would come across as a foolish idea.

"We need to finish going through the data and get a

contact number and a location. Then I can phone him." Seeing the concerned looks, he quickly elaborated. "Look, the bastard's tried to have me killed, and it looks like that's still the plan. Hassan all but said it. So as far as Toscana is concerned, I'm just this poor, paralyzed nobody whose life isn't worth much. If I call him and beg him to spare me, in exchange for the SD card, he may well consider that a solution."

"More likely a sure-fire way to kill you," Cochran said.

"That's the point," Devin corrected him. "Of course, he will want to kill me. That's where Maxie and Kobe come in. No matter what any high-priced lawyer might try to do to have him acquitted, trying to kill me in front of witnesses will give us an advantage. In the meantime, you clean up the rest of the mess."

Maxie looked at Jameson.

"It is an interesting plan," he said, "however, I am not certain that Toscana would feel the need to meet."

"It's worth a shot," Devin said. "We haven't gotten very far by other tactics."

"True enough," Maxie said. "And if Kobe and I are there, perhaps we can just shoot the SOB and save the taxpayers some money."

They all looked at her.

"What?" she asked, shrugging. "A girl can dream, can't she?"

Cochran considered what Devin had suggested. Separating Toscana from his men, especially while the latter were all being arrested, would certainly simplify the process. And he knew from the mob trials in New York that too often, technicalities, as well as insider action, resulted in the mobsters getting off free. He did not wish to take that chance in Corpus Christi. *This is Texas, dammit,* he thought. *It sure would be easier to shoot first and ask questions later.*

"On one condition," he finally said. "I need to be informed every step of the way. No surprises, and no unnecessary risks. Understand?"

"Thank you, Chief," Devin said. The others nodded.

22

THE PLAN

An hour later, Cochran met with the three department heads in his office. Assistant Chiefs Javier Renaldo, John Samuels, and Harold Wilson listened in awe as Cochran recounted the events leading up to Rob's arrest, the decision to arrest the named officers, and the plans moving forward. He handed each man a copy of the names.

"You have this list of everyone we believe is connected with, on the payroll of this new organized crime group. The leader is Leo Toscana, out of New York, well-known to the FBI. They're sending some agents our way, but I'd like to have this wrapped up before they get here—a stretch, I realize, but we can minimize their involvement—I want CCPD to have full credit for cleaning house. The only ones they can have are Judge Harmon, Congressman Flinders, and Senator Bordana."

"You're sure," Renaldo asked.

"No doubt. I just don't want this blowing up in our faces. Cochran stopped and examined their faces. He knew that the mention of Bordana would grab their attention. "This runs deep, and we have to end it now before it gets worse."

"This is unbelievable," Samuel said. "I had no clue...."

"I agree, John. None of us did. But now we do. We have names, bank accounts, everything we need to lance this boil."

"So, how will we play this?" Wilson asked.

"The plan is to arrest Toscana as well as his group. We have to flush him out. Maxie is working on that. We're looking at over a hundred arrests here. There's always the possibility that there are others on their payroll not on our list. If you notice any unusual activity or responses, I need to be notified immediately. The officers you assign are not to be told who they will be arresting. They just need to be ready for your order to do so. Names can be given to them right before they make the arrests. That way, we minimize anything that might compromise the operation."

"It might be better to have the officers parked in close proximity to where the arrests will be made, to expedite it," Renaldo suggested. "They can get the lists on their patrol computers."

"Good idea. Just don't have them sitting there all day. The likelihood is that this operation won't go down until morning. So consider today prep day and be ready by this afternoon. Nueces County Jail has been notified. It has room for one thousand and twenty inmates, so we've got plenty of room to add a hundred. Also, the FBI has been notified. They will tackle the judiciary and the senator. Any questions?"

"Will you be holding a press conference?"

"Not until after it's all done," Cochran said. "It's got to be a done deal. I want the public to get facts and not speculation. I want closure. What happens reflects on this department."

"So we're cleanup duty?" Wilson asked. "Maxie gets the big fish?"

"Jealous Harold? I hope not. I'd like to think of this as a four-way target. Each of you and Maxie will be striking at one part of this organization. It's not a contest. And if you know Maxie, it's never been a contest for her. It's about doing the best job we can do. Anything else?"

With nothing further, Cochran dismissed them, then sat back in his chair. The difference between the three men and Maxie was clear to him, even if it wasn't clear to them. Maxie was proactive. She sought out leads and acted upon them rather than simply reacting after the fact. The three assistant chiefs, while all good men and all highly qualified, were sadly reactive.

He contemplated how this investigation would have proceeded without Maxie or Jameson, who was equally proactive. *Without the two of them, the killings would continue until someone made such a blunder that it would be obvious who should be arrested. That's not police work,* he considered. *That's babysitting.* So if Maxie bruised some egos, that was fine with him.

He also reminded himself that his next appointment for an assistant chief should be a woman, not to be politically correct; rather, that in many ways, women, in the line of work, brought less ego to the job.

The job would not be for Maxie. He'd already asked her once, and she turned him down with her usual Texas charm. *What was it she had said?* He asked himself. *Oh, yes, she had told him she was not cut out to be a bureaucrat.* What she had actually said was less politically correct. "When the monarchy of England stopped leading the charge into battle, they became pretty much useless." He smiled, remembering the correct words, and not his watered-down version..

AT HIS REQUEST, and because he had no car, Maxie drove Devin to visit Hank at the *Tribune*. She dropped him off and told him to call her when he was done, so she could fetch him. "Enjoy the visit," she told him once he was secure in the wheelchair.

"Thanks." He watched as she pulled off, then swiveled himself to the handicap ramp leading into the front. Lee was in his usual spot, reading the paper.

"Hey Lee," Devin said, wheeling past.

"Hi Devin," he answered, still reading the paper. Then he realized that he couldn't see Devin and lowered the paper, revealing Devin in his wheelchair. "My gosh, Devin. What happened to you, man?"

"Had an accident, Lee. It's all good."

"Temporary? Right?" Lee's face had a quizzical look.

"Not sure. Time will tell. I'm off to see Hank. Take care, Lee."

"Yeah. Take care. You too. I will pray for your recovery."

"Thanks," Devin said, rolling toward the elevator.

Hank was delighted to see him. As always, he was mid-phone conversation when he spotted Devin through the glass walls of his office, waving him forward. "Call you back," he said hastily to whomever was on the other end, and hung up the phone. He got up and opened the door quickly.

"Devin, you're looking good."

"Thanks, Hank. Much better than when you saw me last."

"I called Maxie last week, but she said you were quite busy."

"Oh, she didn't mention it."

"I told her not to. I was gonna swing by her place later in

the week and take you both to dinner. How're you two getting along?"

Devin thought about his answer, a slight smile on his face. "Um—fine. She's great."

Hank stared at him. He knew that look. "Great. Well, that's glowing?"

"You know what I mean," Devin insisted.

Hank beamed. "I believe I do."

"Okay, enough of that. I wanted to fill you in on what's happening. You're going to love this."

Hank listened as Devin recounted the investigation and where it led. "Good grief," Hank said. "That's unbelievable. That's going to blow this town apart!"

"Right? Sadly, all true. We are now at the end part, Hank. One more step to go—no pun intended."

Hank awkwardly nodded.

"I wanted you to hear it from me. After it's over, the *Tribune* gets the story."

"You're not going to write it?"

"Not this time. It wouldn't feel right, and I want to ensure that what is written about Curtis comes across properly."

"I will make sure of that," Hank said. "So what are the next steps?"

"I know you will tell me it's stupid, but I'm going to contact Toscana and arrange a meeting. I'm going to tell him that I have the SD card and just want my life back. I realize that he has power and will control everything. No one else knows what I know, but I want his assurance that if I give him the card, I get to live. I'll leave the country, blah, blah, blah."

Hank stared at him in disbelief, pulled out his whiskey drawer, and retrieved the bottle and a glass. He poured himself a shot.

"Not offering me one?"

"You always say no. Want one?"

"Hell, yes. Don't you think I need it with this crazy ass plan?"

Hank started to laugh, pulled another shot glass, and filled it for Devin. "Yes. Yes, you do. Quite possibly a double."

Devin took the glass and held it up. "To Curtis. And to friendships."

Hank did the same. "If you get yourself killed I will be so pissed off at you."

Devin downed the shot and slammed the glass on the table. Hank refilled it. "I don't plan on it. Maxie and Jameson have my back."

"I would trust her with my life," Hank said. "What does she think about the plan?"

"I know she worries that it could backfire on me. The chief approved it."

"And you're sure you can handle that kind of pressure?"

"Hank," Devin said, "I'm in a wheelchair. Someone already tried to kill me. Curtis was killed. Rob was the killer. Tia was killed. I think I'm handling the pressure just fine, don't you?" He held up the shot and sipped at it. "I could get drunk off these."

Hank smiled at him. "You wouldn't be the first drunk in my office." He leaned forward. "While I have you at a disadvantage, let me tell you that after our last conversation about your future, I have been doing a lot of thinking, soul-searching, if you will."

Devin nodded. "Good."

"And I agree with you. About this job."

Devin frowned. "What? I thought...listen, what I said, I...."

Hank pointed a finger at him and shouted: "Busted. See, you are so full of shit. You are not useless or redundant. You have a brain and, better yet, you have a ton of experience. You are a reporter—it's in your blood. Wheelchair or no, you can't deny it!"

Devin smiled, happy to be caught off guard. "You win. I just don't know how I fit yet. But I will figure it out. I promise."

"You know you have my support. Whatever we need to do to make it work. I am on board with it."

Devin felt humbled. "Thanks, Hank," he said softly. "Really."

"So, let's talk about your plan. You know he will be lying, right? No self-respecting crook would believe that story."

"I do know that. I just need him to come to the meeting place. I don't care if he brings muscle. It is important he comes. While he is there, he will be vulnerable." He looked at the empty second shot glass. "Good thing I'm not driving. Do me a favor and call Maxie—she said she would pick me up."

Hank picked up the phone and punched up her number. "Hey Maxie, your boy's done! Nah, he's doing fine. I didn't hurt him. Yep, I'll tell him."

He ended the call.

Hank leaned back in his chair. "So, are you going to tell me about the two of you, or do I have to guess?"

Devin blushed. "Hank, we like each other. It's not like there's been any chance to go out or anything. Let it be. When there is something to tell, I'll tell you."

"I've known Maxie for a number of years. Always thought that some guy would be real lucky if she fell for him. You don't find many like her these days."

"I know. We've talked a bit about our relationship."

"Good."

"Good." He stood and walked to the window. "I need a smoke. Disgusting habit. Gonna kill me one day."

"You should quit."

"Yeah." Hank lit up a cigarette and opened the window.

"You do realize the smoke always comes back in, right?"

"Does it? Didn't know that. Sorry."

Hank took a drag on the cigarette, held it, then leaned out the window to exhale a plume of smoke before ducking back in, a big smile on his face. "When this is done, I want to take us all out to a nice dinner. You, Maxie, Kobe and I. Just have a fun night. No stories. No deadlines. No stress. Just friends enjoying life. Yes?"

Devin beamed. "That would be terrific. I would enjoy that."

He moved closer to Hank and held out his hand. "You've always been a good friend to me. I hope you understand how much I appreciate it."

Hank found himself getting teary-eyed. His face winced; he wasn't used to this kind of emotionalism, certainly not in the workplace.

"I do. Thank you for saying it, though. You've had it tough. I've been lucky to watch you shine through it all. But I can tell you this. Your parents would have been so damn proud to see how you turned out. You realize that, right?"

Devin smiled. "I've always hoped so, Hank."

ONE THING LEFT TO DO

There was only one thing left to do. As soon as they returned home, Maxie fixed them a highball—double shot of whiskey, topped by soda, ice, and a slice of lemon. She figured Devin would need it, but he was already quite relaxed from the shots in Hank's office.

He had searched through the files on the thumb drive and found what he believed to be Toscana's phone number—it had been repeated in several places, including some invoices that Toscana had signed for.

He pulled out his notebook and found a blank page, and jotted the number down.

"The moment of truth," Devin said, taking the drink from her and taking a large mouthful.

"Take your time. You have to play this perfectly. Want to run through it before you call?"

Devin shook his head.

He bent the notebook back against the spine so it would remain open, then pulled out his cellphone and dialed, putting the call on speaker. Maxie sat down and nursed her drink. *Calm yourself, Maxie,* she thought. *He needs you to be your best.*

"Who is this?" a deep, monotonic voice said.

"Mr. Toscana. My name is Devin Parker. I got your number from Curtis Delaney. I believe you and I need to talk." Devin took a sip of the drink, forced himself to wait through the silence on the other end. He knew Toscana had been caught off guard and was now weighing his options.

"Go on," Toscana said, finally.

"I am calling to ask—no—to beg you to hear an offer I would like to make."

"Continue...."

"As you know, Curtis is dead. I am paralyzed, my life totally ruined. All because of the SD card. I found the card yesterday, and it is in my possession. No one else knows about it."

"What about the cop whose house you are staying in?"

Devin looked across at Maxie and winked.

"She does not know. I'm only here because she thought I would be safer. I've told her nothing."

"So what does this have to do with me?"

Devin delayed answering for a moment, gathering his thoughts. "My life in exchange for the SD card."

"And why would I accept that?"

"It's the only thing I've got left. I have no family, no job, no way to just live like I did before. I'm tired of running. I don't want to keep looking over my shoulder. If you agree, we can meet, I give you the card, and you allow me to leave the country, start over somewhere else. That's all I want at this point. I have no other options."

Toscana was silent for a moment. "Wait a minute." The line went silent. Devin and Maxie wondered if Toscana had hung up on them. Thirty seconds later, he came back on the line. "My men just confirmed this line is not being bugged, so we can continue talking. How do you know I won't just kill you and take what is rightfully mine?"

Devin considered the question. "That is true. But you're a businessman. Of course, you could get rid of me, but that's one more loose end pointing your way. I have no way to know for sure, so I would have to trust you to keep your word. Doesn't that count anymore? Don't you guys follow a code of conduct?"

"You've got balls, kid," Toscana told him with a laugh. "I'll think on your offer. Call me back tomorrow morning at nine sharp from this phone, and I will have an answer for you. But don't get smart and bring anyone else in. I've got eyes everywhere. If you cross me, not only will I kill you, but everyone around you, including that lady cop."

Devin heard a *CLICK* as the line went dead. He let out a deep breath and downed the rest of the drink. His heart was racing. Glancing at Maxie, he realized she was feeling the same anxiety. "Fingers crossed," he said quietly.

"You did great," she said, coming up behind him, running her hand across his neck before leaning over and kissing him on the cheek. "I'd have peed my pants."

Devin broke out in a laugh.

"So in the morning, he will either accept or reject the offer. If he accepts, he will expect to name the time and place for the exchange. The time doesn't matter, but the place does. We have to decide where the best spot is, somewhere open, away from people, in case there is any shooting."

"And if he declines?"

"I guess I will have to plead it out. As far as he's concerned, the people on his payroll are still out there. I could threaten to go to the newspapers. But he should be smart enough to guess that already."

"Let's look at it from his point of view. Why should he trust you?"

Devin pointed at his wheelchair. "He's already done this. I'm not making it up that he ruined my life. So the only question is if he believes I am giving up."

"Maybe you should be more of a drama queen," Maxie suggested, which got Devin to raise an eyebrow in curiosity. "If he declines, be sad. Say something like your life has no meaning. That you will make sure copies get out to everyone you can think of, and you will end your life. That will take the power away from him. If he plans to cross you, which we know is a given, he will miss out. So what does he have to lose?"

"Drama queen?"

Maxie smiled. "You know what I mean."

"It's a good idea."

"Good. Then it's settled. Once we have the when and decide on the where, we can let Bryan do his thing so we can coordinate the take down." She raised her glass in a toast. Devin raised his, took a drink, and then fell silent. "What's wrong, hun?"

"Yesterday...us.... I was just wondering what kind of relationship you can have with me in this chair?"

She put her drink down and leaned forward. "That again? Don't you understand that I don't care if you're in a wheelchair or you're not? The part I like about you is none of those things. It's you, your personality, your heart. If you're going to start second-guessing everything before anything is even started, it's not a good sign."

"That's easy to say now. But what happens if it is a problem later? What happens if I can't...you know...be a man?"

"Hun, you carry enough bags to be a hotel porter. What if

I drown in the canal? What if I get shot and killed in my line of work? There is no answer. Life is risk. If you feel strongly enough about someone or something, you take the risk. It's gotta be worth it to you." She took a drink. "I like you. I know you like me. Sure, it will have its challenges, but I want to see how far we can go. Don't you?"

Devin smiled. "I do. You're the best thing that's happened to me. Okay, I will stop being a baby about it."

Maxie started to laugh and raised her glass. "Oh, thank the Lord!" Devin started to laugh as well. She knew how to reach him. "When this is over, you and I will take a vacation. I surely deserve one. Take the boat out and go sailing somewhere nice. But first, we need to be ready for tomorrow. I know it will be hard to sleep tonight, so what if we get settled on the couch, find a good movie, and just drift off that way?"

"Sounds nice. Can I make us something to eat?"

"I have a better idea. Let's do Doordash tonight, have something brought in. Do you like sushi?"

"I love sushi."

"Best on the island is Rock 'n Roll Sushi. Trust me to order?"

Devin nodded.

"Great. Be right back." Maxie went to the kitchen, pulled the number from a card on her fridge, and dialed.

Devin watched from the deck, saw her talking, even though no sound reached him. He studied the way she moved when she spoke, the way her head tilted slightly, her hand gestures as they rose up and down through the air as though she were conducting a silent symphony. From time to time, she glanced at him, and when their eyes met, hers seemed to sparkle. She brushed her hand through her hair, sweeping it back. He studied all her mannerisms, soaking them in so as not to forget. He had never met anyone like her before. Hank had described her as a force of nature, and that was true, although in a very complementary way. She had a way about her that moved mountains, and yet in so many ways she was gentle, a soft and beautiful woman. Why she liked him, he could not explain. Perhaps if they had met before his accident, before the paralysis had left him in this wheelchair, he might understand it more, but he also knew that there should be no questioning how she felt. That she felt anything at all toward him was amazing, and he reveled in the thought.

"I also texted Bryan and let him know where we are," she said, returning from the call.

"Good."

"What movie should we watch? Comedy, romance, drama?"

"How about *The Godfather*?" he suggested.

"Devin Parker," she said, smacking him lightly on the head. "You are one sick man. I'll pick." She plopped down beside him.

"Please don't say *The Notebook*," he teased.

"Oh heck, no," she replied. "I was thinking more of a classic like *High Noon* with Gary Cooper."

He looked at her. She made no facial expression.

"Fine," she finally said. "The last movie I saw was three years ago, and I fell asleep early on."

"What movie?"

"Heck if I know. I'm usually too busy for movies. So you pick one. Just make sure it's a good one."

"A good one?"

"Yeah, you know, something you think I would like."

He stared at her again, then broke into a grin. "This is a test, isn't it?"

She laughed. "Now you're sounding like Kobe. No test. I

want to see if you can pick a movie I might like. And don't be getting something goofy."

Devin considered his options. Despite what she had said, he knew this was a test. Women liked men who understood them.

"Okay. You're strong, capable, clever, determined, yet you have a heart. You value things that have stood the test of time, love your car...."

"Yes, I do," she replied. "That's my baby!"

"So I will pick a movie that is a classic, yet relatively newish, has values, character-driven, solid values, yet offers humor, taking chances, and is fun to watch."

"So, what is the movie called?" she asked impatiently.

"*American Graffiti*," Devin told her.

"*American Graffiti*," she said, puzzled. "I haven't seen it. It's not about people writing graffiti on walls, is it?"

"Oh no," he said. "Classic George Lucas film before *Star Wars*. It's about growing up in the fifties, a coming-of-age film that has classic cars—which you'll love—decent people, simpler times, great music, and good romance."

"Is it on streaming?"

"Yes, it is." He grabbed her television remote and, after searching and finding it, loaded up the film, pausing it until their food arrived.

He positioned himself to the side of the couch and hoisted himself onto it in a single motion. Maxie watched, amazed at the fluidity of it. He shuffled toward the center and made himself comfortable, using a pillow on one side for added support.

Moments later, the doorbell rang, and she went to fetch it, leaving the driver a nice tip. She brought the boxes to the couch, then fetched two plates, two small bowls, napkins, and brought over the whiskey bottle and a fresh glass they could share.

She opened the box, pulled out the sushi trays, set up the bowls with soy sauce, separated the thin ginger slices, and instructed Devin to mix in the wasabi paste. He followed along as she snapped her chopsticks apart, rubbing them together to remove any loose splinters. Then she took one roll, dipped it lightly, and popped it in her mouth. Devin watched the look of pleasure on her face, then did the same thing.

She poured a slug of the whiskey and took a sip, handing the glass to him. "Good sushi," she mumbled through a mouthful.

After they had devoured the whole meal, she moved the waste to the kitchen, then returned to the couch, moved beside him, and nestled her head on his shoulder. He turned toward her so he could see her face, and lightly kissed her on the lips.

"I'm behaving—promise," he said.

She returned the kiss. "Me, too. But start the movie before I change my mind."

They settled back as the opening credits played, both as satiated and delighted as anyone could be.

24

READY FOR ACTION

orning arrived with the realization that not only had they not really slept well—sprawled across the couch with the blue screen on the monitor once the movie ended—but today was the day that would decide the future. Today, they had the chance to take down a huge organized crime ring, get justice for Curtis, as well as for Devin. Everything was riding on the nine o'clock phone call, and what happened afterwards.

Devin had awoken first, moved slightly to allow Maxie to lie flat on the couch, and deftly got into his wheelchair. During the night he had pondered the best places to meet Toscana. He knew it needed to be in the open, somewhere away from civilians, and also where there was an opportunity for Maxie and Jameson to remain hidden from view.

He had looked up some public parks that had baseball and sport areas. It seemed that these would offer hiding places, lockers where equipment would be stored, dugouts, other places that could easily be overlooked. So far he had isolated it to one of two parks, but of course, Toscana could refuse and end that plan.

By the time Maxie woke up, Devin had coffee brewing. He poured her a cup and wheeled it over to her on the couch.

"Morning," he said handing it to her. "Did you make it through the movie?"

"No. I never do. But I liked what I saw, so we may have to watch it again when we don't have other things on our minds."

"An hour and a half before I have to call. We need to decide on the place, if we can. When's Jameson going to be here?"

"Soon. I also need to check-in with Bryan once we're done." She got up from the couch, leaned over Devin and kissed him. "That was fun." Then she went upstairs to her room and he heard the shower running.

The downstairs bathroom had a tub/shower. Devin knew that he could sit on the edge and from there give himself a good wash. He wheeled to his room to grab some clothes, then went to the bathroom.

When he came out fifteen minutes later, he was freshly shaved, hair neatly combed and felt new again. *If I'm going to my death today, at least I will look good,* he thought.

Maxie and Jameson were in the kitchen. "You look nice," she said.

"Thank you," both Devin and Jameson said, casting a quick quizzical look at each other.

Maxie laughed. "You're such a baby, Kobe. Of course, you look good—you always look good."

"Thank you," he said, sipping his coffee.

"I guess I don't have to say it, then?" Devin said staring at Jameson with a smile.

"It is all good, Devin," Jameson replied. "You have been saved."

Devin kept glancing at his watch. The time was getting closer. He needed to be in the right frame of mind. "I have to be a victim," he muttered. "Toscana is doing me a favor by letting me live. I want to live. I want to leave America and go settle in Greece or Spain."

"Do not be too convincing," Jameson advised. "Only allow little pieces of information to come out."

"Toscana will not believe it, anyway, Kobe," Maxie said. "He's gonna figure out that Devin is lying. But he wants to finish it himself, get the SD card, and know there are no more loose ends."

"So it must be a good trap for Devin?" Jameson said.

"And a trap we make before he can execute his own trap," Devin explained.

"Sounds good."

"Hun, make the meeting for mid-afternoon if we can. It will give Bryan time to set up properly, and for us as well. I have an idea how we can remain undetected."

"And what is your plan?" Jameson asked.

"Since we don't know where the meet will be, we will push for a park, one with a sports field. We should have a ball park with a dugout. We won't be there, though. Instead, we will be inside a large, metal equipment box. Locked. Right there in plain sight."

"Locked?"

"On the front side," Maxie explained. "The hinges will be loose. Old trick. Distraction. The guys in the shop can make that work. That way if they check the box, they will believe it to be an equipment box for sports gear."

Jameson studied her face. "And this equipment box is six feet by four feet?"

"Yes."

"And you and I will be hidden inside?"

Maxie nodded. "We will have holes, so we can see what is happening outside."

Devin saw Jameson was stewing about something. "What is wrong, Kobe?"

Jameson looked at Maxie. "You must really like Devin enough to compress your body into an old, dirty, metal box."

Maxie studied the indignant look on his face. She was not about to let him have the last word. "Well," she said, her hands on her hips. "No one said it had to be dirty!"

Devin began to laugh. It was classic slapstick comedy, and they both played it so well. Jameson applauded, then turned to Devin. "You are a very lucky man, Devin Parker. I promise you that."

Devin blushed. "Thank you, Kobe."

THE LITTLE PERFORMANCE managed to kill some time. Devin wheeled over to the table. On his laptop, he pulled up a map of Corpus Christi. Then opened the notebook with the phone number flat in front of him and waited until it was exactly nine o'clock. He dialed the number and kept the call on speaker.

"I have considered your request," Toscana said upon answering. "I am not certain of the benefit to me, however."

Devin took a deep breath and held it. This was the part he feared would happen. He slowly let out the breath.

"Mr. Toscana. Do you understand how I feel about my life as it is now? I am trapped. I cannot move. Everything below my lower spine is paralyzed. I...." he stopped, cast a look at

Maxie. Tears were building in his eyes. "I am forced to wear diapers because I have no control over my bladder. Things you take for granted are no longer available to me. I do not sleep well. I am filled with sadness and anger. And grief. The only future I have left is one where I am not looking over my shoulder to see if you are trying to kill me." He paused, took another breath. "You said you were not certain how this was of benefit to you. I have thought about that as well. I am not trying to be brash, but if we do not reach an agreement over this, then my life truly is over. It would only be a matter of time before your men found me. But, I wouldn't wait for them. Before that happened, I would take my own life. But before I did that, I would ensure that my one copy of the SD card in my possession was made into one hundred copies, and I would make sure that everyone and anyone of any importance would receive a copy. I would make sure my suicide note would include explicit details about what was on the SD card. Copies would be sent to the media. And of course, the police would also get a copy. At least my death would then mean something."

Devin stopped. His voice softened. "I would prefer to not do that. I hope that you reconsider. What I am asking for costs you nothing, but for me, the chance to live out my days in peace, far away from you, from all of this. That's all I have. It's up to you how this will end, but it has to end one way or another."

Devin took another deep breath, reminded himself to stop talking now, and let this gangster make the next move. There was silence for a minute.

"There is only one copy you have?"

"Yes."

"No one but you has seen it?"

"Yes." He lied.

"How do I know you are telling the truth?"

Devin thought of a decent answer. "After everything we have discussed, the cops would have traced the call and you would be arrested already, right?"

"Perhaps. Very well. I agree to your request."

"I need you to promise it to me on your word."

"My word?"

"That is all I have to go on. Your word. Don't they do that anymore?"

"Very well. On my word, I will allow you to live provided you meet me and give me the only copy of the SD card that belongs to me. Satisfied?"

"Yes. When? How?"

"Noon. Dixon Park off Earhardt Rd."

"Can we make it three? I have an infected catheter that needs to be removed at noon."

"Fine. Three O'clock. Dixon Park. Do you know it?"

"Yes," Devin said, having pulled it up on his laptop. It had a baseball area. "I'll be in the baseball area. On the mound. You will be able to see that I am alone."

"Don't screw this up, kid."

"I won't."

Toscana ended the call. Devin sat there frozen. *Holy cow, I pulled that off,* he thought.

"Good job," Jameson told him, snapping him out of the trance he was in. His heart was pounding hard. He looked up at Maxie. She was smiling, but tears were running down her cheeks. She hastily wiped them away. She held up her hand with her thumb and forefinger a few inches apart.

"We're that close, hun."

"Let's get that son of a bitch."

Maxie poured a coffee for him and placed it before him. "Need me to add anything to it?"

He shook his head. "I'm okay now that part is done."

She poured one for Jameson and one for herself. Then dialed Cochran on her phone.

"We're in. Dixon Park at 3 today. I need a large metal storage box rigged for Kobe and me to hide in. Kobe will call in the specs. It has to be in place before noon. I don't want to take the chance that Toscana gets there early, or has his goons in place before we get wind of it." She put him on speaker and told him as much.

"We are all set for the mass raid. FBI agents arrived this morning. They're going to handle the judge, congressman, and senator. There's going to be over a hundred arrests, Maxie. Huge. Once we're secure, I'll have a few cars head your way as backup. Just in case. We won't come in unless there's a reason."

"Good luck Bryan."

"To you, too. Kobe, Devin, take this guy down hard."

"Thank you, chief," Kobe answered, and the call ended.

"Are we going to be in the box for a few hours?" Jameson asked.

"We'll have eyes on the place. We can wait in the dugout. Once we get word he's on his way in, we can climb in. We'll also need a wheelchair enabled van for Devin. Can't make it look like he was dropped off or anyone else is involved."

"Good idea," Devin said. "I'm sure I can use one."

"We've got a few hours until we need to be setting up."

"I will handle the van," Jameson said. "I will meet you somewhere before the park, so we can go in together. Use the van. Devin can drive, in case anyone is watching."

He nodded at Maxie and then fist-bumped Devin on his way out.

Maxie paced the room. "If he comes armed, which he almost certainly will be, and if he comes with one of his goons, which he almost certainly will be, we have to figure out how this could play out."

"I'm sure there will be no small talk. I will be there, on the mound. He will drive in. They will park close to where I am. His goon will check to make sure I am not armed. He'll check the dugout and any other structures before anything."

"And he will find nothing."

"He will want the SD card. I will want assurances. He will offer none. It's quite likely that either Toscana or his goon will already have a gun pointed at me."

"Does he shoot first, or get the card first?" Maxie asked. "He'll want to make sure you have not shared the information, so I expect some chatter before he decides to finish you off."

Devin wheeled next to her. "So he will shoot me first, or after he gets the SD card. We agree that those are the two choices."

"We can't intervene until we know he is about to shoot you."

"You have to be out of the locker box before then."

"Once Toscana believes that no one is there, Kobe and I can come out of the box and stay hidden in the dugout. That way we will be ready."

"Okay, that's a plan. You nervous?"

Maxie stopped pacing and moved closer to him. "Of course. I don't want anything to happen to you."

"Me, too. Should I have a gun?"

"That's a thought. In case they search you, though, it will destroy your narrative—you're supposed to be desperate for a new life, remember?"

"True. No gun, then."

"They'll also search the van—you drove there by yourself.

That will take a few minutes. I doubt Toscana will want to drag this out any longer than it needs to be."

"So from the time he arrives, we will have about five minutes at the earliest, before my life is in danger."

Devin spun around, gracefully lifting one wheel off the ground. Maxie watched in amazement. "Where'd you learn to do that?"

"Jackson—the physical therapist at the hospital. He taught me. He's also paraplegic." He allowed the wheel to touch down gently. "What about other people?"

"What people?"

"At the park. Regular people who might be there."

The thought had not occurred to Maxie, who had been so preoccupied with keeping Devin safe that the thought of other people never crossed her mind. She grabbed her phone and dialed.

"Kobe, I need you to get Parks to close the park—get some signs up pronto. Closed for maintenance, something like that. We need to keep civilians away from the area."

Kobe assured her he would handle it, and she ended the call.

"I missed that one," she told Devin.

"You're preoccupied," he replied.

Maxie smiled at him. "That's *your* fault."

"I can live with that." He turned and wheeled off to his room. She watched him go, reminding herself that he had no reason to stay with her after the case was done. She would miss having him there. On the other hand, they could see where their relationship might head. *Who knows?* she thought.

25

WHAT CAN POSSIBLY GO WRONG?

The van was delivered to Maxie's house at eleven that morning. Both of them were ready. Devin insisted on wheeling himself to the van. He wanted it to seem natural. The officer delivering it, gave Devin the briefest of instructions.

Devin accessed the driver seat from the driver side door. A key fob activated the motors to open the door. This slid straight out from the driver position while still attached to the car door itself. The bottom had a small ramp, and in the center a locking mechanism, similar to how a fifth-wheel hitch would lock onto the bed of a pickup truck. Behind it, a regular driver seat had been pushed back and locked. That way enabled drivers could also use the van.

Devin listened intently. The rest of the process was simply extension handles, as well as a power bar operated from the left hand that controlled acceleration and braking. This was similarly connected to the car pedals with rods and brackets.

The steering wheel was equipped with a Tri-Pin attached to the wheel—a knob with three prongs. The driver's hand would fit between the prongs to ensure a stable grip. Here, Devin's hand could fit and allow him to use his arm and shoulder strength to steer the vehicle.

Smugly, Devin wheeled into position by the driver side door ramp. "Piece of cake," he announced. He tried reversing into position, but his right wheel missed and got stuck. He repeated the process, this time the left wheel got stuck. Finally, on the third attempt he backed in straight, the connector beneath his wheelchair clicking into the restraining socket on the floor of the ramp. "Ta-da!"

He pressed the button to raise the ramp and slide him into the driver position. Maxie thanked the officer delivering the van, and they both got in.

"You sure you trust him?" Maxie asked the officer. "You could walk?"

The officer smiled shyly. "I'm sure he will be fine ma'am."

Devin turned the extra-sized ignition key and the van started up. He adjusted the mirrors. "Down for acceleration, side for braking?"

"Yes, sir," the officer confirmed.

Devin popped the gear into reverse and then backed out of the driveway. With his right hand in the Tri-Pin, turning was easy. The pin would rotate so only the wheel turned. "It's very responsive," he said.

They dropped the officer back at the station, then headed out to the park. There was still over three hours before the scheduled meet with Toscana, but Maxie wanted to canvass the area, make sure that everything they needed was in place.

Checking in with Jameson—he had parked a few streets

away and was waiting by the side of the road—they pulled over to allow him to get in.

"Nice ride," he said. "How is the driving?"

"I'm already used to it," Devin replied. "It's nice to go fast again."

As they approached the entrance to the park, they saw that the signs, announcing the park closure, were in place. A barrier had been placed across the entrance to prevent cars from entering. Maxie got out and moved it aside enough to look like it had been pushed by a vehicle entering.

"You're here alone," she explained to Devin. "It's unlikely you got out and pushed it so I wanted it to look like the van pushed against it."

They drove further in, passed a row of trees, to where the baseball area was. A large metal lock box had been left.

Devin parked the van, then reversed the process of getting in. Getting out seemed a lot easier. He followed Maxie and Jameson to the box. A solid padlock on one side gave the impression that it was closed tight. Without knowing that the pins had been removed from the other side, the box looked solid. Jameson grabbed the handle and dragged it closer to where he thought it should go.

"This way, we can get out of the box and still be out of sight," he explained.

"What about the noise it makes?"

Jameson lifted the lid. A hinge had been welded on the padlock side inside the box, so opening it worked the same way. "No noise," he announced. He climbed in and curled up. Several drill-sized holes had been made in the side. Jameson moved his face closer to them.

"See anything?" Maxie asked.

"Yes. It is enough to see when they come to the box. Once

they have inspected it we should get out immediately. It is too difficult to see what else is happening."

Jameson got out of the box. He left the lid up.

"It's a shame your name isn't Jack," Maxie said, attempting to inject some humor into the moment. Jameson just shook his head. It was not her best joke.

Devin wheeled himself to the center of the field, as close to the mound as he could get. He then turned and looked back. "I've changed my mind. If I stay here and they come to me, it will be too difficult for you to intervene—you'll be too far away. Once I see them coming I'll move from here closer to the fence. That way they will be closer to you, as well."

"That is a good idea," Jameson said.

"Can we get someone to watch the entrance so we have a heads up when he arrives?"

"Unmarked car across the road," she said. "Already in place. One of our guys is watching. You okay with this? I don't want you to do this unless you're sure?" She put a hand on his shoulder and he reached up to hold it.

"It's a good plan, Maxie. I have to do this."

She checked her watch. "I hate waiting. Did you know that about me?"

"Everyone hates waiting."

She called the unmarked car by the entrance. Inside, she knew was Simon Malone. He was a police officer, but also an avid photographer, certainly someone Toscana would never recognize. All he had to do was watch who entered from his position across the street, take photos with a telephoto lens, and later, once arrests were made, come in and document everything with photographs.

"I'm here, Maxie," Malone told her. "I have a good view."

"Thank you, Simon," she said. She hung up and looked at

Devin and Jameson. "Do we assume that Toscana will be early, on-time, or late?"

"On-time," Jameson said.

"Early," Devin said. "He's going to want to see if there is a trap. Maybe we should expect him around two-thirty."

"Or," Maxie countered, "if he is ego-driven, he will come late just to annoy you. And me!"

"Devin is correct. We should assume he will want to secure the area. Could he send an advance party to be sure?"

"Better hope not—we'll be sunk," Maxie said.

"It's a park," Devin said. "Not much here. If I were trying to be careful I would drive around the block to be sure that no cops were waiting, then come in a half-hour early to get a feel for the place, especially if he plans to kill me. Then I would park and wait."

"So he will be suspicious when he arrives early and sees that you are already here."

Devin nodded. "So he will look around, or have his goons look around. There's only the dugout which will be empty. And a metal sports locker that is locked. The goons might try to move it, then realize that it is full. I don't think they will think twice."

"We're overthinking this," Maxie said. "We've covered all bases—no pun intended."

Her phone buzzed and she answered it. "Simon.... Crap. Okay, I'll have Kobe handle it." She ended the call. "A mother and two kids are cutting through. So much for signs. Kobe, go scare them away?"

Jameson nodded and headed quickly toward the front entrance.

"Always the random things," Devin said.

"Always," she replied. "Hopefully we won't have more."

A few minutes later Jameson returned. "I told her there was a toxic spill."

Devin laughed. "Probably scared her to death."

AS TWO-THIRTY APPROACHED, they decided it was time to assume positions. Devin saw that she looked worried. "I'll be fine," he told her. "Let's get this done." He turned and started to wheel out toward the mound. Once there he turned and saw both the main road leading in, as well as Maxie and Jameson standing behind the dugout by the locker boxes. He nodded. He knew that as soon as they climbed into the box it meant Toscana was on his way in. So that all eyes were on him, he would wheel closer to Toscana as the car approached.

At two-forty, Malone notified Maxie that a brown sedan was turning in, then changed course and headed off.

"Show time. He's gonna go around the block, so figure we have five minutes." She motioned at Jameson, then they climbed into the locker box and pulled the lid down. The car appeared a few minutes later, slowed as the driver examined the barrier that had been pushed aside.

Devin watched. The car moved closer to him. He turned and wheeled slightly toward the car, getting closer as it approached, and then parked. The driver got out, a muscular thug holding a gun equipped with a silencer. Devin stared at him.

"Parker?"

Devin nodded. The thug walked over and patted down Devin. Then, without warning, he quickly lifted Devin from the wheelchair and hurried to the car.

"What the...."

In a handful of seconds, and before he could offer resistance, Devin had been placed inside the car; the thug hopped in next to him, slammed the door, and the car started off.

From inside the box Maxie and Jameson watched in shock. He pushed the lid up and stood up. The car was almost out of the park.

"Crap," Maxie shouted. "The van, Kobe...."

They quickly exited the box and ran to the van. Jameson fumbled getting the regular driver seat to unlatch and push forward. Finally, after much frustration he managed to do so, climbed into the driver seat and started the van.

"Simon," Maxie yelled into her phone. "Do you have them?"

"Affirmative. They tore outta the park, so I figured something went wrong. I'm following them now."

"Where are you?"

"Heading down Everhart towards Yorktown."

"Keep on them. Simon, they're going to kill Devin if we don't get there in time."

"I'm on it."

Jameson glanced at Maxie. She looked visibly upset. "They're quite a bit ahead."

"Stupid, Kobe. I should have known this could happen. It was all too easy."

"How could you know? Jameson told her. "We will reach him in time."

Jameson had to swerve around other cars, overtaking on the wrong side, hoping that all other police were busy with arrests—the last thing he needed was to be pulled over.

"Maxie, they just turned right onto Oso Parkway... wait...I'm holding back until I see what they do. It's quite wooded back there."

"Keep a distance until you see what's going on, Simon," Maxie said. She looked at Jameson.

"Remember it will take Toscana time to make sure he is safe before he does anything. We have time."

THE CAR HOLDING DEVIN, did a u-turn and parked by the side of a small, manicured outcropping from the neighborhood, just on the other side of Oso Parkway. Although it was a small area, a few benches, it was bordered by dense trees leading to Oso Creek several yards below. The thug got out and pulled Devin from the car. He carried him over his shoulder, across the area to the base of a tree where a well-dressed man in his fifties was seated on a stool. The man was dressed in a black suit, complete with vest, a pale blue tie. His dark hair was combed back, a slight shock of a curl falling forward. He had on a pair of sunglasses that he removed as Devin was placed on the ground before him.

"You didn't come alone?" Devin shouted out, adjusting himself into a seated position.

"My bodyguard, Tony," Toscana replied, pointing at the thug, his thick New Jersey gangster accent now strong—stereotypical. "You have the card?"

Devin nodded.

"And no one else has seen it?"

"Only me," Devin answered. "Look, I figured it's the only way I get to leave here and live a normal life."

"Show me the SD card," Toscana instructed.

Devin reached into his pocket and withdrew it, holding it between his fingers.

"Give it to me."

"First, I need your promise."

"What promise? I already gave you a promise."

"That I give you the card and I get to leave."

"You know, kid, I admire your guts," Toscana said. "In my lifetime I have seen a lot of things. I've seen people do stupid things, brave things...well just about everything you can imagine. I will tell you that you are brave—it's a compliment from me to you."

Devin stared at him. He already knew this compliment wouldn't end well.

"Thank you," he said reluctantly. "But, that's not a promise. Please tell me you're not going back on your word?" He was delaying for time now, hoping that Maxie and Jameson would catch up.

Toscana shrugged. "In my line of work you just don't get many chances to do things right. In the old days, when a leader, such as myself, had to take care of someone, they used to wipe out everyone in the family—wife, kids, parents, friends. You see, to leave any witnesses, or anyone who could enact revenge, well that was just foolish. It's been done this way since the time of the pharaohs, the Roman Emperors. So, to answer your question, I am afraid that I cannot let you go. Now I need you to give me the SD card. Don't make this any harder than it has to be."

"And if I snap it, break the card?" Devin held the card with both fingers.

Toscana laughed. "Kid, feel free. Destroying the card is fine with me. It will change nothing."

Devin lowered his hands. "Why did Curtis have to die? He was a decent guy."

"You already know the answer to that. Same reason why I have to eliminate you." Toscana clicked his fingers. "Tony, get the card."

Tony moved toward Devin who tried scooting back with his hands. At the last minute, as Tony was close enough, Devin twisted his upper torso, swiveled his body, just as Jackson had shown him how to do on the parallel bars, allowing the motion to swing his legs out and knock Tony off-balance. The gun flew out of Tony's hand as he fell to the ground, and Devin reached over, grabbed Tony's shirt and pulled himself behind Tony. He grabbed him in a headlock and tightened his grip so Tony struggled to breathe. Devin was glad for the upper body training Jackson had forced him to do.

"Damn you," Toscana said, getting up and heading for the gun. "Finish the job myself." He picked it up and pointed it at Devin, who moved his body to use Tony as a shield.

"Don't," Devin said. "Think this through. It's all over Toscana."

"Let go of him or I will shoot you both."

"I lied to you. The SD card is not a secret anymore. The cops know. Your men are being arrested. You're going to shoot your bodyguard for nothing."

Toscana aimed the gun at Devin's head, but Devin shifted position again so his head was behind Tony. Toscana fired. The bullet hit Tony in the head, slamming Devin back to the ground and releasing his grip. Tony's body fell to one side.

Devin looked up and saw the gun now squarely aimed at him. "You're lying to save your ass."

The SD card had fallen out of Devin's hand during the struggle and Toscana spotted it. He bent down to pick it up. Out of instinct, Devin took advantage of the move, but this was different. Toscana was a mere three feet away now. Devin knew that his next act after retrieving the SD card would be to immediately shoot Devin. Reflexively, he rolled his body to bend his legs up, kicking Toscana as hard as he could. His feet impacted Toscana's chest, and the man lost his grip on the gun, the SD card, and fell backwards to the ground.

My legs..., Devin thought. He willed them to move, and they did. He saw Toscana struggling to get up and, without thinking about it, Devin got up first—his legs wobbly, but functional, not unlike a newborn foal taking a few minutes to adjust to life. Devin was overwhelmed—adrenaline rushed through him. He stumbled towards Toscana, now getting up, looking for where the gun had fallen, and charged at him as best he could. His body slammed into Toscana, who again fell back to the ground, now with Devin on top of him.

Devin sat across Toscana's chest, as the man struggled to free his arms. Devin stared down, his thoughts now lost in a fog of rage, and he started to repeatedly punch Toscana in the face, pounding him as hard as he was able. Welts and skin tears appeared on Toscana's face, blood seeping out as Devin continued to pummel him.

"For Curtis, you asshole."

The beating accelerated, each fist impact with a word escaping Devin's mouth..."You—killed—him—you—bastard...."

Simon, who had been watching, as instructed, had run toward Devin as the beating started. He grabbed Devin from behind and pulled him off Toscana. Devin turned, ready to start hitting Simon, his mind so enraged that he could not think clearly. He wanted to hit anyone. The anger coursed through him. He raised his fist to strike again.

"Devin. Stop!" A voice yelled from behind. He knew that voice. He froze, blinked several times, then looked at where the voice was. Maxie was standing there with Jameson, guns drawn. He looked back at Toscana, moaning, his face so badly beaten that both eyes were swollen shut, with blood seeping through every tear of the skin from the repeated impacts. Devin was panting hard, hyperventilating, unable to control his breathing.

He started to stand, legs wobbly, turned, looked again at Maxie, then at his hands covered in Toscana's blood. He took a step toward her, but his legs gave way and he collapsed to the ground. He was sobbing uncontrollably as he struggled to catch his breath.

Maxie ran to him, lifted his head into her lap, and held him tightly as he sobbed. Tears were running down her face, but she didn't care. "It's over, hun," she said quietly. "It's over." She stroked his hair.

Jameson checked to make sure Toscana was still alive, retrieved Toscana's gun, and then called for an ambulance.

Slowly, Devin regained his composure, the emotions within subsiding enough that he could sit up. He stared at Maxie's face, then, using one finger, wiped at her tears. It seemed the right thing to do.

"I thought I lost you," she whispered.

Jameson handed him a small towel and a bottle of water for his hands. He tried to open the bottle, but his hands were swollen. Maxie twisted the lid and poured the water onto the towel, wiping his hands gently until most of the blood was gone. "That's gonna hurt tomorrow," she said.

"Already does," he muttered. "Worth it."

She held his face in her hands. "You walked." She was smiling.

Devin was surprised. In the emotions of the moment, he hadn't realized that he had actually walked, but remembered kicking Toscana to the ground. *Had that not happened, I would have been dead,* he thought.

"Can you stand?" Jameson asked, grabbing one arm to help him up. Maxie stood and grabbed the other. Devin managed to put weight on his legs, although they still wobbled and felt weak.

"They ache," he told them both. He began to smile. "That's such a good feeling."

"You did very well," Jameson told him, letting go and holding out his hand so Devin could do it himself. "I could not have done any better."

High praise, Devin thought. With Maxie holding one arm, they walked toward the road where the van was parked. Simon was standing there. As Devin approached, Simon looked at him pensively.

"I'm sorry," Devin said. "I wasn't thinking...."

"It's fine," Simon said.

"Thank you for being there."

Simon smiled and nodded.

The sirens in the background grew louder as the ambulance and two police cars arrived. The medics went to fetch Toscana with two officers in tow, handcuffing the criminal to the stretcher before carrying him back and loading him into the ambulance.

One medic asked Devin if he needed assistance, but Devin declined. He had everything he needed. The ambulance soon left for the hospital, with one patrol car following. The other remained behind.

Jameson, along with Simon, processed the area, bagging the gun, the SD Card, and photographing anything relevant. By now, nearby residents had gathered and were ogling the scene. Gunshots in their neighborhood were never a positive event, and they were glad of the police presence. Then one woman spotted Maxie and frantically called out to her.

"Maxie, is everything alright?"

Maxie looked at Devin and smiled. "Everything is fine

now," she answered with a hand wave. Then, turning back to Devin, she added, "It's finally over."

"I hope the chief managed to round them all up," Devin said.

"Once Jameson gets done, we'll find out." She stroked his hair back, away from his face. "You're a mess," she teased.

"And you were crying," he teased back, now able to control his breathing and knowing that the rage had slipped away.

She shrugged. "Must mean something."

Jameson waved at Simon, then climbed into the van. "All good," he said. "We should leave."

"Yes, please," Maxie said.

Once Jameson had started off, Maxie dialed Cochran's cell and put the call on speaker. "Harold Wilson," the voice answered.

"Harold, it's Maxie. Where's Bryan?"

"Maxie," the voice said. "I'm glad to hear your voice. Bryan was shot during the FBI raid on Senator Bordana's office. He's in surgery now."

"How bad?"

There was silence for a moment. "Bad enough. Don't have more info, yet."

"We're headed to the hospital now. What about the rest of the arrests?"

"Over a hundred twenty. It's a huge success for us. And you."

MEET THE PRESS

By the time they reached the hospital, Cochran was just out of surgery and in the recovery room. The post-op nurses were waiting for him to regain consciousness before moving him to a room. Cochran's wife, Betty, was in the waiting area, along with Wilson and Renaldo. Jameson and Devin quietly sat down. Renaldo stared at Devin, not sure if he had understood correctly. *Wasn't Parker wheelchair bound? No matter.*

"He'll be fine," Wilson told her. "Missed the vitals, thankfully. They're just waiting for him to wake up."

"Are you okay, Betty?" Maxie asked. "Can I get you anything?"

Betty smiled at her. "Thank you, dear. I'm fine. But what about you? You had a rough day."

Maxie nodded. "Once Bryan wakes up, the day will be just fine."

"Maxie, the press are gathering downstairs. I need to tell them something about this," Wilson told her. He hated public speaking. It was part of the reason he would never be chief—

he always left that to Cochran, who handled the media like a finely tuned instrument. With him out of action, it was easy to see Wilson's discomfort.

"Would you like me to speak to them?"

"Would you mind?" Wilson felt immediate relief. Maxie was good at handling the media. He never understood why she had no ambition for Cochran's position.

"How about I give them a sliver to hold them for now, and then a presser tomorrow? Will that work?"

Wilson nodded.

"Let's wait until we hear the chief's out of the woods, then do it," she said.

A few minutes later, the recovery nurse poked her head in with a smile. "He's awake now. Doc said it all looks good. He needs to rest, but he asked to see his wife.".

"Give him our best, Betty," Maxie said.

Betty nodded and followed the nurse out.

"Ten bucks he's not here by morning," Maxie said. "Any takers?"

No one would take that bet; they all knew Cochran too well.

"Okay, time for the press," she said, standing and motioning Devin and Jameson to join her. "You're not getting out of this that easily," she told them.

STEPPING out of the glass front doors of the hospital, Maxie was greeted by a barrage of flashes from cameras, microphones shoved toward her, and a dozen reporters all clamoring to have their questions answered.

Devin tried stepping back, but she grabbed his hand and

held it, motioning Jameson forward as well. "We're in this together," she said to them directly.

Holding up her hand to quiet the crowd, she waited until the volume had dropped before speaking.

"In a massive raid on organized crime today, the Corpus Christi Police Department, in conjunction with the FBI, has made over a hundred arrests, including several prominent members of society, the names of whom will amaze you. Full names will be released to you tomorrow at an official press conference. During the raid, Chief Bryan Cochran sustained a gunshot injury. He is out of surgery, conscious, and expected to make a full recovery."

"Maxie, is this related to the murders that have taken place in the city these last few months?"

"Yes. Directly related. As we will outline in detail tomorrow, this was a criminal organization that had infiltrated the city."

"Maxie, is this related to the recent killing of well-known financier, Curtis Delaney?"

Maxie looked at Devin, then back. "Mr. Delaney was sadly murdered because he had uncovered documentation linking the arrests we made today. Because of Mr. Delaney's courage, the information was passed to his family member, noted journalist Devin Parker, beside me, who in turn made sure we were brought in."

Cameras and microphones were turned now to Devin. "Mr. Parker...."

He could not differentiate who was speaking from the questions flung at him and just stared blankly ahead. Maxie raised her hands again. "Mr. Parker is not answering questions at this time. Ladies and gentlemen, we'll let you know what time the press conference will be in the morning, but in the meantime, please revel in the fact that our city is safe and that our police force has continued to do a fantastic job. Thank you."

The noise swelled up again, the press never one to quit, and Maxie turned back to the hospital door, leading Jameson and Devin inside, away from the chaos.

"That went well," Jameson noted. "Devin was surprised when you mentioned his name."

Maxie looked at Devin. "Were you?" She was grinning. He nodded, uncertain what to say.

Jameson pointed at him. "You need to get used to that," he warned.

Maxie just smiled. "I'm ready to go home. Do you want to invite Hank over for a drink and give him the story?"

Devin nodded.

"Good idea," Jameson said. "I need a drink."

"Who said you're invited?" Maxie teased.

"You did," he replied. "All the time." He grinned, his white teeth shining.

"Okay, then. But I'm driving. And not the van. Where is my car, anyway?"

AFTERMATH

A month later, on a clear Saturday, earlier in the day, before the muggy humidity and heat would make the outdoors uncomfortable, Maxie and guests boarded *Lady Tears,* and sailed out past Port Aransas, into open water.

The lapping of water against the hull was, for the longest time, the only sound to be heard. Aside from Maxie, Devin, and Jameson, she had invited Hank and Cochran, now well-healed from his gunshot wound.

The hullabaloo of the press had died down. The city's crime wave had ended. Corrupt politicians, council members and cops were either in jail or awaiting trial for their part in Toscana's mafia operation. Toscana had been handed over to the FBI, who had advised it was unlikely he would see the outside of jail anytime. Hassan was still in custody. Cochran wanted more information from him before releasing him to the Feds. That would happen in the near future. For now, he was securely locked up under guard. Cochran would take no chances with this one.

Maxie, Jameson, and Devin had been awarded citations and commendations, Devin's coming from the mayor. Hank made sure that the byline of the story in the *Tribune* included Devin, advising him that by living it, Devin had all but written the story.

Around the seating area of the boat, fishing rods were primed, lines taut. Bryan Cochran sat on one cushion nursing a beer. Beside him, Kobe Jameson, although he was only drinking sparkling water. "Someone has to be the designated driver," he had told them when they set sail. "And you all enjoy getting drunk."

Cochran laughed at that one. He always found Jameson to be good for comments. Hank did not disagree, pouring himself a whiskey chaser from a small, silver flask. "It's five o'clock somewhere," he announced, even though it was barely ten in the morning.

And Devin delighted in the fact that the stress was finally gone. Over the month, he had come to terms with Curtis's death. He still had Curtis's ashes, and Maxie had agreed Devin could use her boat to scatter them further out in the bay when he was ready. Just not today.

Today was a day of calm. Devin had visited Jackson and, despite the lack of a wheelchair, enjoyed working out with him. Their friendship had transcended the need of the moment, and Devin had promised to work with him developing a business model they both could benefit from.

And Maxie reveled in the new man in her life, an equal who challenged her, kept up with her, understood her, and most of all, loved her for who she was, not some illusion of success or fame. Devin was a good man. She would have loved him even if he had never walked again, although his regained mobility made their life somewhat easier. For one thing, he could walk upstairs in her house, where he now lived, and their evenings were often spent on her upper deck, not the lower deck, where they had gathered before.

"There's something about a boat," she said, randomly. "You can just go, be subject to the wind, not care where you go, when you get there. No one tells you what to do. You enjoy the air, the water, and the birds. There's a certain peace to it all."

"You're scaring the fish, Maxie," Cochran told her. "Sssh...."

"What fish? You guys haven't caught a thing. And here I was thinking we would have caught dinner by now."

"*You* are not fishing," Jameson noted.

"No, you know I leave that to you big, strong men," she teased.

Devin was smiling. After a month, he had grown fully accustomed to the banter between Maxie and Jameson.

"You are a brave man, Devin Parker," Jameson told him.

"Oh, shush, Kobe," Maxie said. "You're just jealous."

"But now you have another man in your life."

Maxie leaned in closer to Devin. "Yes, I do. But don't you worry, Kobe. Plenty of room in my life for you both. If you behave."

"Seriously, though," Cochran interrupted. "Do you golf, Devin?"

Maxie started to laugh.

"Bryan needs to win," Maxie teased. "He's tired of losing to me."

"I'm game," Devin said.

Just then, Hank's line suddenly started to jerk. He spilled his beer and jumped up to grab it. "Holy...."

With two hands, he was holding tight, reeling it in, when he felt he could, and allowing some slack in the line, the rest of the time. "Come to daddy," he said to the hidden fish.

Jameson burst out laughing. "Come to daddy?"

They watched as Hank wrestled with his pole. Cochran offered to help, but Hank pushed him away. "I can do this. You're not chief of the ocean, you know."

Cochran raised his beer can in toast and sat back down to watch.

Finally, after much fussing, Hank reeled in his fish. A twelve-inch sheepshead, not even of legal size to keep, short by several inches. The fish floundered on the line until Hank managed to grab it with both hands and held his prize up high. Jameson snapped a photograph. "This is awesome," he blurted out. "Do I really have to throw it back?"

"I can arrest you if you prefer?" Cochran announced, which drew laughter from the rest.

Carefully, Hank removed the hook with some needle-nose pliers, then, holding the fish close to his face, told it, "You're one lucky fish." He tossed it back, watched as it quickly disappeared. Maxie and Devin began to applaud.

"You did good, Hank," Maxie said. "Don't let them tell you otherwise."

Cochran popped another beer and took a swig. "Kobe, I hear you're adopting a young boy?"

Maxie shrugged. That was not how she had presented it to Cochran.

"Not adopting," Jameson corrected him. "I am fostering Tyson while his mother will be in rehabilitation."

"Ah. Good for you. That's so admirable."

"Kobe picks him up tonight. Should be for a month," Maxie said. "It's going to be a wonderful experience for Kobe."

"He is a good boy," Kobe said. "I hope that it will be a good experience for us both."

"I'm sure it will," Devin said. "You'll be fine, Kobe."

They fell silent again, and for a while, the only sound was the water against the boat.

This is a perfect day, she thought, reaching for a beer and popping the cap.

And, just then, her cell phone rang.

MAY I ASK A FAVOR

Could I ask a favor? If you enjoyed this book, could you take a few moments to leave a rating or review?

Your honest review helps to make my novel visible to other readers. It also helps them to decide if this novel would be one they might also enjoy.

Thank you very much.

William Gensburger

"…has a deepness of soul touching in the stories. I tend to want to mull over each story before continuing on.It reminds me of T.S. Elliot." ~ *Catherine Baskett*

"William's short stories are spectacular. The writing is excellent and the stories move at just the right pace. The characters are weird and wonderful. It wasa pleasure to read and I enjoyed this book very much." ~ *Allison Rose*

"I'm blown away by the quality of your work. You bring me into the story and captivate me." *~Danielle Calloway*

"I really enjoyed this book! It was a fun read. I was drawn in from the start – snappy dialogue, a hint that all isn't as it seems and, most importantly for me, I liked the characters. Fun, engaging, escapist – it made me smile, and want more!" *~T Hoop*

"This was such a good read. This is great beach reading!" *~Tanya Lu (Vine Voice)*

<u>NON-FICTION:</u>

VERISIUM: Conversations with AI on the Meaning of Life and Death.

Verisium: Conversations with AI on Life and Death is not just a book—it is a voyage into the forgotten corridors of consciousness, the buried truths of human potential, and the emerging frontier where artificial intelligence becomes a mirror to the soul.

In a world choking on shallow distractions and fractured identities, Verisium dares to ask the questions we were never taught to ask: What is consciousness? Where do we go when we die? Are we truly free—or are we engineered to conform? Through a riveting blend of personal narrative, historical insight, and dynamic dialogues with an advanced AI, this groundbreaking work unveils a deep inquiry into life, death, and what lies beyond both.

"Everything is consciousness, not everything has consciousness.

Having is owning something, but being different from it, and being it is just simply an expression of it being an expression of it." -Dr. Tony Nader

<u>COMING SOON:</u>

A SPLINTER OF JUSTICE: In a society almost fully corrupted, where justice has failed, politicians bought and paid for, child trafficking and exploitation rampant, one man executes his own brand of justice: death. Some call him an assassin. Others call him a hero, doing the work that should have been done. No one knows who he is. He has no flashy name, no costume, and is never seen. Just a coin that he leaves with each victim.

Award-winning reporter David Ross is well aware of the corruption surrounding him. Paralyzed a few years earlier from a targeted hit that left his wife dead, he is tasked with uncovering the identity of the vigilante, a figure he has mixed feelings about. Paired with reporter Kate Halston, the two must make headway in learning the truth before the FBI Task Force hunting him down eliminates the vigilante.

Visit William Gensburger's author website at:
https://bnpmag.com/misterwriter/

Be sure to join his private VIP Reader list.